On
Being
Afraid
of the
Dark

KEN WOOTEN

TRITON PRESS

ISBN: 978-1-936946-40-2

Triton Press
426 S Lamar Blvd
Suite 16
Oxford, MS 38655
662-513-0159
www.nautiluspublishing.com

Wooten, Keneth (1933 —)
        On Being Afraid of the Dark — 1st ed.

Interior design by Sinclair Rishel

Printed in the United States of America

10 9 8 7 6 5 4 3 2 1

For the three great loves of my life:

Margaret, Lisa, and Laurie

PREFACE

In considering these musings of an old man, the reader may choose one of several literary classifications. It might be considered an autobiography since it is the story of my life. However, I have created vehicles to present the story that are fictional. For example, the story of the protagonist charged with a hate crime is imaginary while stories illustrative of character are essentially true. Having the protagonist a widower is contrived; personal encounters with minorities are true.

Were the category of creative non-fiction to find acceptance, it would meet the criterion of truth hidden in illusion that mirrors reality. It is a real story accentuated with non-factual accounts, acceptable if I understand the idiom of adherents to creative non-fiction writing.

It might be thought of as a memoir since it is based on subject matter with which I am familiar and have personal knowledge. Alas, it does not meet the test of objectivity, is not scholarly, and much is subjective relative to my own views and understanding.

In the end, it is to be classified as fiction. Even though based on a true story, it purports to have no relationship to real persons, living or dead. The author does claim credit for the lame attempts at poetry scattered throughout. Finally, it is a love story for romantics.

Growing up and spending my entire life in Mississippi, I have ideas that are shaded by experiences that may be unique to this Southern state. Naturally, work and travel to other venues influence one's world view. Under the veneer of rational progressivism, I have thought of myself as moderately liberal. When defenses for liberality are peeled away, it is instructive to look deeply at the leftover. The question is whether one has built a façade of civility that belies hidden traits that are fundamental in determining who we are. My objective here was to investigate what has been retained and what has been abandoned. Are we awash with good intentions that are compromised by something more basic to our nature?

PROLOGUE

It was a glorious day. Leaves beneath my feet proclaimed the harshness of winter wear, anticipating budding replacements just pushing shades of green faces against an azure sky. The trail snaked past decaying logs secreting that musky aroma so reminiscent of dying life cycles. Irregular rows of lichen, wallpaper mushrooms, stood in clusters like corrugated fans adorning tree trunks. Tall oaks and patches of hickory retreated, expanding the pathway, opening a panoramic view of lake and forest with the house in the distance, beyond spring-fed water. The house, built in my younger days, sat majestically on a hill reflective on a lake of fifteen acres. The A-frame protruded like a Spanish galleon with a breast of glass extending three stories. At my feet, ipomoea, morning glory, climbed up pampas-like grass, thatching the roof of a beaver dam. Sun, topping tall pines, chased the dew. Rivulets of stream water, seeping through a spot where careless beavers had neglected to tighten their span, left moist silage to cushion my step.

Mid-day heat and humidity followed up a high hill into a path of thick white oaks on a downward steepness leaning to a dry creek. Sweat pooled upon my naked arm. The gun I carried slid with the cadence of my stride. The gun, an after-thought, was in deference to Maggie, who had an aversion to cottonmouth moccasins that hang around lake water.

Maggie, long gone now, the love of my life.

Thick dry leaves scattered beneath my boots, leading the way to a huge beech tree marking the depth of an extreme slope. I braced myself with young saplings fighting for hillside space. Slipping and sliding, I sat on my butt to avoid a fall. With my gun held high, tree roots halted my progression as a dark shadow blurred my vision, my last remembrance until she spoke. "But, Poppy, I love him!"

CHAPTER I

The courtroom on the third floor rose atop offices housing Lafayette County officials. There was space for the circuit clerk, tax assessor, and other administrators. Steep polished banisters, circa 1874, wound around rooms to house minor officials and ended on an alcove facing ten-foot double doors. Inside, benches faced a three-foot walnut barrier with swinging doors that allowed admission to a raised platform affording a boxed area for the jury and tables on the north and south sides. There was space for court clerks and a slightly raised chair for questioning those who might testify before the assembly. The second rise accommodated a podium for the United States magistrate court judge.

A uniformed deputy held the door for Lafayette County Sheriff Bert Roberts, who led a small procession, including me, a stoop-shouldered old man of 82-plus years. A dozen all-white citizens sat to my left on hard, straight-backed benches. To the right, across the aisle, twice as many African Americans with a smattering of whites turned to watch our small number proceed frontward through the swinging doors and settle at tables that now included separate lawyers who had appeared from offices beyond the courtroom.

Turning to the white side of the audience, I recognized my two daughters. Valerie was crying. Lois stared straight ahead, unseeing. Tom, my son-in-law, sat straight-laced, his drab brown suit blending with the bench. A few friends, stone-faced, occupied rows of solemn people I thought of as church folk waiting their turn for Communion. The room was still, the kind of stillness that cries for any distraction, a nervous cough, a shift in position, any auditory evidence of cosmic continuance. There are moments before a storm when the sky is still, and we hold our breath, waiting. There is an awareness that a sudden, impending clash is just over the horizon, but now is a pause for preparation.

So instructed, the audience rose for the entrance of Judge Wilmer K. Longest. Settled on the bench, Judge Longest peered over half-glasses and declared the court in session. The clerk of the court announced the docket case number and the subject of this preliminary hearing.

"Ladies and gentlemen, good morning. We are gathered today to conduct a preliminary hearing in the case of the United States of America versus James T. Warner. Is Mr. Warner present in the courtroom?"

I struggled to stand. "Yes, Your Honor." The voice did not seem to be mine. It shook and faltered, echoing from some distant space unknown. I did not recognize that voice. There was the dry mouth and shaking body, but surely I was not present. This had to be some other person standing to face this hostile adversary. I must be sitting in the chair next to this body that speaks so tentatively. After all, I am a lawyer. I have a degree in law, membership in the Mississippi Bar Association, and am licensed to practice by the Mississippi Supreme Court. Admittedly, I have pursued other careers and never tried a case, but I have faithfully attended continuing education classes, paid bar dues all these years and, therefore, I am qualified to represent clients in legal matters.

"Mr. Warner, are you represented by counsel?"

Still standing, holding tightly to the table in front of me that hid trembling legs, I was unable to speak. I could not find a voice.

"Walter Dunbar here, Your Honor, representing Mr. Warner."

Yes, a friend, a lawyer representing me. What was he doing here? We had been meeting—had been talking. Yes, I do remember.

From the bench, "Mr. Warner, you may sit down."

"Yes, thank you," that strange voice I heard again.

"Is the state ready?"

"Yes, Your Honor. Lawrence Greenwood, United States attorney, Northern District of Mississippi, for the prosecution."

Prosecution? What prosecution? Yes, I remember now.

"Mr. Warner, you have been charged with a hate crime, first-degree murder. How do you plead?"

Murder? Hate? Surely there is some mistake. I must defend myself. I attempted to stand, but Walt jumped to his feet.

"My client pleads not guilty, Your Honor."

In the distance, I heard or remembered I heard talk of bond and risk of flight. In my mind's store, I knew how unusual it was to release anyone charged with a capital offense. But the risk of flight or the propensity for a repetitive crime or danger to one's self or others was ridiculous chatter. I ignore these details with the assurance that lawyers must argue for one thing or another. It's their calling, so inclined to extend billable hours.

O n the way home, I stopped at the county library. I needed to know more about this charge of "hate crime." My law books are a bit dated, and what little I know are newspaper reports that sensationalize criminal cases that purport to have been motivated by some intense hatred for the victim. I guess I had assumed that if you decided to kill someone, that person was someone you didn't particularly care about. Unless it was a mercy killing.

The Mississippi Code Annotated was fairly general on the subject and, I gathered, seldom used. Most of the cases I found had been litigated in the federal courts. I quickly found there was no standard legal definition of a hate crime. It might involve any number of misdemeanors, assault, vandalism, murder —all of which might already have penalties. A hate crime adds an extra penalty if motivated by bias against any number of characteristics or beliefs held by the victim. In other words, more punishment than would be the case if the perpetrator was pure of heart.

My question had to do with whether or not a dead man is entitled to more consideration if he belonged to a protected category. Protection seems afforded for bias against race, religion, sexual orientation, ethnicity, national origin, disability, and perhaps others.

Legal "hate crime actions" listed everything from lynching black children purely because they were black to dragging a homosexual man behind a truck because he was gay, to Amish men shorn of their beards because they didn't strictly adhere to the Amish religious doctrine. Evidently, that sect requires a beard to communicate with the Great Master. I asked myself where my action fell among those atrocities. More important to me is why I did what I did and what influence race had on my own action. I must discover what is deep within my psyche, what drives my motivation.

But, I'm getting ahead of myself as I'm prone to do these days.

The incident happened more than a year ago. I have trouble keeping things straight. When I'm confused like this, I just revert back to happier times.

Presently, I am home, back with Maggie—Maggie, on a windy day, ashes spread over the land, lo these dozen years. Sitting on a deck she supervised the building of; I look across hanging wisteria to the distant tree-line, past the little lake house she cherished. Just maybe she is there prone in a hammock, a computer on her lap, working on a project for her business. Perhaps she is in the house, on the side porch with Cheddar, the cat, ever pursuing her passion for creating a better life for groups she serves. I see her on every ripple of water, every shape and form of scattered cloud and in every ray of sunshine.

But, I know it is an illusion. She is gone. I hold these pictures in my head these days. Reality is fuzzy, the past clearly and purely presented in rainbow colors. I see India pink spigelia, cardinal flower, sumac, passion flower, and goldenrod leaning beside a hot, winding, dusty road.

It was on such a day we met, a day when the Texas star hibiscus outside my window limply listed toward a budding seed capsule. August heat in humidity-laced currents spiraled downward. Dispirited dew drops, too dry to reach earth, evaporated mid-air. Even an occasional breeze forgot a path to the small campus apartment building that resolutely held space from new construction invading a scrubby lawn. It was a Saturday. Students who failed to leave on Thursday had abandoned this house of learning for a carefree weekend, the last before summer session ended.

A divorced forty-two year old, mid-level university employee, I sweated in the apartment that pre-dated air conditioning. Supporting my family from the failed marriage left little for an expansive lifestyle. A faded couch sat sadly on a dingy brown rug whose shag lay prone. Side tables and a green Naugahyde recliner positioned in a semi-circle looked to a small kitchen accommodating a plastic-topped table with four straight-backed chairs. The back half of this euphemistically dubbed "square architecture" contained a bath and bedroom. There were eight such stacked boxes with mini-courts dominated by open stairways. My casa on the second floor faced street-side, which provided an opportunity to engage passing fumes and noisy traffic. Avoiding the stack of bills anticipated to exceed numbers on a monthly check carelessly tossed aloft, I watched through the grime of an unwashed window as an older maroon Oldsmobile slowly pulled into a vacant parking spot. Obviously a hippie student, the young girl driver with long black hair streaming down to her ass leaped out to direct a Rent-All maneuvering to the front building entrance. Unshaven, dressed in polyester khakis and a t-shirt with under-arms spoiled from countless deodorant applications, I hastened down steps to offer needed directions. In my haste, I missed that damn last step as my face was unceremoniously introduced to an exceedingly warm sidewalk, all the more inviting from neighborhood cats utilizing that area to relieve bodily morning stress.

"Shit!" My verbal outburst was the most appropriate descriptive expression I could think of at the moment. Unhurt, I struggled to my knees. Dark eyes of concern were focused on me. They belonged to a young person whose short, short skirt from a squatting position revealed a most attractive woman. She was down on her knees with me on the stained concrete.

"Are you hurt?" she managed.

"Noo—no—just embarrassed."

"Let me help you?"

"No!" Scrambling to my feet, I almost screamed, "This is not student housing! These are faculty/staff apartments. You're two streets over, but fall check-in will not be possible for at least two weeks. You'd better talk with student housing, which is near the campus center. Just follow the signs."

I didn't offer to help her up. After all, this kid was fifteen to twenty years younger than me, and her intrusion had caused me to be in hot August sun with sidewalk crud on my face.

"I'm Maggie Boyd, a new instructor. I've been assigned to apartment 2 B."

"Oh! Oh, I thought you were a student—not that you look like—

I'm so sorry. I just assumed—"

A lyrical note of laughter only heightened the deepening blush creeping up my face, augmenting stifling heat.

"It's okay. This is my first teaching job. Fresh health sciences Ph.D. from the University of Oklahoma Medical School. I'll be starting a graduate program in audiology and, probably, will have students older than me. Anyway, I'm scared as hell and, right now, quite as hot."

"I'm sorry. Thoughtless of me. Come on up. I'm across the hall in A. I'll try to find something cold."

"Don't apologize. My parents are helping me move in. We'll be right up, Mr.—er?"

Damn, I hadn't even introduced myself. Suddenly, I was cognizant of my disheveled appearance and, for some inexplicable reason, highly agitated. I quickly uttered, "Jim Warner," and fled upstairs.

The weighty slap of leather on the top step announced strangers invading my space and serenity.

Chapter 2

"Good news, Mr. Warner. The district attorney is not calling for a grand jury. There will be no indictment. It will be ruled an accident —an unfortunate incident but not an act of planned aggression."

I was in the porch swing looking out over a patch of jonquils that suddenly stood taller with a sharper hue of gold butter. "That is good news, Walt."

"We still have to be prepared for a civil action. Preston Howell is in town, making speeches and turning up the rhetoric. I'd recommend you not go in, and I'll ask the sheriff to have a deputy schedule periodic checks of this place."

"Oh, that won't be necessary Walt. People around here know me. They know that I wouldn't willfully hurt a flea. Besides, this is Oxford, not Ferguson. Here, people vote and use political and economic means to settle differences. They demonstrate peacefully. They don't riot."

"Yeah, but we still need to be careful. There's a rumor that others are drifting into town, just waiting to see if the judicial system works."

"Is the judicial system working, Walt? Does the public have a right to know why I did what I did – what was my motivation?"

"Come on, Mr. Warner, that's crazy talk. There is little pressure from the public at this point. You know it was an unthinking reaction. You just made a mistake."

"But why, Walt? These last few days, I've been asking myself why. There are so many questions. I can't seem to get a handle on it."

"Mr. Warner, don't be so hard on yourself. Don't you think we all do stupid things sometimes, without thinking? Don't question your re-action. The sheriff considered it an accident; the district attorney didn't press charges, and you were released by the court."

"I know that I should be filled with relief at all of that, but Walt, deep down in my gut, I wonder."

"Wonder what, Mr. Warner?"

"Can't you guess, Walt?"

"I don't understand."

"I don't understand either, Walt. I don't understand the why of it— and I have questions."

"What kind of questions?"

"Well, for one thing, would the who of it have made a difference?"

"Mr. Warner, I have no idea what you're talking about. But I do know this. You can not change your initial statement that it was an in-voluntary reaction to a mistaken perception of a crime in progress. Stop questioning your motives. They have nothing to do with what happened. Stop second guessing. It only adds fuel for the other side."

"Walt, why is there an other side?"

"Mr. Warner, I don't need to explain human nature—greed, revenge, and the like. If I am to represent you, we must be realistic. The old adage about loose lips sinking ships is applicable here. Just you relax and give no interviews. Let me handle your case."

"I know. You're right. I just wonder."

The following day, I drove up the lane to the main road that curved through pine and hardwood forest to approach the north highway to town. Along the banks, black-eyed Susan spread golden yellow petals in centrifugal array from coffee-colored spheres. Strange, that as a child, we called them "nigger navels" or in country folks' talk, "nigger nabels." These beautiful and hardy volunteer plants lack little associated color or visual structure to deserve such association. Well, that's another question to be pondered.

In the meantime, along the road, I saw violets sprinkled in unplanned isometric patterns. Eleven miles of radio news gave more pause for broadening my concerns beyond a windshield splattered with departed locust parts splayed in isochromatic figures reflecting morning light. God, those boogers appear every number of years like clockwork. They feast on the corn crop, and many end up on windshields.

ISIS in Iran and Egypt, United Nations and NATO meetings, Shiite vs. Sunni, Israel vs. Palestine, Russia vs. Ukraine, Libya, Somalia, Egypt, and other conflicts evade understanding. Talking heads expand on these and other problems, dissecting without any specific solutions, mimicking administration and congressional actions. It occurs to me that this state of affairs might very well be related to the black-eyed Susan. It has been mislabeled and misunderstood, yet it keeps coming back.

Facing the Confederate statute looking southward, I circled the unique Square for a non-existing parking spot, waving Carmen Eagles to back out of her convenient location. I motioned and yelled with no response. Well, Carmen probably didn't recognize me. Down by Neilson's Department Store, I raised my arm to salute Wiley Grant. I've known him for over forty years. Head down, Wiley crossed to the other side of the street.

"Howdy, boys" I said, to a couple of black fellows who sat on a bench near the courthouse. They didn't acknowledge me, but one spat on the grass as I passed. I made note that I had called them "boys," a habit of many years when addressing more than one male of any color. Maybe I should watch that.

The minority circuit clerk whom I had helped to elect left the front counter as I entered. Guess she had business in the back office. I was served with quiet courtesy at Regions Bank, but there was an air of formality I had not experienced before. Must be tired of my corny jokes. All in all, it was not a usual day. The buildings were the same, the streets were familiar, but the air had somehow become polluted. Oh, people were smiling, shaking hands, chatting away, but only shy, uncomfortable eye contact was cast my way. Will Pickings did shake my hand but was too busy on an important errand to stop for a chat. Almost on cue, a willowy dark cloud appeared on an otherwise sunny morning, and rain spattered the sidewalk.

I thought of the illusive nature of reputation, of friendship, perhaps even of love. And I was ashamed. Ashamed of unkind words and deeds I have said or done. I thought of the failed marriage and living apart from children I could no longer provide challenge or direction. Yes, we are deluded into thinking the past is past, that nothing survives. Three categories of shame: that which we do, that we have to do, and that we fail to do. As a sharecropper's son, I had to beg and borrow. Oh, on my own I achieved an education, a modicum of respect, some recognition, modest wealth. But the shame of the past! Youthful stealing of useless trinkets, taking a pocket knife from a neighbor, taking advantage of girls who confused my hormonal lust for an expression of caring, facing the dishonor of my most recent shameful act—these things stamp me as undeliverable correspondence. I have, however, strived for excellence and respectability. Now, all of that effort seems for naught.

I Built My Own Wagon But Gave It Away

Mr. Gordon, Daddy said could borrow?
Taint no difference, today or tomorrow.
Well shore we got a respectable team,
Butch and Nellie, or so they seem,
To git you there and git you back,
Just the family and the vittles we pack.
First in ages Momma had a holiday.
I built my own wagon but gave it away.

Butch would take it, never complain,
Plodding and pulling, content to strain.
Nellie was different, an ornery cuss,
She never was hitched without a fuss,
Balking, her traces hanging slack,
No matter the flailing cross her back.
Knowing her tail'ud be tied single tree,
Ole Nellie expressed her will to be free.

How's that hoss pull with her tail?
Priss'in and pawing, a'crowing the rail?
Her head held high and neck erect,
Every effort in the form of a jerk.
Proving no son-of-a-bitch could,
Force surrender, even for her own good,
Chose resistance, yet had to pay.
I built my own wagon but gave it away.

Say, Ned, gimmie your used nub,
You smoked it down to a pitiful stub.
I'll buy my tobacco when I kin,
Pay you back from top of the tin.
In private to gaze at a faded prince.
Ain't he a dude now, who's to say?
I built my own wagon but gave it away.

Boy, what makes you so proud?
Give a little, take from the crowd.
It don't hurt none to be dirt pore,
God'll return, fourfold or more.
You put in Miss-sippi an extra I,
As if to get bigger pieces of pie.
Chip on the shoulder, high it lay,
I built my own wagon but gave it away.

Everything here belongs to me
House, position, friends I see.
Sharing and loving without thought,
Who's to sell and who's bought.
That image on a Prince Albert can,
Where's the boy and where's the man?
Why lose it all now, did you say?
I built my own wagon but gave it away.

I realize now that I must cast aside all illusions about friends and legacy. Face reality. For myself, I must discover the truth that may go back generations. Still, I presently ignore the truth of calcified bones, arthritic ankles, and inner ear equilibrium issues. I fantasize an adagio of constant grace as I walk in the falling rain to my chariot that will take me to Wyldewoode, my land, spread with the ashes of my greatest accomplishment, Maggie, the young Ph.D. who moved into the apartment on the Ole Miss campus.

Off-and-on showers played on gutter spouts, issuing mournful copper tunes, whirling a vortex of sorrow to my receptive ears. Ordinarily, this would be restful music for a nap to escape a lousy day. Today, I sit long hours in an easy chair, lost in a series of hard reflections competing for reason and understanding. Why do we make assumptions based upon appearance or language or where one lives or their friends or habits or any number of factors entirely unrelated to who a person really is?

Recently, I shopped at Kroger, and as I was putting groceries in the car, someone came running across the parking lot shouting at me. It was a muscular young black teenager with a cap turned backward and pants dragging the pavement. My first thought was that I should jump into the vehicle and lock the door. I assumed that this person was up to no good and probably made his living attacking old men in parking lots. But, I noticed that he was waving something in his hand. It was a twenty dollar bill.

"Mister," he said, "I was behind you at the checkout counter, and you dropped this twenty dollar bill." Handing the money to me, he ran back toward the store displaying the crack in his butt that showed just above his underwear.

I was so taken aback that I didn't even offer a reward! Without any evidence, I had pre-judged that young man. I had to ask myself if that was a manifestation of prejudice. Had it been a white gentleman in a business suit, would my reaction have been the same?

This "judging a book by its cover" has been a part of my experience in observing people from whatever walk of life or area of the world in which I have had the opportunity to visit. When I was a professional traveling for the university or acting as a consultant during the 1960s and '70s, hotel clerks might glance at my Mississippi address and feel compelled to express solidarity with what they considered my feelings about race. From Chicago to New York or Los Angeles, I might expect a remark that they understood how I felt about blacks and for good reason.

In 1963, shortly after the enrollment of the first black student at the University of Mississippi, the institution sensed a need to reach out to the larger educational community to repair some of the negative perceptions attendant rioting and political interference threatening the heart of independent thinking in higher education. Various staff members were asked for proposals to approach regional and national organizations and seek membership that might give us an opportunity to show the world that some Mississippians actually "wear shoes." The assignment was to become active in the professional groups associated with our particular area of university employment. One of the areas for which I was responsible was student financial aid. A few years later, after some success in becoming involved in that group, I was asked to seek membership, on behalf of the University, in the College Entrance Examination Board. The CEEB membership, at that time, was primarily composed of Eastern and West Coast colleges and universities. By and large, they were private colleges. With the development of the American College Testing program, CEEB had competition for its array of college entrance testing and need-analysis systems for student-aid programs. The Board was anxious to expand the market of products to state institutions, land grant, community colleges and others. All this coincided with my appointment as dean of admissions and registrar at Ole Miss.

My first venture into the culture of the College Entrance Examination Board was an annual meeting in New York City at the Waldorf-Astoria Hotel. For a country boy, this was an astounding experience. The first luncheon meeting was held in the hotel's voluminous ballroom with a couple of thousand representatives from throughout the nation. There were huge round tables seating perhaps fifteen people. Someone suggested we go round the table and introduce ourselves and name the institution we represented. There were people from all over, some government officials, but primarily large and small private schools. Everything went well until my turn. In the best "northern" impression I could muster, I announced my name and that I represented the University of Mississippi. Immediately, from a small table-mate to my right, there was a loud "awhh" followed by an even louder expiration of air.

The outburst was followed by what I considered an inappropriate harangue castigating the South, our racist attitudes, and moral values. She threw in "outrageous" and "evil" and other words I considered unfriendly.

When the venom slowed, and she had not yet introduced herself, I spoke. "I'm sorry, ma'am, you sound so well informed. Who are you and what do you do?"

She raised her chin from her white bib and said: "I am Sister Catherine from Holy Mother, and I teach history—but not from your perspective, of course."

"I'm sorry," I said. "I was not aware that history was taught from a perspective. How do you know what I think or feel?"

Other folks at the table were embarrassed, but almost all gave my retort a polite clap. The little nun tucked her chin in her bib and ate her soup.

I made a vow to myself to remember never to judge someone by where they were from. I also promised myself that I was going to become an important part of this "chicken-shit" organization. It never occurred to me that an entire group could not be judged by one of its members. I had broken the vow just made.

Actually, The College Entrance Examination Board was and is an outstanding organization that has provided needed services to higher education over the years, and it gave me opportunities for development that might never have been possible had the confrontation with Sister Catherine not occurred. Three years later, I had the good fortune to be elected nationally to the eighteen-member Board of Trustees of The College Entrance Examination Board.

An acceptance of rumor in the absence of evidence has been a part of my dealings with people. Perhaps it is the fear of being wrong in our assessment of others that drives this total rejection of logic.

When I was ten years old, my little Feist dog and I were inseparable. He followed at my heels by day and warmed my feet at night. I loved the mutt and shared food intended for me in the scarcity of the times. Poochie was my companion and confidant. We ran the path and drove the cow and roped the mules for plowing. There was a rumor that a "mad" dog was sighted in the community. It seems that none could be identified as hearing dog fights, seen a dog suspected of being infected with rabies, or indeed, observing a strange dog attacking human or animal. Still, there was the anxiety, the uncertainty, the fear that the rumor might be true. It was daybreak, and I awoke to find Daddy taking down the shotgun from a bedroom rack. (Back then in a relatively large family, children and parents might sleep in the same room.) Daddy loaded the gun and slipped out to the corncrib to search for a rope. He had planned to take care of the problem before the rest of the family were awake. I was on the ground holding Poochie around the neck when Daddy came around the smokehouse with gun over his shoulder and a plow line in his hand.

"Don't do it, Daddy!"

"Let me have that dog, boy."

"Look, Daddy, look—Poochie ain't seen a mad dog. I been with him most all day long every day."

"Your Momma thought she heard dogs barking last night."

"Look, Daddy, Poochie ain't been in a fight—don't have a scratch on 'im. Please, Daddy!"

Momma was up by then and grabbed me to her.

"Son, we can't take the chance," she said without feeling.

"Please, Daddy—Please—Please—Please—Please!"

Struggling and squalling uncontrollably, I watched the rope circle Poochie's neck and Daddy lead him away, passing the barn, over the pasture and into the woods beyond a patch of Kudzu bordering the field of cotton.

Like a swirling tornado, the roar traveled through the circle of trees, beyond the cotton house and up the dusty road delineating the dog trot shack where I stood transfixed. In the echo, I clearly saw buckshot shattering nearby bushes while Poochie, tied to a tree, awaited his fate.

I hated my parents for a long time after that. It was also moving day for us—to another sharecropper's cabin half a day away by wagon. Just as well, I supposed. I was never able to visit Poochie. Later, even though I never understood the reason, I did realize that determining the health of a dog was unrealistic in that day and time. Even if doing so could be justified and afforded, the county had only one veterinarian, and his job was to treat horses and pluck after-birth from heifers that had just dropped what would someday be a milk cow to feed hungry bellies. My parents had been practical in eliminating a potential risk. However, even today,

I wonder how we can act, not on the basis of any scientific information, but rather on the fear of uncertainty.

Now, I try to think of my family. Valerie, my first born, a delightful child with an unusual capacity to accept and understand. With an unconditional love, she considered the frailties of her father. She had one daughter, Summer. I thought it an odd name, but it rolled off one's tongue like a breath of spring or a crisp winter snowflake. Summer, blonde and beautiful with skin touched by an angel. Bright blue eyes that shined on Poppy and melted his heart.

In the present, my vision sees puzzlement and hurt.

"But Poppy, I love him!"

Another major reason to look at the "who."

Trying to push that image to the subconscious, I sought to think of happier times. Maggie had moved into an apartment across the hall. Another bachelor friend, Ishmael, completed our triangle on the second floor. The two of us strained at unloading the van, including negotiating stairs with a battered piano, the general condition of which served to negate new chips and scratches. Her mother and father pitched in, and Mom mastered unfamiliar kitchen appliances to prepare dinner. They left the following day with an admonition that I was to take care of their little girl. Ishmael and I took the job seriously. The three of us became best buddies, ate alternate meals at each of the three apartments, and bummed around together. There was seldom an activity that the three of us attended separately. By that time, I was traveling frequently to represent the university at regional and national organization meetings. I had met a lady from Raleigh, which was a convenient stop-over to Washington or New York City. She was nine years my senior, very intelligent, and well-traveled. And she taught me many things. Meanwhile, with the twenty-five-year age span between her and Maggie, I had no romantic attraction for the kid. I'm not so sure the same went for Ishmael.

One night there was a Philharmonic Orchestra performance in Memphis. Ishmael couldn't go.

Having returned from Memphis, we sat on my brown shag rug and listened to Neil Diamond tunes. No wine in the place, we shared a lemonade. In the shaded light, I suddenly realized that Maggie was a beautiful, mature woman. For some reason, still a mystery to me, we both reached for a bowl of popcorn. Each hand hesitated in mid-air, and each altered progression as a race driver might negotiate a ninety-degree curve. Fingers touched—first the thumb and, as if automated, each finger sought that of the other—not to grasp, but to come within proximity. Neither spoke, feeling electricity like a connected plug speeds current over space to produce an immediate shock. Our extended digits touched and lingered, sending magnetic charges. Perhaps the spark was generated by movement over carpet, perhaps some hidden electrical cord or some cosmic calamity elicited the jolt. But it was strong and sure and lasting. The kiss and progression of intimacy was slow and natural.

Sheepishly, I confessed that I did not have a condom. Maggie ran across the hall to return with an unopened package, a diaphragm kit. Nervous laughter accompanied the slitting of plastic to read instructions. At that point, we stopped and looked at each other. We decided to enjoy just being close this night in a warm bed. I visited the drug store first thing the next morning

Ishmael was a Palestinian who was sponsored by Saudi Arabia to come to America for graduate study. Pennsylvania State University was a long way from the small West Bank community of his birth. I can only imagine the strength of character and courage that prompted him to leave that culture and adopt a new country. He arrived at Penn State to receive orientation by a Jordanian Arab. Unfortunately, that individual had only one day on campus before he left for California. They went to a restaurant and ordered Salisbury steak. For the next three weeks, Ishmael ate Salisbury steak. Even though he was not a practicing Muslim, he was attuned to his cultural background that included an aversion to pork. Not understanding English food titles, he was deathly afraid of eating pork. The only food he was damn sure he couldn't eat was ham or hamburger. After Ishmael's being associated with me, his culinary tastes broadened, even to a great appreciation for turnip greens. I never disclosed to him that, in the South, a basic ingredient for turnip greens was a healthy slab of sow belly.

More than friends, Ishmael and I became more like brothers, each engaging in practical jokes. After Maggie and I became an item, Ishmael began dating Betty and fell in love. Once, when I knew that she was in his apartment, I called imitating a campus policeman. I informed Ishmael that he was violating law and university moral responsibility by having someone of the opposite sex with him alone in his apartment. It was not a very nice thing to do. I had not thought of customs in his home country and his fear of authority. He finally forgave me.

Maggie and I watched the flowering romance with Betty and anticipated that both wanted marriage and family. By chance, I saw him at the campus health service and deduced that he might be having a blood test for the marriage license. I called Ishmael assuming the identity of the health service doctor. I told him there was a problem, evidently a result of his being with loose women. He nearly choked before deciding that it was one of my practical jokes. Looking back, it was a fairly sick joke and wasn't nearly the fun I expected it to be.

All was forgiven. Betty and Ishmael married with me as best man and Maggie as bridesmaid. They enjoyed a beautiful life together and raised two great kids. The four of us remained close, and when Ishmael passed away, I was honored to speak at his celebration of life service. I loved the little Arab. Now, I wonder if my practical jokes might qualify as hate crimes.

Recalling incidents and people who are a part of my life and those I care for, I find myself in the midst of a melancholy mood. It was early evening, and I decided to go to bed. Sometimes, living alone, the hassle of preparing a meal is not considered important. So, I skipped supper. I lay in my bed, not caring. Sleep was fitful, dreams terrifying, even more frightful than the smell of smoke drifting through an open window. Flames were lilting toward the night sky, dancing in an effort to catch dazzling sparks cascading ahead. Springing from my bed as fast as an old man springs, I surveyed a lighted lawn dominated by a huge illuminated cross in contrast to a moonless sky.

CHAPTER 3

"But, what does it mean, Walt? Where is this nonsense going?"

"I really don't know, Mr. Warner."

"You're my lawyer, Walt. You must have some idea."

"I'm your attorney, but I don't have a crystal ball. I thought this thing had died down. There had been some loose talk, but no one could have anticipated what developed. Remember, I told you that civil rights advocates were about. Evidently, they fanned the flames, and with record unemployment, poverty, and a sense of the lack of political empowerment, the minority community is responding."

"But, the violence, the stuff I'm seeing on TV."

"So far, Mr. Warner, it's confined to the outlying areas of the city and with relatively minor damage—a few windows smashed and limited looting. Bisett Drugs was likely the work of addicts looking for pills. Someone just wanted food from Jones Grocery. Protest marches are small and organized by people who live somewhere else."

"Why would anyone not from the county be involved?"

"Oh, there are sincere people who see an opportunity to advance a cause, there are mere opportunists advancing their own agenda, and there are those who want to be a part of the action irrespective of any commitment to a particular ideology."

"Will it get worse?"

"We'll just have to wait and see. A petition has been filed with the justice department. Mind you, I don't think it likely, but a federal grand jury could be called. Mississippi has a statute dealing with what some classify as a "hate" crime, but that doesn't mean the Federal Government is not empowered to act on its own even if a local entity fails to indict."

"What are the chances?"

"In my opinion, small, but you never can predict public pressure or the political ambition of a federal prosecutor."

"What should we do?"

"Just wait. We have no choice. Already action has been taken to secure your property. The sheriff is most cooperative. I've been in touch with state officials who will take measures to keep things under control. Plans have been made to move you to another location if that becomes necessary."

"My Lord! But, what about that cross? I can't understand using that kind of protest—that KKK symbol of repression visited upon black people. A cross burned on my lawn!"

"Mr. Warner, you forget that burning crosses were also used against white people who sympathized with minority causes. I don't need to remind you of the white attorney in Vicksburg who died when his office was bombed or the white students who ended up in a muddy grave in Philadelphia or any number of atrocities aimed at Caucasian citizens."

"I know, Walt, but in this day and time—and on my lawn!"

"The motive is the same, Mr. Warner, to strike fear."

"Well, I'm not afraid. I'm mad as hell!"

Walt's tires made crunching sounds on white driveway rock, reminiscent of sounds visited on a plastic bottle by a white German Shepard puppy Maggie brought home. Those were the early years when career building balanced with frugality. As the sound of the automobile faded in the distance, I took a blood pressure pill and contemplated the fading visual evidence of her being. The garden was still bare save some herbs wrestling with Bermuda grass that had grown brown above the deep green. Smooth sumac and goldenrod at the edge of my shop had already succumbed to early frost. Only the beauty berry, sans leaves, cast a purple glow against the clump of cedar.

We married in the home of a mutual university friend, a plantation farmhouse thought to be the model for Faulkner's "Frenchman's Bend," located near the Yoknapawtapha River. Shelloy and Ben were determined to saw the house in half for moving ten miles north to be restored beyond a levy road on a hill by the lake. A full moon rose as we crossed the dam to white columns with only candlelight peeking through. A small group of friends and family together with a professor who at one time had been a minister awaited us. Maggie in her long, twenty-dollar white dress looked every bit the glowing youngster, exacerbating the fact that she was seventeen years my junior. Having written our own vows, we quoted liberally from *The Prophet* by the Lebanese poet, Kahlil Gibran.

Love gives naught of itself and takes naught of itself.
Love possesses not, nor would it be possessed;
For love is sufficient unto love.
When you love you should not say, God is in my heart,
But, rather, I am in the heart of God
And think not you can direct the course of love,

For love, if it finds you worthy, directs your course.

Love has no other desire but to fulfill itself.

But if you love and must need have desires, let these be your desires:

To melt and be like a running brook that sings its melody into the night.

To know the pain of too much tenderness.

To be wounded by your own understanding of love;

And to bleed willingly and joyfully.

To wake at dawn with a winged heart

And give thanks for another day of loving.

People wisecracked about the age difference and speculated about how long the marriage would last. Still, after almost thirty years, it was ended by an unpronounceable micro-organism. It had no regard for me or the fact that this woman had gained the respect of my two children and made them her own, that she loved them and cared for them until the end. What advice would she have for me now that I see the daughter of one of those children standing along a creek by a huge beech tree sobbing—"But Poppy, I love him!"

I awoke from my reminiscing of happier times with the realization that the present was disconcerting. Reluctantly, I made my way to an appointment with my attorney.

"Well, Mr. Warner, at least the federal grand jury indictment stopped the rioting and calmed the natives. Now we have to concentrate on defending our action and establishing a reasonable explanation for what occurred."

"Is there a reasonable explanation for what occurred, Walt?"

"Mr. Warner, let's focus. We're here to identify folks who are steadfast friends and can create a positive image. Forget about setting any record straight or attempting to establish reasons or motivations. You've got to be the guy in the white hat, the upstanding citizen, the squeaky-clean fellow who, when placed in a stressful situation, chose to react in a completely reasonable and understandable fashion. You have been a community leader and never accused of any crime or behavior that would constitute a threat to law and order. You are a model of discretion and consideration for your fellow man."

"I completely understand your strategy. But Walt, tactical maneuvering does not change the facts. I am no hero. I am not a perfect human being. I am an average person with average warts. I am interested in the bigger picture, a broader interpretation. It's not that I really care about what people think of me, rather, it's what meaning I can make of it for myself."

"Mr. Warner, are you going to let me conduct this trial or not? I am unable to defend someone who is set on self-destruction."

"I'm sorry Walt, I'll try to be good—but, I do reserve the right to testify."

"We'll cross that bridge when necessary, but I do strongly advise against you taking the stand."

I left Walt's office resolved to face the reality of what I had done by visiting again that sandy stream meandering by a huge beech tree.

Turks-cap, hearts a bustin', and wild hibiscus lined the pathway now. It has been over a year, and New England aster spreads a hillside. For the first time, I attempt to re-create a scene I've tried to repress. Now, the trail is littered with fallen branches and leaves with sticks breaking through, accusing neglect. With so much litter, wildflowers diminish in the mind's eye. There is no gun, no bounce to my step and only a casual acknowledgement of the beauty of the day.

I must have studiously observed the ground to escape any appreciation of the landscape for, at the bottom of a hollowed sweet gum tree, I spied a pink blob. Kneeling, I retrieved the baby possum and observed a newborn, "kitten-sized" animal. Convinced that the possum is the ugliest creature inhabiting my kingdom, I was surprised at the beauty of this small bundle. Too young for hair and with un-opened eyes, the delicate pink flesh and intricate structural features reminded me of the beauty of nature and the relentless progression of the life cycle. Ordinarily, I would think of the possum as a predator to be destroyed. Its ancestors invaded my hen house and were forever tipping a garbage can as they foraged for scraps. But this little fella was so pretty and so vulnerable. It had probably fallen from the belly or tail of the mother as she scampered to avoid my tramping feet. I've seen before at least a dozen holding fast as their parent ran to avoid danger. This one was quite young and possibly was unable to hang on. Reasoning that Momma would miss one of her many, I gently placed baby by the hollow tree. Surely, she would return and care for her own. In my state of mind, I left it there without thought of any responsibility.

My attention diverted to a blazing star and a liatris aspera plant with a huge monarch butterfly stealing milk from its flower. Is it really stealing, or is the wildflower dependent on that sucking mouthpart to propagate its image? Somewhere in the eerie land of evolution was there a pact which read—"you share your milk, and I will be your semen." Maybe that's why we're told to be our brother's keeper, that the universe is somehow built on a shared responsibility, that our very survival depends upon interaction with others. Maybe it means that I should have done something other than leaving that damn possum.

The beaver dam had collapsed, water rushing over upturned sticks, carrying silt into the lake. Ignoring my wet feet, I trudged up the bank and into the forest. White oak, cedar, hickory, red oak, post oak, persimmon, pine, and more shadowed my path. But it was the unseen barrier that brought me to a halt. An apparition. She stood, her blonde hair catching sunlight dispersed through the branches in radiant color.

"But Poppy, I love him!"

Retracing my steps, I retreated to the sanctuary of a house that love built. I sat in the deck shade watching a retreating sun and desperately tried to tell myself that I was merely preparing for a trial that begins tomorrow.

CHAPTER 4

The lawyers were at their respective tables. Clerks scurried around like scared chickens, scattering papers over mounds of legal briefs and books already stacked in neat rows on polished tops. Jurors, previously selected from a voir dire of eighty-seven, sat in the elevated box, stretching twelve necks to locate family and friends who had dropped by to observe their exercising of their sacred duty. The twelve included five black and seven white citizens of Lafayette County. There were eight men and four women. One, an African American lady in her mid-thirties, gazed at me, the one elderly gentleman sitting with one attorney at the nearest table. Across the way, five others sat at the second table, leaning in for what appeared to be a serious discussion.

After the callings of "hear ye, hear ye!" and the standing, Judge Wilmer K. Longest seated himself, raising his haunches to smooth pleats in his long robe. Judge Longest announced the reason we were here, as if it were breaking news, and addressed the jury with platitudes as to their forced participation. He laid out for them the list of rules. Then it was the proper procedure to turn to the attorneys and call for opening statements.

"Good morning, ladies and gentlemen of the jury. My name is Lawrence Greenwood, your United States attorney for the Fifth Judicial District of Mississippi. As you are aware, this branch of our federal judicial system is designed to protect the citizenry, the people, by prosecuting those who would break federal laws that were enacted for their benefit. We are charged with righting wrongs, enforcing justice, and holding lawbreakers to the standards set by the nation as a whole. We strive to fulfill that purpose without regard to age, sex, race, creed, economic, or political standing or other impediments to a fair and equal treatment of individual citizens. This treatment extends to the constitutional rights of life and liberty of the dead as well as the living. Likewise, that philosophy applies to those who would break the law. Social standing, influence, personality, age, or other characteristics of one who defies the laws of the land are not a consideration. I am sure that each of you will keep those standards in mind as you consider the facts of this case.

"Having alluded to the overall purpose of this trial, I would like to briefly touch on the authority vested in this office and our responsibility to pursue this action. I would refer you to the Civil Rights Act of 1964, 18 U.S. Code 249(a)(1). It is our contention that the accused, James T. Warner, violated 18 United States Code 249(a)(1), willfully causing bodily injury with a dangerous weapon because of the actual and perceived race of one, Artise Bradley Washington. In addition, we contend that The Violent Crime Control Act of 1994 equally applies. That act requires in federal sentencing an increase in penalties for hate crimes committed on the basis of actual or perceived race, color, religion, national origin, ethnicity, or gender of any person. In 1995 the United States Sentencing Commission implemented guidelines that provide increases in penalties applicable only to federal crimes. The perpetrator did not know the victim and could have only acted upon a visual identity of a young black teenager. We contend that Mr. Washington was denied his constitutional right to life, liberty, and the pursuit of happiness; that the accused, James T. Warner, did intentionally, maliciously and without cause shoot and kill Artise Bradley Washington.

The U.S. attorney prosecutes such cases in conjunction with the civil rights division of the United States Department of Justice. Some states have their "so-called" hate crimes statutes. Mississippi has chosen not to invoke such legislation in this case. The United States Justice Department may assume jurisdiction in states where appropriate, and supersede any state statute inconsistent with federal law.

"These actions are not unusual, nor are they confined to those based upon racial discrimination. Contiguous states, as well as Mississippi, have litigated "hate crime" cases. Race-based cases are currently being pursued in Memphis, Jackson, and Panola County.

"In 2009 The Matthew Shepard and James Byrd, Jr. Hate Crimes Act expanded the hate crimes law to include crimes motivated by a victim's actual or perceived gender, sexual orientation, gender identity, or disability and removed the requirement that a federally protected act be involved. Such actions are often brought to address the Shepard Act when a local jurisdiction has chosen not to act. Justice demands that wealth, fame, political influence, and the like are not present to impede fair and equal treatment of victims.

"I call this to your attention and provide this information as background for you, the jury. I want you to understand the authority and purpose for pursuing this action for a more fair and just society. Thank you very much for your attention and for accepting the responsibility to hear this cry for justice."

I paid little attention to the rhetoric, but I did recognize that Larry Greenwood had impressed the jury. He was quiet and grave in his presentation but emphasized his points with appropriate pauses and modulated his voice at all the right places. As a lawyer myself, I could see that Greenwood had, with poise and confidence, identified with the twelve who were to determine my fate. Personal future? What the hell do I care? I'm just an old man with a fading memory who is interested in understanding self rather than measuring life.

Walt was addressing the jury in his opening statement.

"Ladies and gentlemen of the jury, thank you for being here to exercise your civic duty. It is especially laudatory in cases such as this that speak to the very heart of democracy and the relationship between peoples of different ethnic, cultural, racial, economic, and religious backgrounds. Hate crimes by definition must ascertain, beyond a reasonable doubt, the motive of the perpetrator. Ascertaining motive can be extremely difficult. It cannot be shown by forensic or laboratory evidence. To look into the mind and soul of an individual to determine motivation, one must look to circumstantial evidence. The circumstantial evidence in this case is a lifetime of activities and action that speak to a responsible individual who never expressed any prejudice for any human being. Paradoxically, his life could be described as one who fought for equality. As he has lived for over eighty-three years, his contributions to racial harmony are legion.

"Through the course of these proceedings, we will prove that James T. Warner had no motive to act on the basis of race, creed, or color. Instead of exhibiting hatred or bias, this man has spent a lifetime upholding the personal and civil rights of all people. Race was not the reason for this unfortunate, tragic accident—I say accident because no harm was contemplated and no thought of injury to anyone was planned. He did not know the victim, nor did he process his color. He only reacted to what he perceived to be a crime in progress.

"In the course of this event, James T. Warner had no intent or purpose based upon race. His action was race neutral. It was an automatic response. He had no time to set goals, form a racist motive, think of results or the analysis of a thoughtless moment. He did not seek a defined, pre-planned result. Mr. Warner's reaction was visceral, responsive to a perceived violent act—the rape of his granddaughter."

After lunch, the prosecutor called his first witness, a county deputy sheriff, Willie Eagles. Through laborious effort, Greenwood traced events from a call the deputy received from me, informing him that someone had been shot. No, he had not thought to inquire as to the extent of the injury or other details. He did hurry to Wyldewoode to be led by Mr. Warner into the woods to where the body lay by a dry creek bed. He ascertained that it was the body of a dead black male, a bullet hole through his chest, age about grown. Relaying that information to his office, he waited for other officers and the coroner to arrive.

"Did Mr. Warner tell you what happened," prompted Greenwood?

"He just said the boy got shot."

"And did Mr. Warner remain there in the woods with you?"

"No, sir. He said he needed to go and see about his granddaughter."

"Mr. Eagles, what was Mr. Warner's state of mind at that time?"

"Sir?"

"How was he acting—was he nervous, upset, agitated?"

"I'd say he was in a daze—he walked into branches on the path and mumbled some."

"What did he say?"

"Nothing—just mumbled."

In his cross-examination, Walt asked, "was the word 'accident' ever mentioned in any of the conversations?"

"I don't remember," Willie said.

Sheriff Bert Roberts explained to the court the lay of the land where the incident occurred and reported on the questioning of the accused, Mr. Warner.

"In my judgment, it was an unfortunate accident when Mr. Warner came down a steep embankment on his wooded property and suddenly saw his granddaughter thrashing about on the ground with another person. Without thinking, he assumed it was a rape in progress. He didn't seem to remember how it happened, but when he came to his senses he found that his rifle had been fired, and the male participant in the scene had been shot. He still maintains that he has no memory of the actual shooting."

Lawrence Greenwood asked, "I assume you arrested Mr. Warner immediately and proceeded with the questioning?"

"Well no, not exactly. Mr. Warner was shook-up, as might be expected. We let him be with his family until next day."

"You let a suspected felon go?"

"Where was he to go? Around here, we know people. It was not risky to give him some time to adjust to the tragedy."

"And perhaps to gather his privileged friends and create an alibi?"

"We treat people as people here, regardless of status."

By that time Walt had objected to that line of questioning, and the objection was sustained, but the damage was done if the jurors sensed that special treatment had been given. There were a few inane questions left for the prosecutor to use to whittle the day away.

The following morning, without much fanfare, the coroner was called to establish that indeed a bullet had pierced the heart aorta. Greenwood made a big deal about how accurate the shot was for it to have been an accidental aim. Experts came and went to project trajectory of the bullet, distances, what kind of weapon, spent projectile compared to the gun used, ownership of the weapon and other specific evidentiary details. There was even an expert who re-enacted the scene to include timing and positioning of participants. Days were wasted on matters not in question. The simple answer was that I was present, it was my gun, and Artese Bradley Washington lay dead in my woods.

CHAPTER 5

"Your Honor, the prosecution calls Allen Sims."

Mr. Sims was an attractive middle-aged man with dark hair and horn-rimmed glasses. He had bulging muscles and a face reminiscent of the Marlboro Man. He carried himself with an air of confidence, a long stride with large hands swinging by his side. Although his countenance suggested strength, his brown eyes were gentle and seemed to be smiling.

"Mr. Sims, I am Lawrence Greenwood, U.S. attorney. How are you this morning?"

Mr. Sims merely nodded.

"Mr. Sims, would you tell us a little about yourself and what you do?"

"I own the Argus Arms Restaurant in New Orleans. I am married, no children. Have lived most of my life on the Gulf Coast. Always worked in the food and beverage industry."

"Mr. Sims, were you ever acquainted with the victim in this case, Artise Bradley Washington?"

"Yes, Sir."

"Please tell this court what you know about Artise."

"I knew his mother."

"Why don't you just, in your own words, tell the story of your involvement with the family and with the son, Artise?"

"I'll try. Back then, I was a bartender. I had just completed my service in the navy and was working in Pensacola. Thelma was a young pregnant drug addict that hung around the bar. I listened to her story and slipped her food now and then. Sometimes, she slept out near our dumpster, where she took some of her meals. Even without a fix she acted irrationally. As her situation became worse, I let her sleep on my couch. I don't know where she got the gun, but one night she blew a hole in the ceiling of my small apartment. I didn't know what to do with her, so I took her over to a Pascagoula mental health center. The director of that facility, a lady named June, got her a place to stay and arranged for hospitalization. I don't know if I was so concerned about Thelma, but I was attracted to June and had this excuse to go by the center to check on Thelma. A couple of weeks later, Art was born. June took me by the hospital. As we stood by the nursery window, she remarked that she thought I needed to see my baby. It took a while to convince her that I was not the father just because Thelma put my name on a form she completed. When the window curtain was opened, I saw a bundle, hooked to all kinds of tubes and monitoring equipment. It was twitching and shivering and fighting the covering. June said quietly, "Crack baby.""

"But it was not your child?"

"No. The proof came three months later when the baby was to be released from the hospital. It was a week before the scheduled release to foster care. Thelma pitched a fit to let him go early so that some guy named Washington could see his son before he had to go to prison where he was to spend twenty years."

"What happened to the baby?"

"Oh, Art was placed in several homes, never adopted. June and I kinda kept up with him. Did I tell you we were married less than a year after taking Thelma to the clinic? Anyway, at ten, Art was hustling on the streets of New Orleans. I saw him once. He would accost a male and say for a quarter he could tell the man where he got them shoes. Of course, the answer was 'on yo feet, on the streets of New Orleans.'"

"Did you hear from him after that?"

"We heard that his grandparents from north Mississippi had found him and that they took him to Oxford. We understand that they got him in school and that he became quite a wonderful young person, straight A's in school, football squad, and all."

After listening to that tale of overcoming the odds, Walter Dunbar had no reason to cross-examine. I leaned over and whispered, "Walt, I'm getting closer and closer to testifying!"

A swarm of similar-minded individuals followed the lead of the bartender, much as geese form in a "V" behind the point bird. Counselors, coaches, and other school officials joined preachers and Sunday school teachers in extolling the character of one Artise Bradley Washington. And from all I heard and knew, Art was a bright young man with a brilliant future whose life was cut short by a single rifle shot.

Walt did not make objections. There was no way to besmirch the positive reputation of the victim even if we had cared to. We had previously agreed we would not even try to impugn the stellar character of this young man. Not only would it be inappropriate, but it would also have to be manufactured. We could find no fault in this person and could be only repulsed by the thought that such a life had been wasted.

"Your Honor, the prosecution calls Dr. Pamela Brown."

Pamela Brown was a lady in her fifties. She was dressed in a black business suit and a white blouse covered at the long neck by a patterned scarf wrapped haphazardly around her throat. Large, horn-rimmed glasses perched on her thin nose. She sat on the chair cautiously and observed the crowd in quick, nervous jerks of her body, like a squirrel in heat.

"Dr. Brown, would you state your name, employer, and position held?"

"I am Pamela Brown, Ohio State University, director of the Neural Science Center in the department of psychology."

"That is an impressive title, Dr. Brown. What exactly do you do?"

"I teach graduate courses and engage in research that deals with emotion and motivation. I have written books and delivered papers in my specialty, amygdala."

"Please explain to the court in layman's terms what that specialty is—amygdala, you are saying?"

"Of course. Nuclei—I guess you could say cells, located in the temporal lobe of the brain have a role in the processing of memory, decision making and emotional reactions. They are a part of the limbic system that may trigger an automatic response, usually as a result of fear. Emotion and motivation are affected in some kind of response."

"Dr. Brown, I am a country lawyer not familiar with such an academic explanation. Could you provide an example of an action that might follow some event, without thought—automatically."

"Well, it's not quite that simple, but I can provide an example that might elicit what might be described as instant response. A sudden loud noise may startle one to react automatically. He or she might jump, run, be gripped by fear, have an increase in blood pressure or heart rate, and experience any number of physical changes in the body. The specific response and the severity of the biologic reaction may be attributed to collective negative experiences of a similar nature. It is primarily a response to danger—self-preservation, real or imagined."

"Are you saying that bad feelings can build over time and result in some spontaneous act?"

"That's putting it simplistically, but, yes, that is a possibility."

"To help the jury understand the process, let me form a hypothetical situation. Much has been suggested in this case that one, automatically, without thought or reason can take a gun he is carrying, release any safety measures, point, aim, fire and kill another person. Is it possible that such a precise act could be an immediate response that is done automatically, without thought?"

"My research has uncovered no such case."

With a half-assed satisfied smile, the prosecutor bowed and said, "Thank you, Dr. Brown."

Walt almost jumped to his feet to cross-examine.

"Dr. Brown, did I hear you say that if one is prejudiced, he or she might have an automatic violent response?"

"Well, it was all hypothetical—"

Walt interrupted. "Do you have any prejudices, Dr. Brown?"

"I—pride myself—"

"What does the term 'prejudice' mean?"

"The accepted definition, I believe, is to pre-judge something or someone."

"Then, let me propose another hypothetical. I don't like broccoli. I have never tried broccoli. I avoid buying broccoli. I leave the kitchen when I smell broccoli cooking. Have I pre-judged broccoli?"

"Well, yes. We all have prejudices of one sort or another, sometimes because we have no experience with the particular person or thing, or our experiences have been negative."

"And bigotry?"

"Normally that refers to one who holds blindly and intolerantly to a particular creed or opinion and is so narrow-minded that it becomes a part of his or her personality. Such a belief may result in hating anyone or anything that does not correspond to that creed or opinion."

"What about discrimination?"

"That is a bit different. It denotes a positive action—to distinguish, to differentiate, show partiality. For humans, bias in the treatment of an individual or group."

"Dr. Brown, are all these attitudes learned behavior?"

"That is the conclusion of my research."

"So, if a person has learned none of those bad habits and exhibits none of those tendencies, there is no possibility of an automatic reaction to outside stimulus?"

"Oh, I didn't say that. There are the involuntary and spontaneous reactions I explained earlier—like a response to a loud noise or some other unfamiliar or frightening stimuli."

"Could it be that one who had no learned discrimination or hate for a particular person might respond without thinking to an abhorrent action that he or she observes, an action that is contrary to his or her belief, creed, or religious conviction?"

"I have no knowledge of a specific instance, but the research indicates that this might be possible. It may be stretching a bit to say 'without thinking,' but theoretically, it might be possible. The mind and body sometimes act in mysterious ways."

"Thank you, Dr. Brown."

"Your Honor, the prosecution calls Dr. Steven Carter."

Carter was a jovial character, middle-aged and academically typical with a plaid coat and green tie. He was rather plump but not seriously overweight. He moved with a wobbly gait that shook long, curly hair that matched a twitching mustache. He settled into the witness chair with a flourish. Twinkling eyes first acknowledged the federal jury and then fixed on Lawrence Greenwood.

"Please state your name and occupation," Greenwood intoned.

"Steven Carter. I am a genetic anthropologist. I teach at New York University in the department of anthropology."

"Dr. Carter, would you explain to this jury exactly what a Genetic Anthropologist is?"

"Yes. My degrees are in anthropology, which is the study of us humans. It involves man's cultural and physical nature, his customs, social relationships, language, and other characteristics. My research has concentrated on biochemical factors that establish the characteristics of the human organism."

"Could you be a bit more specific?"

"I'll try. We could talk about nucleic acid and chromosomes and cells, but let's just say it's what we are made of and what makes us different from other animals and, indeed, different from other groups of people or individuals. We inherit through this make-up of physical differences and other unique features."

"Dr. Carter, would you say that these differences are the basis for prejudicial treatment of individuals?"

"Well, I don't know that I would go that far. Let's just say our differences are important elements in creating prejudice, just as mental and physical abilities might influence how one is perceived."

"And, are there categories of people who are classified on a biological or inheritance basis?"

"Over the centuries there have been many attempts to do just that, normally based upon the continent of origin such as European, Asian, African, etc."

"So, Dr. Carter, race or ethnic background are factors in establishing a pecking order of importance among peoples because of inherited traits?"

"That is the theory, at least, although it could be that a status could improve over a period of time through combining gene pools, a process called eugenics. There may be environmental factors also that impinge upon the development of certain characteristics, a survival-of-the-fittest doctrine."

"Can the results of such a process be measured?"

"Many have tried, from phrenology, skull shapes that differ, to arrangement of teeth, to trials of ethnic cleansing. Some have given examples of superior physical prowess developed through survival of the fittest. Although short in terms of evolutionary time, an example has been postulated that Africans, the fittest of whom survived the slave ships to work on plantations, make up some of the best of the world's best athletes. From a more practical evolutionary viewpoint, those who survive in a hostile environment over the centuries may develop a physical predisposition to athletic skills.

Perhaps I shouldn't have said that. It seems to me that not long ago a sports prognosticator lost his job for a similar statement. Ordinarily, evolution involves eons of time as is the case of our own species linkage to the genus *Homo*. Recently, a jawbone found in Ethiopia dates back 2.8 million years."

Walt jumped to his feet. "Your Honor—relevance."

Judge Longest, suddenly alert, scowled at the prosecutor. "Mr. Greenwood, all this is very interesting, but please get to the point."

"Yes, Your Honor. Dr. Carter, you have indicated that there are genetic differences among groups of people?"

"Yes."

"What kind of differences?"

"Oh, things like size, appearance, hair color, skin color, prone to certain diseases, obesity, and so on."

"And could such biological distinctions include personality differences as well, such as temperament or the predisposition to act violently?"

"I am unable to say with certainty, but it is possible that certain groups have varying tendencies for social interaction."

"Dr. Carter, if XX or XY chromosome variation determines one's sexual orientation regardless of physical body characteristics, why hesitate to validate other perceptions relative to human differences?"

Walter tilted his chair in his haste. "Objection, Your Honor. There has been no hint of the defendant's sexual orientation. This line of questioning is entirely irrelevant and insulting."

Greenwood shot back. "Your Honor, no reference to the defendant was intended. I was merely—"

Judge Longest stopped Larry in mid-sentence. "Sustained. Mr. Greenwood, you are hereby warned to stick to pertinent facts that are in evidence and refrain from offering testimony yourself. The jury will ignore the question."

Humbled, Greenwood said, "Yes, Your Honor. Dr. Carter, in your opinion, what is racism?"

"I believe that racism involves two factors. First, a perception of biological differences between people, perhaps enhanced by environmental experience, coupled with the power to exert attitudes and practices of superiority and control."

"Dr. Carter, are you saying that prejudice and discrimination result from a belief that one race or ethnic group is superior to others?"

"Yes. It can be a matter of social action, political systems, or individual assumptions that different races are inherently superior or inferior because of inheritable traits."

"Does one who lives in a political system or environment where such attitudes are prevalent adopt racist attitudes?"

"That is likely the case."

"Is the individual aware of such racist attitudes?"

"Often, one takes the attitude or practices of his environment for granted—it's just the way it is, and little thought is given to understanding alternatives."

Walter asked Carter one question. "Dr. Carter, assuming that all these biological inheritance theories are correct, can environmental factors and commitment to humanity overcome any animosity toward those who are perceived as different?"

"I would say so. Yes, environment and circumstances may alter the way we react."

"No further questions, Your Honor."

"You may step down, Dr. Carter."

"Your Honor, the prosecution calls Dr. Harry Grossman."

Grossman, dressed in a tan business suit, looked as though he had slept in his clothes for more than one night. His hair was frizzled; his tie hung loosely around a large neck. The only neat characteristic he displayed in his appearance was a closely manicured goatee hiding the chin in an otherwise seriously pock-marked face. Darting eyes surveyed the jury, lawyers, and audience.

"Please state your name and occupation."

"Harry Grossman, research sociologist. I have my own firm. Have published five books and numerous articles."

"Are you active in professional groups in your profession?"

"Yes, The America Sociological Association, The Association of Applied and Clinical Sociology, and other groups. I have received top awards from AACS, and a recent book received a Silver Cross award."

"Dr. Grossman, what does a research sociologist do?"

"Well, the simple answer is that we study the relationships of people living in groups, their activities, customs, beliefs, family life, organizational structures, and other ways in which an individual adapts to live and work in an integrated association. It also includes the way in which distinctive groups relate to others who adopt alternate lifestyles. This is my own explanation of what I consider to be my calling and perhaps not a complete definition of specialties in the field."

"Is what has been termed 'racism' within the scope of your studies?"

"Yes, but racism has been defined in so many ways that it is difficult to design studies that reflect the complexity of discrimination. Everything from xenophobia, the unreasonable fear or hatred of strangers, foreigners, or anything foreign, to sexism or other 'ism's.' We talk of institutional and economic and other forms of racism in all their varied implications. My studies deal primarily with race hatred as a result of one's feeling of superiority because of color, ethnicity, religion, or sexual orientation. I'm more interested in individual overt action than societal implications."

"In your studies, do you find that individual racist action as you have described it, is the result of irrational hate powered by a feeling of superiority?"

Walt rose to object to prosecutor testifying.

Judge Longest muttered, "I'll allow it with the admonition that the prosecutor refrains from leading the witness."

"You may answer, Dr. Grossman."

"Yes, that seems to be the case. A feeling that the object of the action is indeed inferior."

"Dr. Grossman, might the color of one's skin evoke a racist response?"

"Absolutely. Racial identification is a primary ingredient in a majority of such incidents."

"Why is skin color such a motivating factor?"

"It goes back to ancient times and the tendency to support that with which you are familiar. There was danger in the unknown, and skin color was the easiest way to identify that potential risk. A lighter skinned individual would naturally feel superior if his or her group were all of that color and, conversely, the reverse could occur."

"Then why has the cradle of civilization, the African people, suffered most in this exchange?"

"Although in ancient times great African civilizations emerged, for some reason, many of those dynasties perished as European and other societies advanced. Africa was more tribal in nature and became categorized as savages, sub-human, ape-like cannibals. It became easy to think of them as animals—hence, inferior slaves."

"Dr. Grossman, are there other theories relating to whites feeling superior to blacks?"

"Well—yes. There have been attempts to classify individuals from various ethnic groups based upon differing genetic structuring. Social, intellectual, moral, and other characteristics have been assigned based upon those supposed chromosome arrangements. Most of those theories are debunked as a result of discoveries that show differences between racial or ethnic groups are no more pronounced than differences among those belonging to the same racial or ethnic grouping. A hierarchy of races based on heritable traits that dictate one as superior or inferior is highly problematical."

"Are you saying that inherited traits are unimportant in terms of what we become?"

"Of course not. Things like color, physical appearance, proclivity toward certain diseases, and the like are definitely inherited. I believe that those characteristics are molded and directed by environmental factors that determine our societal action as individuals and groups. Regardless of when and how it began, racism is the result of living in a racist society."

"Your witness, Mr. Dunbar."

Walter Dunbar rose slowly from his chair and stood by the desk, looking directly at the witness for a full minute.

"Dr. Grossman, did I understand you to say that one is not born with some predisposition to act in a certain way? Say, become a racist?"

"That is my position."

"And, Dr. Grossman, did I hear you say that racism is the result of living in a racist society?"

"Well, perhaps it is a bit more complicated than that—but, well—yes. One may be born less than five feet tall. That might limit him or her from being an NBA basketball star, but they can become a fan of the sport. There are other physical, medical, or psychological tendencies that are passed down from generation to generation that affect what one is to become. Most of these conditions are not specific to one race or culture."

"Are there studies of identical twins reared in separate environments that retain similar traits?"

"Yes, reports emphasize similarities, but few to the differences developed over a number of years."

"So, the conclusions of your studies are that racial attitudes are gathered primarily from one's environment?"

"Yes."

"And, can two people subjected to the same environment develop entirely different beliefs and societal attitudes—say one becomes a Democrat and another a Republican?"

"Of course. People react to situations differently. They can even change over time. Remember, they didn't inherit a strict set of rules."

"Thank you, Dr. Grossman."

As an old man with limited hearing and only a country common-sense understanding of the nature of human interaction, I miss much of the nuance in these arguments. I did pick up on the idea of two people subjected to essentially the same environment following entirely different paths. Some time back, there was a report of identical twins who were separated at birth but reunited some forty years later. They looked alike, had the same hair style, the same mustache, and many of the same mannerisms. Perhaps I should consider their differences when subjected to different environments. It might help me to understand whether or not I might have inherited prejudicial tendencies.

The year was 1921 when bulwarks of drifting snow-quilted, abandoned trenches were now slipping into oblivion. The Austrian-Hungarian Empire was gone, Germany only a global shadow, there over the horizon. A Polish peasant girl trudged a frozen path to the war-torn cathedral left asunder as if mimicking the victor's division. Times were hard, food was scarce, and death was a present possibility. As if anticipating freedom, two identical womb-mates rustled as falling leaves in a stiff wind. She felt the movement and slid down a balustrade supporting the skeleton remains of stained glass. Failing to see truth, she framed, in her mind, an illusory virgin wrapping the young in swaddling blankets. Her vision faded, and both she and the ghost were gone.

Mothers, grieving the loss of their own, sought out the placid chapel standing resolute against the ruins. Neither could afford two. Each took one.

His adoptive mother was from the town of Poznań. To find work, the family moved to Podolian, where Heinrick Lublin was reared in a Jewish home. He attended the Temple synagogue and the Jewish day school. The invaders came again in 1939. In the midst of the Depression, the peoples of Germany had turned to a phantom of hope, Adolph Hitler, whose aim was to restore the nation by appropriating neighbor lands. Poland was soon in his sights. The local prison was now filled with Polish politicians and soldiers. Along with many of his schoolmates, Heinrick was a member of the Szaye Szerigi, a Polish scouting organization. They became a part of the underground resistance movement and, as their first mission, attacked the German garrison and released a number of freedom fighters, who were a part of Armia Krajowa, the largest organization in opposition to the fascist regime.

Assuming the role of a Nazi spy, Heinrick was able to get into Auschwitz, where he set about organizing resistance plans while reporting atrocities to British and allied forces.

As the new commandant of Auschwitz, Rudolph Ost had obtained the pinnacle of personal achievement within the third Reich. He had attended the most prestigious grade schools, been selected for a top military secondary education, and attended the German war college. He was an officer in the German Workers Party, an anti-Semitic political organization.

Ost was on the job only a few days, inspecting the facility, observing the staff, checking for regulatory violations. He was a stickler for hygiene, and the facilities for relieving oneself were utterly deplorable in his estimation. He noted that the officer standing in the next stall flushed the toilet before urinating just as did he. That officer walked ahead of him with the same jaunty step. In line at the mess, Ost observed the other selecting the same variety of food that he enjoyed. At this point, the two came face to face. Ost was staring into a mirror, the other an exact reflection of himself. They had exactly the same glasses, the same, well-trimmed mustache. Thinking that he must be hallucinating, Ost removed his cap as the other removed his. Both had the same hair color arranged with the same cut that revealed the same receding hair line.

Ost called for guards who, upon observing the higher rank of the two, conceded the winner to be Ost. Rudolph Ost demanded that the imposter drop his pants. With strong guard arms holding Heinrick, Ost probed private parts with the tip of his Swastika-encrusted officers knife. He muttered three words, "damn nasty Jew," and plunged the dagger deep into the victim's chest.

I have a friend who thinks of Nazism as a form of fundamentalism, a focus on a perceived rightness and purity as opposed to the evil in others. The "other" threatens the righteous, giving the pure a right to destroy. He relates that to the present-day ISIS, as well as other societies that act on the basis of their superiority, their righteousness, and purity.

One of my book club members made a statement recently that has caused me to think a lot about Nazism:

"The more I read about the rise of a political party and its fanatical leader in Germany, the more I am convinced that the treaty of Versailles was the real culprit. If the 'victors' of WW1 had not required Germany to pay for WW1 and totally destroyed their economy with the ridiculous reparations, Hitler would have been a flash in the pan and forgotten after the failed Beer Hall Putsch in the early '20s."

These little day-dreaming scenarios are something I do a lot these days. Guess that's why there's an old saying, maybe a Bible verse about "old men dreaming dreams." I dream dreams to help me understand a situation like arguments in this trial. That's why I talk to Maggie while the mist hangs lazily over the lake, and pine trees sway in harmony.

I sit at the table for a long time after today's testimony. After the jury was dismissed, after the judge and court officials abandoned their posts. After the observers filed out. After the lawyers gathered their files and dismantled their exhibits. After the janitor appeared with sweep brooms, bags, and garbage cans, I sit.

The elderly janitor, perhaps a generation younger than I, runs the wide brush between rows of benches, starting in the back. When he comes within the swinging doors to the action area, I speak.

"Guess you need to chase out the useless trash so you can do your job?"

"Oh, nosir. Stay as long as you like. I'll jest sweep a'round ya. I'll be real careful not to sweep under yuh feet. Wouldn't want to keep somebody from marrying."

"Thanks, at my age, don't think it would make a difference. It's been a long time since I heard that old wives tale about sweeping under someone's feet. Where you suppose that came from?"

He leans on the broom handle to look carefully at me.

"Don't rightly know. I jest always heared it."

He sweeps a few strokes and looks at me even more closely.

"You one of dem lawyers?"

"Not really. Have you had a chance to watch the trial?"

"No, but I heared a smart bit about it."

"What do you hear? By the way, I'm Jim. What's your name?"

"Buster. Pleased to meet'cha, Jim. I hear that it's a rip snorter. Hear a black boy got shot gittin' a little white nooky."

"Who do you think shot him?"

"Some white dude. Some old man. Boy on top of his granddaughter. Just up and shot him."

"Buster, do you think the grandfather would have shot if it had been a white boy?"

"You know he wouldn't—probably have pointed the gun and invited him into the family."

"So, you don't think there was any possible reason to kill the boy?"

"Hey—you sure you ain't one of dem lawyers?"

"Just thought you might have an opinion, Buster."

"Yeah, I got an opinion. Don't know you and don't mean no harm in saying it but—I think they ought to cut his balls out."

"Well, I guess the question is did he do it because the boy was black?"

"Sho' he did."

"You're pretty sure of that?"

"As sho' as God made dem little green apples."

"Good talkin' with you, Buster."

"Good talkin' with you. Say, Jim, you think that white guy will get away with murder?"

"Can't tell. Don't know, Buster. Just don't know."

CHAPTER 6

After my encounter with Buster, I began to reassess my approach to the question of racism. For a full year, I have been concentrating my research on the broad category of racism. To date, this trial seems to focus on discrimination based on skin color. I suppose this is natural since the basis for the alleged charge of my hate crime hinges on the color of skin. Throughout recorded history, a predominant group enslaved those it considered different, labeling them infidels. One could consider this fact the foundation for all hate crimes. For countless centuries skin color has provided an easily recognizable and distinctive feature to accentuate that which is divisive in human relations. As I lay in my bed that night, these thoughts spun around as flashing lights behind tired eyelids.

To sleep—to dream.

He was as tall as the first bud of the box tree in the center of a temporary camp and had seen not nearly as many suns as most of the clan. The entire group was his family. He realized that one of the big-chested mothers had acquired a swollen belly and spat him out like the spent chew of a landrace plant. In addition to providing recreation, this hallucinogen had medicinal application much appreciated during the birthing process.

The tribe plied the forest for fruit and animals and fished the nearby Atbara River. All worked and played together in the idyllic setting. He noticed the difference between animals and naked human bodies, but he was too young to appreciate sexual orientation. Rooster-like couplings frequently occurred with little sense of exclusivity. It was an open society with few taboos. He had no reason to know that he was heir to the ancient Bronze Age kingdom of Kush, alternately conquering an Egyptian dynasty or being subjected to it, or being a colony of that governing body with intervening wars involving Assyria, Libya, and other groups.

He heard the noise, the crackling of dry twigs, the crush of salient grass turned crisp in the pervasive summer heat. He had wandered from the protective circle to chase a black butterfly with orange wing spots that suddenly transformed into a sea of black, obliterating the sun from his crouching position amid a leafy cover. The dark cloud dispersed with stealth, delineating each black part that brandished a long spear or a bulbous limb from an ironwood tree. Some carried short sticks embedded with rock. Each was painted with neighboring tribe colors, the only covering an animal skin thong strip pulled around the buttocks to hang loosely down front. The dark cloud advanced to the camp, running and screaming unintelligible barbaric chants.

The tribe matriarch was first to fall, followed by a contingent of unarmed warriors. Others were surrounded and submitted to pleated bark ropes bound tightly behind arms and legs. Women and young ones huddled at the foot of a ceremonial calamite pole erected to ward off the unknown. Younger women and girls of six hands' height were attacked and forced to the ground, an aggressor lifting his thong to expose a straight member, which he plunged between the legs of the struggling victim.

Concealed in his leafy sanctuary, he observed the spearing of the very young to be bound on spit poles set between tree forks and the stoking of fires for a giant feast. For hours he watched the drinking and dancing and the lying with women of the tribe. Night suddenly dropped its cloak of light. He lay wrapped in insomnia until the eastern round ball spattered shades of purple on an opaque horizon. Drifting into a troubled half-sleep, he awoke to a huge foot pummeling his mid-section.

In the camp his world lay dead, their naked bodies spread in fetal, child-like fashion, lying in heaps of scattered piles. The visceral pit of his stomach, the scene of debauchery and mayhem, created pain that made him double with dry heaves of cataclysmic proportions. He was joined with other young men whose hands were tied with grass ropes to skinned saplings. They were arranged in rows of five fingers.

Together, the combined groups were marched through the jungle, across the plains and through the marshes, past high rises of earth in geometric design. At the entrance to a large settlement, representations of men stood in stone. One towering above all the rest showed close-cropped hair with a broad headband displaying painted cobras on the front. It was hovering over a group of mounds with a crude circle of stones. From captor chatter, they learned that this was a "Pan Grave," a place for keeping departed great men.

In a city he heard called Meroe, the captives were paraded before in-dividuals with the lightest skin they had ever seen, halfway between white and black. They were forced to kneel before this swarthy new race of men and caged for an unforgettable trip across a broad body of water. Many died of starvation or the beating regularly administered by these new captors. Survivors crossing desert land for the first time were brought to an open space where giant rocks were being laid as foundations for mon-uments that would reach the sky. Working in the shadow of a superior's whip, they constructed building blocks for these new masters. Day in and day out, under the searing sun, they toiled without rest.

He developed bulging muscles and was resourceful in understanding the will and emotions of his handlers. He even began to understand their language. Some of the curious papyrus markings apparently referred to him. Grunts were directed his way with appropriate sarcasm for a lowly slave. That grunt ended in a snarl that sounded like "ha-mmm". The only name he had ever known, Ham!

Ham so pleased his captors that he was, surreptitiously, slipped extra rations and, occasionally, he found oil for sun-exposed skin. He grew to be a handsome teenager.

From across the sea, invaders came. He heard of Greece and others who had come here in the past, even his own tribe, the Cush—but that was long ago. Those who came now wore metal armament and carried metal spears. They were as white as Ham was black. They were confident, in charge, superior. Some soldiers wore short skirts instead of robes. They selected a dozen workers to be given to their emperor, evidently a great king. Ham was among the group taken away.

The huge water was rough and stormy. The trip took many days, and some failed to survive. Upon arrival, Ham was pampered and given white tunics to wear. Eventually, he was brought to a great chamber where an individual dressed in gold and rainbow colors looked down at him from a raised platform throne. Words were spoken and, evidently, fate sealed. He was locked in a small room for a few days while being examined by bearded men carting bags of instruments. His mouth, teeth, ears, throat, and rectum were closely studied. His head was measured, and he was made to stand by a wall with reflective light for a profile drawing. Led to a room with long tables covered with clay pots, knives, and other unfamiliar instruments, he was disrobed and strapped securely to a flat platform. Accompanying agonizing screams and excruciating pain, Ham watched as his testicles were carelessly tossed into a wooden basin.

Recovery was slow, every turn a measured movement. Ham survived to wonder what his future might be. Wonder morphed into anxiety as time passed. One day he was led through cavernous halls of castle splendor to a barred door that opened to a sea of drapery. A gaggle of women servants scurried about, singularly attentive to a young female named Augustina. She was seated upright in the middle of a satin-laced bed comparable in size to the entire room he had just vacated.

Augustina was the most beautiful human he had ever seen. Coppery skin adorned her slim body and long legs. Large pointed breasts parted hair of charcoal curls that reached halfway to strong curves of buttock. All these treasures she displayed through a silk of lavender with a smile of innocence.

From habit, Ham dropped to his knees and bowed to stone floors. A soft hand lifted his face to her starlit dark eyes that met his trembling stare, her eyes, he thought, reflecting a hint of sorrow with a shade of passion. She bade him stand and turn and turn again before she ventured a curt nod he interpreted as approval. Female attendants ushered him from the room.

He learned that his job was to clean the room, empty bed pots and run errands at her command. She ignored Ham as she amused herself and dressed for seemingly constant parties. He would watch from a balcony as she whirled across the dance floor with the attention of a crowd of admirers, including the great man who had approved Ham's position in this great house. She sat on the lap and kissed the cheek of this crowned person, but often pressed herself closely to one particular dancing partner and let her hand slip to his backside in a squeezing motion.

One night, that dancing partner failed to appear. Augustina was ceremoniously escorted to the crowned man, who placed her hand in that of an old bearded gentleman. She danced unresponsively with the gentleman and later fled to her room. Ham followed to find a terrified young woman standing among packing crates of clothing and other articles suitable for travel.

He walked behind the carriages, one occupied by a weeping Augustina. Through virgin forest and dry sand they traveled far to a series of small stone cabins. Augustina was housed in the largest of the lot, with Ham ensconced in a nearby hovel with other servants. Still, he continued to serve the despondent lady who secluded herself in her prison. Ham spent hours performing stints and coaxing her to eat her food. She lost her appetite and her smile. But one night as shadows of midnight approached, Ham was summoned. Augustina gave him a curious glance and bade him approach her bed and bare himself. Reluctantly, Ham turned around before her, his flaccid member swinging hopelessly. Like an ocean storm, a wave of frustration and hate lay on her face for only an instant. Loud screams alerted guards who led away the naked man. Portending an act to be observed over the centuries to follow, a body swung in all its absurdity from a tree limb shattering streams of morning light over a glistening darkness.

I sat upright in the bed, heart racing. Fully awake now and shaking, I visited the bathroom, looking at the frazzled old face in the mirror. Why, I asked the reflection, when we think of slavery, we often think of the black man? The history of mankind is filled with people enslaved without politically correct color consideration. I'm fairly certain that ancient nomadic Turks and Mongolians, incorporating lands and people, failed to employ indiscriminate practices. In fact, slavery existed before written history, some authorities dating it back as far as eight thousand years. It has been documented in art forms and grave sites. The Bible as well as the Code of Hammurabi, a Babylonian law of ancient Mesopotamia dating back to 1754 B.C., validates the established practice of taking slaves.

In an attempt to control the thoughts racing through my brain like an out-of-control roller coaster, I turned on the light. There on the bedside table lay a forlorn object, a King James Bible. It had remained there untouched for years, a surrender to a tradition that permeates the South. Everybody has one; few read it.

When I had a summer job in college selling Bibles door to door, I discovered a trick that helped me make a sale. After inquiring as to whether the homeowner had a Bible, I asked to see it. Most ran to the night table or a chest drawer and returned, dusting the jacket with a shirt tail or an apron. The embarrassment of treating one good book so carelessly created a need to have a new one.

Thumbing through the leather-bound edition from my bedside table, I remembered something of my early childhood country religious experience. Although I was never a Bible scholar, I did hear a preacher once who talked about the reason for black people. I don't remember the context in which it was mentioned but I do recall that it had something to do with the children of Israel disobeying God, wandering in the wilderness and such. Anyway, it involved the prophet Noah. Since sleep was not an option at this point, I went to a trunk where I knew a copy of the Naves Topical Bible from my Bible-selling days had languished all these years. That volume contained meticulously arranged verses under specific topics. I was able to locate verses I'd heard a preacher use to touch on an old story about the origin of black persons. My opinion was that the story had been promulgated to justify slavery, but I did find scripture from which this notion apparently evolved.

I have never understood the family progeny of Adam and Eve after the apple incident. It would seem that ole Cain and Able needed to find a female companion somewhere. However, somehow, there were enough people around to accommodate the great flood. Noah and his sons apparently survived with an admonition to re-populate the earth.

Genesis 5:32 After Noah was five hundred years old, Noah became the father of Shem, Ham, and Japheth.

Genesis 9:18 The sons of Noah who went forth from the ark were Shem, Ham, and Japheth. Ham was the father of Canaan.

Genesis 9:19 These three were the sons of Noah, and from these the whole world was populated.

Genesis 9:20 Noah was the first tiller of the soil. He planted a vineyard.

Genesis 9:21 And he drank of the wine and became drunk and lay uncovered in his tent.

Genesis 9:22 And Ham, the father of Canaan, saw the nakedness of his father and told his brothers.

Genesis 9:23 Then Shem and Japheth took a garment, laid it upon their shoulders and walked backward and covered the nakedness of their father; their faces were turned away, and they did not see their father's nakedness.

Genesis 9:24 When Noah awoke from his wine and knew what the youngest son had done to him, he said:

Genesis 9:25 Cursed be Canaan; a slave of slaves shall he be to his brothers.

Genesis 9:26 Blessed by the Lord my God be Shem, and let Canaan be his slave.

Genesis 9:27 God enlarged Japheth and let him dwell in the tents of Shem, and let Canaan be his slave.

Genesis 10:6 The sons of Ham: Cush, Egypt, Put, and Canaan.

Psalms 78:51 He (God) smote all the first born of Egypt, the first issue of their strength, in the tents of Ham.

Psalms 105:23 Then Israel came to Egypt; Jacob sojourned in the land of Ham.

Psalms 105:24 And the LORD made his people fruitful, and made them stronger than their foes.

Psalms 106:21 They forgot God, their savior, who had done great things for them in Egypt, wondrous works in the land of Ham, and terrible things by the Red Sea.

Psalms 106:23 Therefore, he said he would destroy them—had not Moses, the chosen one, stood in the breach before him, to turn away his wrath from destroying them.

Psalms: 106:24 Then they despised the pleasant land, having no faith in his promise.

Psalms: 106:25 They murmured in their tents and did not obey the voice of the LORD.

Psalms: 106:26 Therefore, he raised his hand and swore to them that he would make them fall in the wilderness, and would disperse their descendants among the nations, scattering them over the lands.

My understanding is that Shem, a son of Noah, was the father of the Israelites and Canaan, the grandson (son of Ham) founder of the Canaanites clan. Enmity existed between the two groups throughout the ancient world. Some authorities believe that the Noah story is meant to justify the enslavement of the Canaan group. According to some biblical scholars, there is evidence that Noah divided the world among his sons, and Canaan did go to Africa and perhaps did serve to populate that continent. Many current-day authorities maintain that this area actually was the cradle of civilization, that a fish first crawled from an African sea. There seems to be no research indicating that it was a white fish.

Many rationales are suggested in the literature as to why the curse was placed on Canaan, the grandson, rather than Ham, who saw Noah naked. Some maintain that Canaan behaved badly on the ark, including having sexual contact with his mother. Some suggest that Ham had informed Canaan of his grandfather's drunken state, and Canaan had entered the tent and performed sodomy or some other act that, at the time, was considered homosexual. There are even claims that Canaan castrated Noah and give as evidence a quote from Noah: "You caused me that I should not father a fourth son, another one to serve me." Considering that Noah is portrayed as being over five hundred years old, that might be a miracle or a blessing. What do I know? These are biblical scholars. Some do think Canaan had merely subjected his grandfather to ridicule. At any rate, Canaan got the curse to pass it along to his heirs forever. According to my preacher, that curse encompassed being black and becoming African slaves.

Somewhere I saw definitions that indicate the Hebrew word for Ham is "burnt" or "black," while the Egyptian word for Ham is "slave." In the final analysis, there does not appear a reasonable rationale as to why Noah placed the curse on Canaan, nor is there an understanding of the patronymic extension of the curse for future generations. Some, even my own ancestors, may have seen this as a justification for slavery or racism. That stretch of religious or moral reasoning fails to meet any standard of humanity.

I fell into a restless sleep in my favorite chair.

Next morning, taking a garbage pot to the compost pile, I discovered that yellow ladies slippers and ragged orchids had sprung up in the heap. Shoveling around the beauty among the waste, I noticed spring coralroot next to the tree line. Like all of life, they will soon wilt away, sooner as a result of their fragility. But, somehow, they'll return next spring. Makes one wonder about dust collection for another human tomorrow. Is man's destiny extinction, or do we keep popping up?

Engaged as I was with the prospect of ultimate human survival, I almost forgot that today was another day to hit the road to engage in witnessing a continuing drama of personal survival. I was a little late arriving but still got there before the jury. In the courtroom, I waited for the next government witness to be introduced. He was a skinny dude with a black goatee and horn-rimmed glasses. He wore a brown tweed jacket and an air that he was an expert on damned near everything. One would expect that he might pull a briar pipe from his coat pocket at any moment and start pontificating. Larry Greenwood gave him his seat with the proper enunciation of a name that suggested authority. Larry looked at the witness as if he were about to disclose that the witness had just announced a cancer cure.

"Dr. Zarcosky, please state your full name and tell us a little about yourself?"

"My name is Archibald Zarcosky, president and CEO of Amnesia Solutions, a national research organization. I am a psychiatrist with twenty years of practice and research dealing with amnesia. Medical degree from Johns Hopkins coupled with several residencies. I am considered an expert in dissociative amnesia. I am a fellow in the American Psychiatric Association and a member of the American Academy of Psychiatry."

"Dr. Zarcosky, in layman's terms, what is amnesia?"

"The simplistic answer is loss of memory."

"And the cause?"

"Normally from brain damage due to accident, disease, or drugs that can produce the inability to recall."

"Dr. Zarcosky, in this trial it has been alleged that the defendant, James T. Warner, committed a heinous crime but cannot remember the act itself."

Walt had to object. "Your Honor, prejudicial. A crime, let alone a heinous crime, has not been proven."

The judge peered over half-glasses. "I believe the term 'alleged' was used so the objection is overruled with an admonition to the prosecutor to avoid such descriptive adjectives in his questioning."

Greenwood straightened his tie and proceeded.

"Dr. Zarcosky, is it possible for one to commit a crime and not remember the act?"

"Yes. Under specific circumstances. This is my specialty—psychological trauma. Dissociative amnesia is brought on by some tragic or horrendous occurrence as perceived by the victim."

"What sort of occurrences are we talking about?"

"Well, it could be anything that causes a drastic reaction—a violent robbery, seeing a loved one killed, a tornado or other disaster, even action during a war—anything that so terrorizes or is considered by the victim as an act that cannot be faced. Repressed memory may occur. Normally, it is stored in long-term memory but repressed by psychological defenses. It happens when some event is so meaningful to an individual that the mind forgets rather than acknowledging or facing that event. Unlike brain damage from accident, alcohol, or drugs, this is the brain choosing to forget."

"What do you mean by 'choosing to forget?'"

"Probably a bad choice of words. For the individual, rationality is non-operative. He or she is not in control of the process. There is no physical damage or disease involved in dissociative amnesia."

"Is it a permanent condition?"

"Usually not. Normally, it is temporary, although, in some cases, it may return."

"Could it last for over a year?"

"The time span varies, but it would be unusual for the condition to last that long in the absence of brain damage from some source."

"Is there one reliable test of the authenticity of a claim of associative amnesia?"

"In my opinion, the best information can be derived from observation by a qualified professional."

"Dr. Zarcosky, have you had an opportunity to observe videos of depositions conducted with the defendant, Mr. Warner?"

"Yes."

"In your professional opinion, is Mr. Warner suffering from dissociative amnesia?"

"No."

Walter was ready for the good doctor on cross-examination.

"Dr. Zarcosky, is a victim able to function normally during a period of dissociative amnesia?"

"Yes, in most instances, one maintains intellectual skills and continues to learn."

"And do emotional ties remain, say the desire to protect the ones we care about?"

"Yes."

"You have testified that certain events that are so devastating to the mind of an individual to the extent that it cannot be faced. Rape for example, could precipitate a state of dissociative amnesia. Is that correct?"

"Yes."

"Could the perception of the rape of one's granddaughter and the subsequent shooting of the perceived transgressor induce such a state?"

"Yes, but—"

"No further questions."

It was rather late in the afternoon, so the judge indicated that testimony of remaining witnesses would be delayed until tomorrow. I was glad to have time to run some errands.

When I got home, my attorney was sitting on my porch, rocking.

"Where do we go from here, Walt?"

"We're just going to have to lay you bare—show that you are a man of principle and regretful of your snap judgment in perpetuating this calamity, more sorry than anyone could imagine. We have to show that you are not a racist and hope that fair-minded people will believe it. But, Larry Greenwood is far from through—he has a star witness yet to vet. You do realize that, other than yourself, there is only one other witness to the event."

"Oh, no! There's no need—no purpose—nothing to be gained! Why would he do that?"

"Mr. Warner, think about it. If you were the prosecuting attorney, would you call the only eyewitness to a capital charge?"

"Noooo—not Summer!"

"Yes. Summer."

CHAPTER 7

My two daughters followed different drummers. Lois married after a successful career in real estate, and, I guess, she and Sid were too busy to have kids. Valerie had worked as a nurse and married Tom just after college. Soon she was pregnant with Summer, the first and only grandchild.

I remember she and Tom, together with another couple, were having dinner with us at Wyldewoode. A discussion ensued as to what the baby would call us grandparents. "Poppy" had been settled for me when Valerie and then Maggie echoed the moniker "Wick," short for wicked step-grandmother. The two had the kind of fun relationship that permitted joking around. Wick stuck.

Valerie excused herself and left the table. Moments later she waddled from the bathroom with a shocked look on her face.

"I can't stop peeing," she cried as a puddle dripped around her feet.

Tom simply panicked. Maggie wrapped towels around Valerie, and we were off to the hospital.

Babies are red, screaming monsters. Your own is beautiful. Summer grew to become a lovely child, all energy and inquisitiveness. By the time she was six, we were walking the Wyldewoode trails and fishing together in the lake.

"Poppy, where did fishes come from?"

"Well, as I understand it, there were these little parts in the sea, and after a long time they got together and we had our first fish."

"How did they get here in our lake?"

"Fish lay eggs like hens do, and sometimes birds who play in the water bring eggs that stick to their feet into lakes and rivers. Then the birds go to the water in another river or lake; they lose the eggs that then hatch in their new home."

"Is that how I got here?"

"I guess, in a way. After a very long time, some of the fish grew legs and came onto the land. That fish on land had to be different, and so it grew into animals and birds."

"Like bunnies and kitties?"

"Yes."

"Mommy said I came from inside her stomach."

"That's the way it works."

"In Sunday school, they say we all came from God."

"Well, if I were God, I might do it anyway I wanted."

"Oh."

"Pull your line tight. You may have a fish!"

Summer and I had lots of talks over the years, swimming in the lake, walking the woods' trails, having lemonade or ice cream on the porch. She had loads of friends and tended to gravitate to activities with her peers. But, even as a teenager, she would call and say, "Poppy, let's walk in the woods."

She loved the wildflowers, the Indian pink spigelia marilandica, passion flower, fringeless orchid, New England aster and more. When she found a new one, she would run to Maggie's wildflower book to authenticate her discovery. She delighted in geese that veered into the water to join blue heron and wood ducks. She would suck in deep breaths of crisp pine and cedar-scented air, declaring, "Poppy, this is special."

I remember her blonde hair filled with sage straw, flirting with a summer breeze. And I now, in my mind, see that beautiful blonde hair so disheveled and windblown on an early spring day—that day.

"But Poppy, I love him!"

That day! As I was tucked under a blanket Maggie purchased from the local sewing circle, sleep became a marathon chorus of flying neurons competing for brain space. I thought of that day and the relationship the third party, the slain hero, may have had with Summer and others, including his own grandfather. What was the new life like for Artise Bradley Washington? I began to dream.

H̲e looked uncomfortable in the freshly pressed gray slacks and brown sweater with irregular patterns of gray wrapped around a scrannel-shaped body hardly filling crosswise threads. The unpretentious banality of jeans and decorated pull-overs clashed in evident disharmony. He was an oddity, not only to the white but also to Afro-American students constituting about one-third of those present. A year older than his classmates, he had a slight build that did blend well with the smattering of Asian, Mexican, and Indian learners. His skin was lighter than some of the local black students', but otherwise, his features were such that one would not question his classification ascribed on his enrollment documentation in the office of the principal. He stared straight ahead, his dark eyes bright with defiance.

Mrs. Dana Wiley stood at her desk, her fingers rifling through a sheaf of papers.

"Class, today we have a new transfer student from New Orleans. Let's welcome our new class member, Artise Bradley Washington."

Mrs. Wiley ignored the titter of laughter and snide looks to address the newcomer.

"And what would you like to be called? Brad, Art, or what?"

"My name is Artise," he stated in a strong voice that was a few decibels louder than necessary.

Thus began a long day of contradictions. He had literally been snatched from the streets of New Orleans, a truant from a placement school that he avoided as often as possible. Police cornered him in an alley just off Canal Street after a lengthy chase. He was yelling that he had done nothing, but these were "Big Easy" city cops who couldn't care less what he had done or not done. He was returned to the current foster home where his assigned parents had determined that he was more trouble than the few dollars they netted for his upkeep. His apprehension was immediately heightened by the unusual smile on their faces when the officers deposited him at the front stoop. The house mother, Mrs. Dabbs, opened the door.

"Artise, come on in. We have a wonderful surprise for you," the house mother gushed.

Sitting at the barracks-like table where some fifteen or so normally took their meals, was an elderly white couple. They both arose and took a step toward the boy who, warily, retreated as much. He had seen this before. Well-intended people who lacked anything close to a satisfying life were trying to fill the void through a mistaken quest to fill that void by saving a child. Well, hell, he was not about to be carried off to some shitty ghetto in some shitty little town where he would be expected to become a model shitty adult. He liked it here. Nobody cared if he behaved, went to school religiously, or watched his P's and Q's. He lived by his wits, caring for no one and bearing the burden of having no one who gave a rat's ass about him.

The house mother beamed with feigned sincerity. "Artise, I know this is a complete shock to you, but these people—these people are your grandparents."

He turned to run, but house Daddy grabbed him and pushed him toward the astonished couple. They did not speak to him. They just stared, a soft, bemused examination by the female and a more disciplinary countenance on the face of the male.

Grandpa spoke first, a deep baritone with just a hint of repressed sorrow and the softness of fall cotton, ginned of debris. "Artise, your mother, Thelma, was a daughter we lost many years ago. God knows we tried to find her, but never a trace—from St. Louis to California, we followed rumors that ran out as fast as crossties are pulled from abandoned train track. Never thought she'd have stayed in Mississippi. One disappointment after another lessened our search. Last year, a cousin on her deathbed hinted that she heard about a Thelma who had been on the Gulf Coast. We finally found a bouncer at a Biloxi casino who remembered a girl by that name left a baby at a Pensacola hotel. All the social service agencies we looked into! Finally found a former social worker who remembered."

The woman spoke up. "Son, we're your only kin. According to the records, your mother passed away a few years ago. You're all we have of her. We're not here to force you to do anything, but we would like to try to give you a home. And, I promise—lots of love."

He answered in measured syllables. "I don't need no love from strangers. I'm happy right here."

House Daddy grabbed the young man by the shoulders. "Boy, don't you know these white folks are trying to help you? We're kicking you out; social services are fed up with you—playing hooky from school—hanging out on Bourbon Street—picking pockets. They're ready to take you to juvenile court. You'll be sent to detention and locked up if you stay here. Is that what you want?"

Grandpa took house Daddy's arm. "Mr. Dabbs, let the boy go. Artise, I'm Homer Bradley, and this is my wife, Agnes. We live in North Mississippi, Oxford. This is a new experience for us too. When we discovered that you existed, we didn't know what to do, but we decided to make a trial run—that's what this is about. A trial run. Just like all the trials with all the families where you've been placed. You may not like us, and we may not like you. It doesn't have to work out. All we're saying is that we have a connection and that we might consider seeing if it is enough for some kind of a relationship."

"I've got all the relationships I need. Oxford? What kind of podunk town is Oxford? Never heard of it."

"It's right down the street from Ole Miss. Ever hear of Ole Miss?"

"Yeah, they were just down here—won the Sugar Bowl."

"Are you interested in sports, Art?"

"Naw, except that I bet on 'em—and don't forget, my name is Artise."

"Sorry, Artise."

"Bet you want to change my other name too."

"Bradley is the family name I inherited—just like you were given Washington."

"I don't like anybody messin' with my name."

"Don't blame you. You can have any name you choose."

Grandmother broke into the conversation. "We're certainly not concerned about names—well, I was happy to change mine. My grandparents' last name was Street, and my mother named me Agnes but wanted to keep Street as a middle name. She had taken my father's name in marriage. That family name was Walker. You can imagine having to give my full name, Agnes Street Walker."

"Say, Artise," Grandpa interrupted, "We don't want to make any quick decisions. We can take as long as we need. In the meantime, I haven't been in New Orleans for years. Would you mind showing me around?"

The streets of New Orleans led to the streets of Oxford and the new life.

Grandmother chattered away on the trip northward. Grandpa drove, attempting to point out landmarks. The new son was unresponsive and showed little interest. He quietly accepted the lunch break sandwich and immediately fell asleep. He showed no emotion in entering the little town or the house situated on a dead-end street. He barely looked at his neat, new room.

And now he was in his new school, the subject of laughter and snide remarks. The class was finally over, and the newest student just sat. This was a mistake. He missed his torn jeans and sneakers. He missed the putrid smell of the streets. His new home, this room, all had the antiseptic aroma of a bottle of wood alcohol. Just then, someone was standing in front of his desk.

She was snowy white with long, blonde hair and the bluest eyes he had ever seen. Man, this was blue, bluer than those in the Gulf tourist posters portraying Gulf waters that were as brown as his own skin. She even looked poster cool in her plaid skirt and soft white sweater.

"Art," she said, "welcome. It's okay. You'll like this school, these kids. Your parents will learn the dress code so that you can be a regular guy. You'll have loads of friends, and I hope you will let me be the first."

He did not exert energy in shaking the extended hand. His hands were already shaking. It didn't matter that she had called him "ART."

They became fast friends over the next eight years. She was a cheerleader and, after a couple of years, he became active in sports. They worked together in school organizations and shared the high school experience. They attended parties and other social events, he dating Afro-American girls and she the heartthrob of white student leaders.

It was the final game for state championship. Jackson Prep scored early and often. Oxford matched their effort, which became a battle of the quarterbacks. Down by one point, seconds on the time clock, the Oxford ball handler faded back and threw the longest pass of his career. Moans and boos commingling with equal whistles and cheers rocked the stadium as the football sailed into the hands of a Prep defender.

With pandemonium vibrating the stadium and goalposts bending like a roller coaster, the Oxford quarterback sought a back bench apart from the crowd spiraling onto the playing field. With head in hands, he sat, suddenly becoming aware that someone was standing over him. The cheerleading uniform and the long, blonde hair were unmistakable.

"Art, it's okay. I'm here for you!"

They embraced in a seamless hug that excluded all. He felt something never before experienced, a warm feeling of being home.

Long discussions, long walks, and the sharing of innermost thoughts led to intimacy and a picnic in the woods by a huge beech tree.

My dream of the life experiences of Artise Bradley Washington served only to exacerbate my anxiety about what this day would bring.

Awakening, I realized that I was running behind and rushed to get to the courthouse. This was the day I had been dreading. It came with an abruptness that an old man cannot fathom, just like Christmas that is always so far away that it slips up on me.

Tom and Valerie were on the next-to-last row with a smattering of other relatives. Lois was with them. Apparently, Sidney had chosen not to attend. The court was deathly silent as our little girl responded to the summons. All heads swiveled to watch as she walked briskly to Lawrence Greenwood's side. Her conservative suit adorned at the neck with a pink scarf mirrored an attitude of confident maturity. When she sat in the witness chair, under oath, a small child with tear-wet eyes stated her name, "Summer Alexander."

Larry Greenwood struck a fatherly pose.

"Miss Alexander, I know this is extremely difficult for you. Those involved in this proceeding understand your anguish. You do, I hope, realize our reasons for bringing you here before this jury. It is not to embarrass you or to strain family relationships. It is merely to learn circumstances surrounding an incident in which you were intimately involved. In fact, with the exception of the accused, you are the only witness to the violence that occurred. I assure you that we are here only to seek the truth and pursue justice."

Summer daubed her eyes but had no response. I could see her lips twitch, and my heart cried out for her. Since that spring day when both our worlds had dramatically changed, we had not seen each other often. We had no conversations, no discussions. When we were together, we only held each other and cried.

My daughter Valerie had treated me as the broken man I was. She looked at me with that trusting wonder that was her nature. It was even more devastating than the seemingly vacant stare received from Lois, who merely pecked me on the cheek. What could I say to these, my daughters? What could I say to anyone?

We would sit on the sofa hanging out in embarrassed silence. Lois would ask how I was doing. Valerie would ask if they could do anything. I would answer, "O.K., nothing, thanks." Staid talk about weather or obituaries boxed the room in claustrophobic oppression. It was as if a giant syringe had sucked life from the living. Having talked without talking, we sought our separate ways as negative ions resist accommodation.

"Miss Alexander, how old are you?" the prosecutor asked.

"Nineteen."

"Miss Alexander, do you remember where you were on May 3 of 2015?"

"Yes."

"And do you remember the kind of day it was? Clear, cloudy, rainy, cold?"

"It was almost the first spring day that was warm and sunny. It was lovely."

"No fog or haze—a clear day?"

"Yes."

"Do you remember what you did on that clear May 3, 2015, day?"

After a bit of hesitation, Summer answered in a small voice, "Yes."

"Would you tell us where you were and why you were there?"

"I went out in the country to walk in Poppy's—my grandfather Warner's woods."

"You were just going for a walk?"

"No, we were going to have a picnic lunch in the woods."

"You say 'we.' Was there someone with you?"

"Yes, my boyfriend, Art."

"You mean Artise Bradley Washington?"

"Yes."

"Did you and Art have a picnic lunch down by the dry creek near a huge beech tree?"

"Yes."

"And then?"

"We lay on the leaves in the sun."

"And did the two of you lay on the leaves and have sex?"

"NO." She almost yelled.

"No? I'm puzzled, Miss Alexander—I was led to believe that you two were engaged in a sexual encounter."

In a voice that could be perceived as a whisper, Summer softly replied. "No, we were not having sex —we were making love. I loved him."

"I —I stand corrected, you were making love."

"We were making love," she quietly reiterated.

"What happened then?"

Another long pause. "I heard leaves rustling and branches crackling as if a large animal was heading for us. Art jumped up."

"What happened then?"

"There was a loud noise."

"What kind of loud noise, Miss Alexander?"

"A gun shooting."

"Miss Alexander, who fired that shot?"

"I didn't see the shooting. I just saw Poppy."

"You mean Mr. Warner?"

"Yes."

"Was Mr. Warner holding a gun?"

"Yes."

"A rifle."

"I guess, I didn't pay attention to the kind of gun."

"What did you do at that point—just try to describe the scene and your reaction."

"There was blood—all over. Poppy tried to stop it. Art stopped breathing. I tried mouth to mouth. He died in my arms."

"Thank you, Miss Alexander."

W alter approached cross-examination in a slow, deliberative manner.

"Miss Alexander, did your grandfather, Mr. Warner, know you were in the woods that day?"

"No, he was not aware of our being where we were."

"So, your being on that path was a complete surprise to him?"

"I assume so—yes."

"Was he aware that you were dating an African American?"

"No. It's a small town, and we didn't advertise or flaunt our relationship."

"That is a peculiar way of expressing it. Were you ashamed of it for any reason?"

"No, it was a private thing—nobody's business. Some bi-racial couples evolve just because they want to prove they can. Ours was a caring thing—we had a lot in common and shared dreams. We both felt that it was what it was, and the future was way out there. It was now, and nothing beyond had meaning."

I was following her every word and struck with her expression of feelings that, over the years, old Jim Warner had felt, even though I had never shared them with Summer or anyone. In a folder of past scribblings, I had come across a similar sentiment.

Love is not to be likened to any process of logic or thoughtful concentration, for it defies the mental process and that is the very magic of it—magic that makes the heart to dance and fills the soul with thanksgiving.

How shall love be defined? Far more easy it is to say what love is not. It is not a spoken word or legal scroll. It will not be confined to tradition, blazoned in stone, locked in diamond or rolled in gold. It is not a flower or a blade of grass or any object great or beautiful. It captures without chain and permeates without destroying—for it is a nymph of thought, a spirit of joy, a moment of tenderness, a feeling of feeling.

One does not acquire love, covet its happiness, nor scheme its finding. Rather, love is—because it is—existing in a state uniquely its own. Some confuse love with infatuation, desire, wont or selfish purpose. But true love is a transcendent phenomenon of selfless commitment—a moment to itself alone. Love defies words or expression. It is to be accepted with joy and guarded with tenderness. It is not forever, but for a moment forever. It cannot be stored away, wrapped in fine linen, or hidden under a bushel. It is to be ravished as an enchantress, enjoyed in princely mirth, appreciated as fine wine, relished with bliss, charmed with delight, savored with devotion.

Love must be free as the dainty thistle floating on a carpet of invisible breeze. Its permanence is in its fleeting transcendence. It is love because it makes no demand, exacts no toll, and builds no wall. Take love to your breast, luxuriate in its warmth, bask in its pleasure. But do not ask from whence it comes or question its direction—for love is love for only so long as it is!

Walt had paused for a moment before his next question, so my attention was brought back to reality and the fact that my Summer was baring her soul before her parents and the entire world. Walt moved closer to the witness and softened his tone.

"You did, in reflecting upon your dating, say that Oxford is a small town. What did you mean by that?"

"You know, it doesn't matter if it's a small town or a big city, racial intolerance exists. It's just more noticeable in a smaller setting."

"Is that why you couldn't discuss this relationship with your grandfather?"

"No, no, Poppy is one of the most tolerant people I know. Both of us had been busy. We had just not found the time to be together to talk about things. My earliest memories are of times spent with him in deep conversation about fairness and justice. He is a good man, a principled man, not one with prejudice for anyone."

Larry Greenwood came back to re-direct with a dynamite question, one that I have pondered for a long time, especially these last trying months.

"Miss Alexander, you have just painted a rosy picture of the defendant, understandable since he is your grandfather. Assuming all that to be factual, I have one question. Why did he do what he did?"

Summer lowered her head for a full minute and then fixed flashing eyes upon Larry Greenwood. "Mr. Greenwood, I honestly don't know."

Larry Greenwood stood before the witness for a long time before addressing the Judge. "Your Honor, the prosecution rests."

CHAPTER 8

The testimony halted for the day. The crowd scattered like geese on my lake at day's end, wings spread against an iris sky to return to a nearby refuge. I hurried outside to comfort my granddaughter. As we embraced, Lois left her car to come over.

"For God's sake, let her alone."

Valerie, standing nearby, just cried softly.

Summer was totally exhausted and drained emotionally.

"Poppy, I'm so sorry. I didn't mean to say anything that would hurt you."

"You didn't, baby. You were wonderful."

With her head on my shoulder, she whispered, "Poppy, let's walk in the woods."

"I'd like that, baby."

The weekend was upon us, and I wondered what this pause in the judicial process would bring. My day was suddenly brightened as a small car pulled into the driveway. Summer melted into my arms, but there was little conversation.

Avoiding the trek around the lake, we took the north trail filled with hundred-year-old hardwoods, cedar, and pine. Boneset flower and dog fennel at the trail head attested to my neglect in clearing the pathway, but they dissipated under a canopy of hickory as we entered the woods. Past an old home place, dating to the early 1800s, crumbling remains of a log cabin with foundation made of sandstone gathered from the surrounding area prompted a pause. Still, with the exception of arrival greetings, we had not spoken.

Ordinarily, we might have shared spontaneous imaginary stories of people who lived in this wilderness, miles of forest from the nearest road. We would also take license with historical facts to fashion our own interpretation of early visitors to the region. A favorite character, as I recall, was Hernando De Soto, the Spanish explorer who arrived in 1540. History indicates that De Soto did spend a winter with the Chickasaw Indian tribe in Tupelo. These Spaniards may have been the first white persons the Indians had ever encountered. According to local lore, a misunderstanding developed when pork was introduced to the Indians. The tribe had never seen a hog. Apparently, Chickasaw custom was to share everything; personal ownership was discouraged. Spanish soldiers didn't understand when Chickasaw warriors helped themselves to a few pork hams. A couple of those warriors were shot for stealing. So, the Spanish expedition force was chased out of Tupelo. They proceeded northwest. There are no records of the route taken. Lafayette County was inhabited by the Choctaw Indian tribe, and there was a popular trail from Tupelo along the Yoknapawtapha River through Lafayette County.

Although there is no evidence that the Spanish group came this way, Summer and I decided that they camped at the exact spot where our rotting cabin had later stood. When Summer was about seven years old, she would run through the woods pretending to be a Spanish pig.

Recorded history has ole Hernando De Soto going only from Tupelo to a spot near Memphis and discovering the Mississippi River, which may have been difficult to explain to the natives who had been plying that water for centuries. Anyway, the textbooks all give De Soto credit for the discovery.

Summer had a lot of questions about what happened in our woods. We talked about the struggle for dominance in this new territory, even before the American Revolution, or the war between France and England when the Lafayette Choctaws sided with France, while the Chickasaws supported England. When England finally defeated France in 1736, it seems the Choctaws were invited to move south, leaving the Chickasaws to give up their land in 1832. They were forced to join the 1836 Trail of Tears to march westward.

Today, looking at the destroyed home site in the woods, I suspected that Summer might be remembering our invented games. I thought of Indians and what must have been a "hate crime" to expunge them from their homeland, a theft of their heritage.

Abandoning our private thoughts, we walked the path to a valley of beeches by a clear water that ran in the open for a space and then disappeared underground only to reappear a few hundred feet downstream. For a few moments we just sat on a log, staring at a continuum of fall leaves floating majestically, casually without haste, to a surface of ground covered already with the splendor of fall. Falling leaves of golden linear, orbicular, elliptic, and other shapes with pinnate, netted, and palmate veins, formed glittering patterns in open spaces of blue sky background through giant trees.

Summer spoke first. "Poppy, I don't blame you. I don't understand, but I don't blame you."

"Thank you, baby. You don't know how much that means to me. I don't understand either. But I am so—so sorry."

"Poppy, let's not talk of regrets. Let's just say we're alive—we're alive.

We're alive, and it's a wonderful day."

We walked the mossy banks by the creek, admired patches of smart-weed, touched lyre-leaved sage, and marveled at a variety of fern plants. Before turning homeward, we dipped tired toes in the clear creek water. Our sorrow was still there, but it had found a resting place. As I watched the back of her little red and white Mini Cooper disappear up the drive-way, I knew we were soulmates reconciled to fate.

Still, the question of "why" pulsated in my brain.

Monday morning I faced life with much more vigor. Summer was tucked snugly in my heart, and it was the day my defense began. The jurors appeared fresh, and Walter had lined up a bunch of witnesses, some of whom turned out to be a complete surprise to me. Walt opened the questioning of witnesses for the defense.

My friend Wiley was the first witness to be called to the stand. Wiley Grant squirmed in the chair. Although a large man, he appeared diminutive in the witness spot. Walter Dunbar in his opening statement had proclaimed that I was a model human being. The federal prosecutor had depicted James T. Warner as a cold-blooded murderer. Now, the defense would have the opportunity to prove, not that the defendant was a perfect citizen, but that he was guiltless in the killing of a young black man. My question was how anyone could feel justified in taking the life of another.

After the swearing-in, Walt stood before Wiley.

"Mr. Grant, how long have you known James Warner?"

"Oh, I don't rightly remember, maybe fifty-years."

"And how did you come to be acquainted with Mr. Warner?"

"We came to work at the university at about the same time. I was in the business office. We were associates. Friends over the years."

"And how many years was that?"

"Oh, I don't rightly remember, maybe fifty years."

"And, would you say you know him well?"

Wiley went on and on about how great I was as a person and as a responsible employee. He spoke of honesty and integrity and other qualities to the extent that I was sickened.

Greenwood, the prosecutor, fired a cross-examination volley in quick succession. "Mr. Grant, you testified that you have known the defendant well for many years?"

"Yes, sir."

"And would you say you know many of the same friends?"

"Well, yes, I would say that."

"And would you say he has many friends and associates, black and white?"

"Oh, yes, Jim is well liked, he has loads of friends."

"Black friends?"

"Sure, people he worked with, those political associates he met with—he was into community activities, voter campaigns and the like. There were meetings, dinners—other gatherings."

"Mr. Grant, would you say Mr. Warner had black friends who dined in his home, partied with him, were close, exchanged holiday gifts, and the like?"

Wiley was obviously rattled, shifting from one side of his haunches to the other.

"Mr. Grant, we're waiting."

"Well—well, he may have—that is—I'm sure he did, but—"

"Can you name five minorities with whom Mr. Warner socialized?"

"Not exactly."

"Can you name two? One?"

Wiley was shaking his head and looking directly at me in frustration that he had not been a positive witness.

The prosecutor turned and fixed a long stare at the jury. A couple of them were shaking their heads. All seemed to be conceding that Jim Warner had only business friends, not people with whom he formed social relations. They sat stone-faced as if they were examining their own attitudes toward other races. It was impossible to determine if the test engendered a positive or negative reaction.

Why don't people like me have close social friends from the African American community? I cannot recall the number of committees, organizations, and contacts with minorities, many of whom I felt were friends. Still, it was more business and less close social ties. Maggie and I attended black funerals, a few weddings, and sent graduation presents. We did invite a few black couples to our annual woods walk and picnic at Wyldewoode, and half the number came. Among the seventy to eighty attendees, we might get half a dozen of our black friends. I always assumed that some would feel uncomfortable with so many white faces, and others just didn't care for the activity. I did go into homes of my black acquaintances for conferences from time to time, and a few visited with me, but it was for purposes other than purely social.

I fail to recall any time a black friend invited me into their world for any purpose other than business. I did speak at black churches that time I ran, unsuccessfully, for the state legislature. There were a handful with whom I became close over the years. We could share ideas, feelings and almost any thought, but those occasions were always on a neutral turf.

The same was true of the growing Spanish community. Minorities are generally employees, business associates, or mere acquaintances. We eat at the same restaurants, work side by side, and our kids go to the same schools, but an unwritten and unseen barrier encompasses all colors. The exception is foreign university students whom white families invite to dine once in order to demonstrate open-mindedness at Rotary or the garden club.

I did have one special friend from the African American community. For years, Leonard Thornton and I shared the chairmanship of the local Democratic Party committee. I was the "hothead" who wanted to challenge immediately any perceived attack on political positions; Leonard was the cool one who thought through more seasoned and productive responses.

I remember once, when I was running for state senate, Leonard provided sage advice. My adversary circulated stories that had elements of truth but were taken totally out of context. One had to do with my divorce. The story was that I had recently left a sick wife and two little children for a younger woman. It was true that my wife and I had parted, but that was some twelve years before, and the wife had been quite healthy. She had re-married, and I had married a younger woman. The two little children referenced were grown up and out campaigning for me.

A second story evolved around my listing Unitarian as my preferred religion. It had a young university student visiting my home and, upon searching for a bathroom, opened a closed door to a room which was full of skulls and bones. That branded me as Satan's helper. It was said that "Unitarians don't believe in Jesus, anyway." The element of truth here, I finally concluded, was that the student must have seen some hanging African art.

Another Unitarian reference indicated that I was the culprit in the passage of legislation for a county unit system that many local country people opposed. Forever, five county supervisors had been able to operate independently of any fiscal responsibility. When elected, they built buildings on their own land to house county equipment that could be bought without going through a bidding process. If not re-elected, elaborate buildings were left on their property while a new supervisor built more. They could hire relatives or friends without qualifications and buy supplies from whomever they chose without any accountability. But the most politically beneficial asset for the white landholders was the offer of county equipment and supplies to build and gravel private driveways.

Somehow, black homeowners had difficulty getting these perks. At any rate, I supported the new legislation that provided for a county unit system banning the use of county equipment for private purposes, setting up a permanent central garage for storage of county-wide equipment and supplies, a verifiable accounting system, bidding for all purchases and other requirements for transaction transparency. For many country voters, seeing the word, "Unitarian" meant that I was for that damn "county unit system."

I wanted to climb up on the roof of the courthouse and scream "lies," but Leonard counseled calm.

Leonard reminded me, "People who know you are aware that all this is purely political and untrue. You only belittle yourself by responding. You are bigger than that." I knew that it was good advice, but I lost the election for senate anyway. The positive thing was that I didn't break my neck crawling up on that courthouse roof.

Leonard Thornton was probably the most gentle and decent person I have ever known. Bright, fair, and consistent were the personality traits that are validated by all who knew him. We actually were more like brothers than merely working associates. I never thought of Leonard as a black man, only as a person with deep moral values who was an honest and true friend. We worked together with others through the integration struggles in which he was a real leader and confidant. Leonard died of a wasp sting long before his time but left a legion of accomplishments in the community. He was the epitome of quiet service to humanity with absolutely no thought of personal gain. He was the manifestation of a good man.

The few black citizens who respond to organizational recruitment in traditional white groups here are hounded to become members of everything. Most interested in such activity find community service divided along racial lines and choose to serve their own. History has a way of perpetuating isolation and distrust. That cycle lays heavily on me at this time.

A friend from Indiana testified about my involvement on behalf of financial aid for needy students who were seeking a college education. Mentioned were state, regional, and national organizations. In the late 1960s, a few college financial aid officers paid our own way to Washington and formed the National Association of Student Financial Aid Administrators. We had met for several years as representatives of regional groups, but this was the formal establishment of a national organization. Primarily because no one wanted the initial responsibility, they chose me as the first president. That was 1969, and until this day, NASFAA has worked through legislative lobbying and other means to develop a comprehensive national package of programs in an effort to assure educational opportunity for qualified students regardless of race, creed, sex, etc.

When that friend ended his testimony, I leaned over and whispered to my lawyer, "Walt, what the hell has this got to do with hate crimes?"

"Relax. We just want to establish your leadership in helping others, especially minorities."

More testimony was presented relating to my being a nationally elected trustee of the College Entrance Examination Board, consultant for the College Scholarship Service, National Merit Scholarship Corporation, several colleges and universities, the U.S. Justice Department, and other organizations. They named roles in community civic groups. Rotary, chamber of commerce, arts council, theatre, museum, library, and so on. They even made me a hero for starting a manufacturing company after retirement from the university.

During a break in the testimony, I chastised my attorney. "Walt, this is pure bullshit. I won't agree to any more of it. It has absolutely nothing to do with the charges. It has no relevance to what I actually did—why I've sat in this courtroom for these past three weeks, why I've agonized these past eighteen months trying to understand my motives, why I've studied half-assed social journals and histories of race relations. Walt, I don't care what happens to me—I just want to understand why."

"Mr. Warner, you're obsessed with the reason instead of the action itself. It simply was a reflex motion taken in response to what you saw. Anyone might have interpreted the situation just as you did and responded just as you did."

Walter Dunbar was relentless in making the defendant a certified saint. Little incidents of common courtesy were highlighted as perfect examples of a lack of discrimination. The prosecutor made few objections. All the mundane minutiae of a diminutive nature had the jury nodding. Judge Longest hid a yawn or two behind a sheath of papers. Witness after witness extolled my many virtues.

Finally, Walt called a person who had all, including the jury, sitting up and taking notice. In particular, minority jury members appeared taken aback. It was apparent that none expected to see the individual who walked briskly to the witness chair.

A tall, immaculately dressed black lady settled in the witness box and lifted her chin with a confident air of sophistication.

"Would you please state your name," Walt intoned.

"Lenore Price."

"And what is your occupation?"

"I am director of Student Financial Aid at Columbia College in Illinois."

"Ms. Price, are you acquainted with the defendant, James Warner?"

"Yes."

"And what is your relationship to Mr. Warner?"

"He is a former employer and long-time friend."

"What kind of work did you do for Mr. Warner?"

"I started as a field representative recruiting students. Later, Mr. Warner appointed me financial aid counselor and then associate director of student financial aid."

"Ms. Price, was there anything in particular about your employment that this jury should know?"

"Yes, I was the first-ever black person employed by the university in a professional capacity. Traditionally, there were black grounds keepers, cleaning employees, cafeteria workers, and the like. Two years before I was hired, Mr. Warner employed the first black clerical person to work on campus."

"Did you also say that Mr. Warner was a friend?"

"Yes, and a mentor. He gave me the opportunity to expand my world, to gain confidence, and pursue a satisfying career. He recommended me for my current position."

"And how has he treated you over the years?"

"As a person—as a lady."

"Thank you, Ms. Price."

On cross-examination, the federal prosecutor rose, walked within a few feet of the witness, paused and attacked.

"Ms. Price, you have given a glowing account of how the defendant influenced your life. Would you say he influenced your moral and legal decisions while you were a student?"

"I—don't know what you mean."

"Ms. Price, is it true that you have a criminal record?"

The courtroom buzzed with whispers that grew in intensity until Judge Longest rapped his gavel.

I thought that Walt would object to this line of questioning, but Walt just smiled and patted my knee.

"Ms. Price, you hesitate to answer my question. Do you have a criminal record in this county?"

Lenore had a quizzical look on her face and, for a moment, seemed unsure of herself. Focusing a dagger-like stare on the prosecutor, she said. "I really don't know—I probably do."

"Do you remember that you were arrested for a criminal act—yes or no?"

"I remember being arrested. I don't know if there is a record."

On re-direct, Walt approached the witness with a wounded look as if the prosecutor had pulled away a bandage on an open wound.

"Ms. Price, isn't it true that the only crime for which you have ever been charged was for disturbing the peace?"

"Yes, sir."

"Would you explain to this court exactly what you did to deserve that citation?"

"Well, this was a couple of years after integration. There were about a dozen of us—African Americans enrolled at the time. We were harassed, subjected to racial slurs, and generally ignored as a part of the university. We had complained to administrators. They listened but took no action. A northeastern speaker from a college —the name I don't recall —was scheduled for a program in the chapel. Eight of us prepared signs demanding equal treatment and marched down the chapel aisles, interrupting the program. Campus security arrested us immediately and dragged us from the building. We were turned over to the local authorities and placed in jail cells. It was considered an unlawful demonstration."

"And was your mentor, Mr. James Warner, complicit in planning this demonstration?"

"Oh, no. I didn't know Dr. Warner at the time —I take that back. When I first came to the university, a friend and I sat in his office to request financial aid. He was director of placement and financial aid at the time."

"And what happened at that time?"

"These two little black girls—"

Greenwood objected, citing relevance.

Judge Longest scowled, peering over his half-glasses. "Mr. Greenwood, you opened the discussion by questioning complicity by the defendant in actions by the witness. I think it might be advisable to permit Ms. Price to continue her story."

Lenore Price picked up where she was interrupted.

"These two little black girls were so afraid. Our parents had scoffed at the idea that we, residents of the same town, should enter the mostly white institution. We applied for the fall semester and looked for summer jobs. There were none. Summer enrollment at the university was the following week. So, without the knowledge of our parents, we walked the two miles to campus and found the office of placement and financial aid. It was housed on the third floor of this building that, to us, looked exactly like an old plantation mansion. Asking for directions elicited stares and grimaces that assured us we were in the wrong place. Little did we know that it was past the deadline for aid application.

"The man behind the big desk rose and asked us to take a seat, but we were so intimidated that we stood shaking in our boots. He had a kind face. He explained that all the summer aid had been awarded. He was very sorry, but most of the fall semester aid had also been committed. He told us we could apply, and he would try to see if he could find something for fall.

"I began to cry from embarrassment. How could I think of rushing out here to this office three days before classes expecting to get help? Anyway, my older brother had already told me, 'that whitey school wasn't gonna help no black nigger.'

"The man got up from his chair, came around and placed his hand on my trembling shoulder. I braced myself because I knew that he was about to throw us out of his office. Instead, he led both Tricia and me to a seat.

"'Now', he said, 'why is it so important that you start immediately rather than making plans for the fall, September?'

"Tricia spoke first in a halting speech that would conjure up a vision of a baby in diapers. 'Cause we scared.'

"'Scared of what?' the man said.

"Tricia couldn't talk, so I had to. I told him about how hard it was for us to decide, even against family objections, to apply to the white school. We'd agonized over and over about how safe and reasonable it would be to go to a black school where we could feel secure and be accepted. The decision had been so soul wrenching that sleep was difficult, the stomach cramped, and rashes appeared on our bare spots. So much had been overcome that one more delay would kill the desire, dig a black hole as black as I am.

"There was a silence as long as ten heartbeats, and then he spoke. 'Why do you want to go to college?'

"A small voice from deep within my chest answered. 'I want a good education. I want to make something of myself. I want to be somebody!'

"The man averted his eyes. I didn't know what he was thinking— what excuse he would give to send these colored gals on their way. But he turned back and in a low voice told us to go home and pack our bags. We arrived on campus the next Monday with enough Educational Opportunity Grant, work-study, and loan money to barely scrape by summer school. Tricia didn't make it, but, with help, I was back in the fall and graduated four years later."

Greenwood objected but was overruled.

Walter Dunbar blew his nose and approached Ms. Price.

"After meeting with this man in the financial aid office, where and when did you next encounter him, in person?"

"In the Lafayette County jail at four a.m. on the morning following our march at the chapel."

"In the jail?"

"Yes."

"Why in the world would he be in the Lafayette County jail at four a.m.?"

"To get me and the others out!"

"And who was that man?"

"Dr. James Warner—that man."

And she pointed at me.

The next witness was also a former student with whom I had worked. By that time, having another black person to testify on my behalf was not such a shock. Tim Haley was especially expansive in relating stories of his university experience and his relationship with Dr. Warner. Tim, a black kid who never knew his father, needed only a little encouragement to become a student leader. He was elected president of the Black Student Union. This was during the early days of integration when the entire community was involved in adjusting to this new reality. Naturally, the majority of students were apprehensive as was the minority, who were suspicious and reactive to slights, real or imagined. Tim had a broader perspective. He never gave the impression that he differed in any way from any other student. He was, however, cognizant and sensitive to the plight of minority students and tenacious in his efforts to make them a part of campus life. He was interested in recruiting more minority students, which happened to be a part of my job at the university. We spent long hours together developing strategy, and Tim sometimes traveled with me to all-black schools. Public secondary schools at that point were all-black or all-white.

The prosecutor rose to cross-examine.

"Mr. Haley, what is it that you do—your career?"

"I publish a newspaper and am a Baptist minister."

"Would you say that you were very close to Mr. Warner during the time you were in school?"

"Oh, yes, sir."

"And what was the nature of your association with Mr. Warner?"

"I guess he became my counselor and friend. "

"How did that come about?"

"I was in line to process my financial aid package, and he showed some interest. Asked where I was from and what I intended to study. We kinda hit it off, and that encounter led me to seek him out after registration. I was homesick and considering dropping out of school. Dr. Warner convinced me to take it week by week. I promised to come by his office on Friday to report my progress. We discussed my feeling of isolation. He asked what could be done about it. I told him we needed more minority students at the university. His response was a question. 'What are you going to do about it?' My answer was that there was nothing I could do. He motioned me to go with him. We walked down the hall. When he turned into the chancellor's office, I almost fainted. He introduced me to the chief executive officer of Ole Miss. He said, 'Dr. Fortune, this is Tim Haley. He is going to help us enroll more minority students.' The chancellor was more than cordial and expressed appreciation that we shared one of the major goals of the university. I left the office of the chancellor with a sense that I could make a difference. After that, Dr. Warner and I had strategy sessions including my own involvement as a student as well as planning for the recruitment of minority students."

"And during these strategy sessions you describe in your testimony—would you say that you discussed racial animosity?"

"Yes, I would say that."

"In these moments of discussions, do you think you got a feel for how Mr. Warner really felt about racial discrimination?"

"Well—yes."

"Mr. Haley, did you and Mr. Warner always agree about racial prejudice?"

"Well, no. Not always. People don't always agree on everything. Mr. Warner was always open and willing to question his own deep-down, gut, feelings."

"What do you mean by that?"

"Well—I don't know exactly how to explain it."

"Are you saying that Mr. Warner had prejudices?"

"I'm only saying that Mr. Warner searched his heart for anything he did that might be unfair or unjust."

"Surely, Mr. Haley, you can provide an example of that."

"I don't know. I just sensed it."

"And why is this sensitive nature of yours unable to recall one single incident that shows Mr. Warner examining his own prejudice."

"Well—this is nothing—it doesn't mean anything—no, I can't be more specific than how I see it."

"Mr. Haley, why don't you open up about what you thought just now? Let the jury decide what it means?"

"Well, it doesn't mean anything."

"Mr. Haley—Mr. Haley—"

"All right! But it doesn't say anything about the man—it's irrelevant, but—"

"Go on, Mr. Haley."

"Well—one time Dr. Warner admitted that—that whenever someone in a big car cuts him off, he automatically looks to determine the race of the driver. He couldn't explain why he is inclined to do that and asked me if I thought that was inborn prejudice. He didn't mean anything by it—he even joked that he had the same reaction to see if it was a student from Texas—either an African-American or a white student from Dallas."

The prosecutor had no further questions.

Walt studied his notes for a moment and then announced, "Your Honor, the defense rests. We have no additional witnesses."

CHAPTER 9

Before Walt Dunbar sat down, I arose to address the court. "Your Honor, I rise to lodge a request. I would like to testify on my own behalf."

There was an audible exhalation from the audience, including members of the jury. Walter was objecting, and people were chattering. Judge Longest rapped his gavel, asking for order.

"Mr. Warner, have you discussed this matter with your attorney?"

"Briefly, but each time he has disagreed with my proposal to take the stand."

Walter took three steps toward the judge. "Your Honor, I have not adequately discussed this with my client. I would like to file a motion for a recess to have that opportunity."

The prosecution objected strenuously to that proposal.

Walter shot back. "If it please the court, I request that a delay of trial be permitted and an order issued that Mr. Warner be subjected to a psychological examination to determine his competency to testify before this court".

Judge Longest peered over his half-glasses, first at Walt and then at me. There was a long pause while, collectively, onlookers held their breath. The Judge frowned his displeasure, each wrinkle resembling the pathway of a drunken sailor.

"Ladies and gentlemen of the jury, it is rather late in the day. I am dismissing you until nine o'clock Thursday. All of the admonitions of this court still apply, including the order not to discuss this case among yourselves or with others. Both prosecution and defense lawyers will immediately go to my office for a private conference. Court dismissed."

Later I learned that when the group assembled in chambers, Judge Longest turned his displeasure to Walter.

"Mr. Dunbar, what is all this drama about?"

"Judge Longest, as you might understand, my client has been under a great deal of stress since this incident. He still has no memory of the actual event itself. He has not provided adequate assistance in preparing his defense. He has spent countless hours researching psychological journals for information about hate crimes. He has consulted social media, sociologists, and psychologists. He is obsessed with theories about discrimination and different forms of prejudice. His entire focus during these last eighteen months has been his personal motivation for the incident rather than his defense of the action. I submit to you that he is mentally unstable and incapable of contributing to his defense. He is eighty-three years of age and has some loss of present reality, Alzheimer's or worse. He has been known to speak of his wife in the present tense, a wife who has been dead for ten years. His competency to testify is certainly in question."

Larry Greenwood interrupted. "Judge, there has been no insanity plea introduced as a defense. Mr. Warner's mental state has not been suggested or questioned in the record. Not a single witness has testified that Mr. Warner has lost any of his intellectual skills or his ability to communicate. I am sure that all concerned would appreciate hearing any explanation that Mr. Warner has to offer for his murder of an unarmed black boy."

"Mr. Dunbar, is there any medical or other recorded evidence of mental illness, loss of communication, or other skills that would severely handicap Mr. Warner's ability to answer questions?" the judge asked?

"Nothing of record of which I am aware, Your Honor, but my observation and that of people who have known him for a long time could testify to his current difficulty in understanding reality."

"Then why didn't you call some of those witnesses?" Greenwood snapped. "Judge, this is just a delaying tactic and an effort to distort the reality of this murder that was prompted by the color of the victim's skin."

Walt raised his voice as he turned to Larry Greenwood. "And you just want to get an addled old man to crucify on the witness stand."

"Boys! Boys!" Judge Longest showed his ire at the lack of judicial and professional courtesy shown by these personal attacks from both lawyers. "I'm tired of hearing this wrangling. Tell you what, I'm going to give Mr. Dunbar forty-eight hours to convince his client not to testify. When court convenes the day after tomorrow, if Mr. Warner insists, it will be his right to offer testimony. I could put something in the charge to the jury that they are to assess the competency and reliability of each of the witnesses."

I watched Walt drive down the lane, past the pokeberry bushes and holly trees to sit in his car for a bit before he slowly got out and came up the walk. He wasted no time as he stood on the porch.

"Mr. Warner, why did you blindside me like that? I thought we had a good shot to convince the jury that this was a horrible accident, not related to race or discrimination."

"Walt, I guess I'm not convinced. I just want to tell my story—to share with ordinary people, to see if there is any sense to be made of it. I feel that the record should include a defense that can be questioned and reconciled."

"Don't you know, Mr. Warner, Larry Greenwood will take that attitude as a guilty plea and challenge your right to live—or, at least to live free? He will label you as a murderer, a rabid racist who has no regard for the life of a black child. This is serious business, Mr. Warner. It's not just my case to lose; you are my friend. I don't want to see you in jail or executed."

"I'm sorry, Walt. This is important to me. As they say, 'a man's got to do what a man's got to do.' Walt, do you really think I'm incompetent to testify?"

"I think you're confused, Mr. Warner. I intend to renew my petition for a psychological examination and continue to object to including your testimony."

"What if I propose replacing my attorney with one who represents my views?"

"You have every right to do that, but for your sake, I hope you don't."

M y lawyer and former friend backed out and drove up the driveway at a considerably faster pace than when he came down. As twilight deepened, I spoke with Maggie, who appeared in the fall haze hovering like a gray sheet at the western horizon. These days cotton dusting of chemicals by plane leaves a residue that drifts like balloons in the air. Not unlike when I was a boy turning a hand crank on a gadget strapped to my back. The crank sucked poison from a cloth sack to spew it out a tin tube onto cotton plants near the squaring and blooming stage. Much of this work was done by the young since all you had to do was carry a few pounds and walk the straight rows with overhanging stalks. As often as possible one walked the row middles on moon-lit nights. The wind normally died at day's end, which meant that more of the arsenic-laced powder would land on the cotton bolls rather than floating about to be breathed in open nostrils flared with exertion. All to kill that little black bug, boll weevil, fighting for food.

But, then again, their food was our livelihood. As a pre-teen youngster, I remember the fright at rows' end bordered by trees or fences that tended to include bushes or tall grasses. Somehow visions of "boogers" and other monsters lurked at those darker spots rather than in an open field. It was just like a black night when ghosts were said to romp about. I wonder if that cloud left by the crop duster on the western sky has its own demons drifting down on an unsuspecting audience. Nature seems to provide choices as to what and perhaps who might be killed.

Talking with Maggie on a night like this, after wrangling with my attorney, seems a reasonable thing to do. I know she is only a spirit, but it's a comfort to the old to have someone to listen. Being alone may sometimes be a pleasant sensation, but, especially in times of trouble, it's reassuring to have a partner. True, a vision never speaks, but the expressive nature of the apparition speaks volumes. You really don't have to provide information, it's already floating out there in the mind's cloud like thought dust.

Maggie, I know that common sense would advise quiet and docile submission. I have made every effort to understand for myself, but there seems to be no standard, no measure by which a definitive enlightenment could be discovered. I wonder if in sharing with others, there might be a clairvoyant moment for psychic revelation that gives motivation a clarity. I understand that you're saying to follow my heart, but I do not know my heart. Why did I act as I did, and why does my memory fail me?

A Lewis Carroll conundrum has a confused Alice meeting a Cheshire cat at a fork in the road. When asked which way to go, the cat replied that it depends on where you want to get to. I don't know where I'm going, Maggie.

It's not as if I'm not trying to find the path, Maggie. That's why I went to Kentucky back last fall. In Mississippi and other states, it has always been a question of time as to when racial reconciliation might be accomplished. To some, the answer is never. Others claim it a process of education and association. I wanted to get a feel for how one educational institution that has a history of overcoming some of the early challenges met those goals through association in an educational setting.

Berea College in Berea, Kentucky, is a small private institution in a small community in central Kentucky, just south of Lexington. It was founded in 1855 by abolitionist John Greg Fee as the first interracial and co-educational college in the South. In fact, there were very few such institutions in the country that admitted black and white, male and female students in an integrated setting. At Berea, students are expected to work along with their studies, but tuition is free. Today, work, scholarships, loans and federal aid provide for other educational expenses. With the approaching Civil War, slaveholders forced the closing of Berea, but it reopened in 1866. In the early years, over half the student body were black. In 1882, the student handbook proclaimed that dating and interracial marriage among students were not prohibited. In 1904, the Kentucky legislature passed a law, the Day Act, to make integration illegal. Not until the 1950s when the U.S. Supreme Court in Brown versus Board of Education of Topeka ruled state segregation statutes unconstitutional did Berea again became interracial.

Settled in at the Boon Tavern, a historic hotel on campus, I walked under the beautiful trees and observed students hurrying to their assigned jobs and classes. I tried to picture an 1882 campus with interracial dating and marriage. At that point, I was surprised to observe the make-up of the student body. In 1866, the opening year following the Civil War, there were more black students than white, 96 black and 91 white. Today a statistical report indicates that about one-third of the student body is an ethnic minority or international from the United States and fifty-eight other countries. I saw mixed-race couples and black students, but predominately a white population. It seems that Berea is like many other colleges now—competing for minorities.

I visited the quaint shops where students work and marveled at the artistic talent shown by their creative endeavors. Berea must be meeting the educational needs and aspirations of many students. I may be wrong, but I did not find it different or more progressive than other colleges with which I am familiar in bridging the racial divide.

My assessment may be clouded by a decision of the Berea administration in 1964 to refrain from participation in a Mississippi project for voter registration. Students were prohibited, according to the then President, due to an assessment that they would "do more harm than good." I am unable to argue with that position, but it does make me wonder if we all wish a result but are afraid to face the problem.

I left a beautiful campus with laudable goals and an admirable history, but I was still without a clue as to how a society so diverse can breach the color barrier. I can appreciate the contribution of abolitionists like John Greg Fee and others who worked tirelessly to right the wrong of slavery. I envisioned a connection from stories told about an 1850s plantation, Strawberry Plains, located in Holly Springs, Mississippi, about twenty-five miles north of Oxford. I imagined a slave whose dreams included a better life.

Three square miles, 2,500 acres with antebellum houses and out buildings joining the south bank of the Coldwater River, constitute boundaries of the Strawberry Plains Audubon Society. One of the largest gifts ever made to Audubon, it is a showcase for the conservation of birds and their habitat. I stood in the midst of thousands of migratory hummingbirds being nourished, studied, and tracked. The meadows are home to sparrows, chats, and other songbirds. A rookery of great blue herons stalk the Coldwater bottoms. It was not always so. In the 1850s, it was the Strawberry Plains Plantation.

Fourteen-year-old Lizzie Turner rolled out the "longer-than-her" sack, adjusted the strap to her shoulder and bent to the row of fluffy white. She was not alone. Twenty or so, each commanding a separate row, constituted a swath of black against the sun-bleached earth and cotton snow. She felt nothing for the person to her left or right. She had vowed not to feel since they had parted. She was only four when young Master Turner lined up men on the "Big House" gallery. Her daddy was bought by the Pidgeon Roost farm not far to the south, near the Tallahatchie River. Daddy was permitted to visit Strawberry Plains every few months, but Momma scooted the children out of the shack, so Lizzie never really got to know him. Plantations swapped labor depending on when cotton opened in their various fields. Daddy was now on her right, a result of a swap day, and Momma was to the left. Brothers and sisters were scattered over the field like blackberries.

That didn't bother Lizzie. Others cried and talked to the fare-thee-well about missing family; Lizzie thought only of escape. Ever since the first tie was laid on the Holly Springs-Grand Junction Railroad line, she knew it would be the golden mist that bore her away from this rat hole. She lay at night among arms and feet invading her space, listening to the whistle and imagining smoke from the giant train pipe turning amber to lift her up and over—over the fields, over the Coldwater River, even over the bluffs of Memphis. She had seen runaway slaves being punished, the bull-whip dripping crimson, rending the naked flesh. But she would be above all that. She was flying.

She hated picking cotton. Sharp burs on bolls seemed to relish plying into tender spots around her nails. Hands never toughened to black splinters invading soft tissue. Already puffy and sore, fingers bled again to stain a handful of white. Still, the sack must be filled. At weighing-up time, if the sack was a few pounds under, the overseer, Mr. Thames, had a razor strap eternally hooked over his arm, and he was not judicious in applying it to tired shoulders. Not meeting your established limit would mean punishment. But it was not Mr. Thames who was riding up the picked row on a sorrel mare. It was Master Turner, now toward his middle years and bearing a bouncing belly just beyond the saddle horn. It was evident from eyes as red as the horse that he had not yet made the night nor lost a bourbon buzz.

"Hey you, Lizzie, the miss'es took the kids to Bible School. Come down and make my breakfast."

"Massa Turner, don't I got to pick cotton?"

"Hell's bells, gal, forget the cotton. I want breakfast."

She looked at Momma, and Momma looked over at Daddy.

Daddy was a couple of yards ahead and didn't look back. He flung it over his shoulder. "Shet up, Emaline. Jest shet up."

Momma went back to picking.

Lizzie passed by the six-posted portico to the back door and into the kitchen. She was just cupping flour from the bin and pulling a bucket of lard down for blending when he came through the dining room.

"Just make coffee," Turner said.

"Yessa." And she reached for the pot to empty old grounds.

He just stood in the doorway looking at her. She took down the busting bowl and smashed the roasted beans, placing them in the straining tin above a pot of water. Stoking up the fire with stove wood strips, she turned to a cubbyhole that held everyday cups. She was aware that he was still standing in the doorway looking at her.

"Lizzie, you're a pretty young nigger," he said.

"Yessa."

He moved into the kitchen and opened the door to an anteroom where the regular cook slept. "Come in here."

"Massa Turner, no—No!"

"Listen, I had a bad night, lost a lot of money—I need a little nigger pussy. I want yours before it gets all dirtied up by those coons you run with."

"Laudy me, Massa, I ain't never done such!"

She suddenly began to heave violently, wiping her mouth on her sleeve.

"Don't matter," he said, "It ain't like I'm gonna kiss you. Just get on that cot and hike up your dress."

Out that back door, she ran. A little voice inside yelled, "Run, Lizzie, run—run, Lizzie, run—run, Lizzie, run!" She ran past the smokehouse, past the outhouse, past the stables, past the garden, and on through fields of cotton and corn. The track was before her, the train engine gulping water from a tin draped to a water tower. She had no way of knowing that a train had to stop every so often to take on wood or coal and water to produce the steam that powered the train, nor did she care to know. Her whole purpose now was to slip past the flat cars loaded with bales of cotton and find an open door to a cargo coach. She had to settle for a bin car filled with seed gleaned from the cotton locks she would normally be packing into her cotton sack. Trembling, she took an iron rung and climbed to the top where she slipped under the canvas topping meant to hold cotton seed in place. Puffing smoke filled with soot failed to project her dream of golden mist, but as the train moved she knew that she was flying.

At Grand Junction, she held her breath for the great crash. Another train was headed directly for her iron monster. In an instant, another track appeared, and her train had the good sense to veer to the side. While both trains were stopped, she slipped into an empty boxcar headed west to Memphis.

Since the Holly Springs track had been laid, she had been talking with every slave who chanced to move through Strawberry Plantation. One returning slave who had been caught explained that there was a group of crazy white folk that helped slaves get out of the South and become people in another state. Dried whelps on his body attested to the fact that such a run was pointless. His advice was to make the best of what you have and forget escaping. He did tell her about a place in Memphis to go if she ever decided to get away.

Lizzie ate some cotton seed that made her sick. When bailing out as the train slowed in Memphis, she landed near a patch of good eating sweet potatoes. It took two days to find the place, to find Mr. Abol. That was not his name, and he never told it to her. He did tell her that the route north of Memphis was too dangerous. Patrollers filled the roads, and bad treatment by these vigilantes who received pay for returning runaway slaves was well known. A young black girl would be subjected to much evil.

"But what to do?" Lizzie wanted to know.

Mr. Abol stroked a chin of mustache and replied. "It is better that you make your way back home and face your punishment."

"I can't—I won't!" she cried.

"What are you willing to sacrifice? Your very life?"

"Yes, my very life."

"There may be another route —It's a long way to get to a safe place, and it may not be safe for long."

"A chance I take."

Mr. Abol rubbed his face and smoothed his hair. "I'll get you some food. You stay here tonight and be ready to leave tomorrow."

The stoop-shouldered, middle-aged white man and his young black slave appeared on the station platform the next morning. He was grumbling and treating her badly as she dragged a huge suitcase almost as big as she was. He gave her a vicious slap as she struggled to place the bag on the station cart. She was admonished to crawl into the baggage car while he rode first class to Knoxville. They had rehearsed the journey well. At Knoxville, he would hire a carriage to take her to the Kentucky border. At that point, she was to walk along the high road for many miles to a place called Berea. She was cautioned to stay somewhat off the road but to use the road as her guide. A knapsack of food had been prepared to last a part of the arduous journey. She would be on her own to scavenge food along the way.

The train made stops to disgorge and take on passengers. Once, her benefactor had, without speaking, poked food through iron bars on the baggage car door. Lying on a bed of straw, she felt convulsions of fear course through her veins at every pause in the progress. On the second day, twilight fell as she waved to Mr. Abol from the back of a wagon. Mr. Abol was standing by the station frontage. He turned his back, ignoring her presence, now and forever.

Besides the knapsack packed with hard tack and bread, her only possession was a row of crooked lines on brown paper. When she was dropped just outside the city of Knoxville, she knew that it was nowhere near the X spot indicated on her paper. Anyway, she had just as soon walk. She was pointed toward Kentucky, and the cool darkness was her friend. She scaled to the peak of a rocky point by the side of the road, where she lay on a mossy ledge and watched the blinking lights below.

An awakening sky invited her to stretch sore limbs toward a beckoning goal. Her pace was hindered by having to scoot off the road to avoid fellow travelers on horseback, wagons, or in fine carriages. Sometimes she would skirt entire villages and towns. That gave her the opportunity to gather an ear of corn or pick juicy peaches. There were plenty of rivers and creeks in which to drink and to soak her tired feet. Finally, she saw the big K on a roadside sign. Kentucky. Kentucky, this meant freedom. Freedom, freedom, freedom! She raised her hands and wallowed in the dirt, relishing the idea. But, she remembered the warning of Mr. Abol. He said, not yet. This was a little safer, but somebody had to decide which way to go. In the next village, she tried to sound out the letters. It was 'E m l y n'. She had been taught some spelling, but never encountered such a word. It must be a place of wonder, she thought, as she bedded down by a huge sassafras tree near a running stream.

The wonder evaporated immediately as she awoke to a huge farmer standing over her. "Who are you, gal?"

"I'm nobody, Massa."

"Whatcha' doing?"

"Nothing, Massa."

"You one of them run-aways?"

"Oh, nosir, I'ze just Lizzie," as she started to cry.

For six weeks she washed the clothes, took care of babies, hoed the garden, and cooked the meals and scrubbed the floors of the shack. She was carefully watched and rope-tied at night. The young couple had five young'uns and, now, one slave. They were kind enough to her, but Lizzie was still a slave.

One night Lizzie slipped the ropes and was thirty miles away when they awoke. Several thirty-mile days brought her to the outskirts of Berea.

From a lofty perch, she observed the big buildings. She had been told to go to a big building, but there were several about the same size clustered in the middle of huge oak trees. It was early morning, and people began moving about going in and out doors. Strange, there were young white people and niggers making their way through those front doors. She ventured closer and found a black boy who had come to a stable where horses were kept.

"Hey," she spoke.

"Hey, yourself," he answered.

"I need the big house."

"You mean the office?"

"I guess."

The young man looked closely at her. "You look like you've come a long way."

"Yeah."

"Well, the horses can wait. I'm Will. Come along with me."

They moved into the center building, across an impressive atrium, to a tall door. Lizzie was literally shaking in her worn clodhoppers. A small, gray-haired, white gentleman opened the door.

"Dean Woodall, this is Lizzie, I found her down by the stables," Will announced.

"Well, Lizzie, where do you come from?" Dean Woodall asked, scrutinizing the dirty waif in his doorway.

"Mississippi, Massa," Lizzie replied hesitantly.

Dean Woodall chuckled pleasantly. "I'm not a master, Lizzie; you may call me Dean Woodall. Come on in."

Lizzie had turned to run. This man was too nice. He must want something.

Will stood in her way. "Don't be afraid," he said. "Go on in. I'll see you later."

Woodall waved her in, and she followed him into a dining room, just now noticing her own body odor. She held her arms close to her ribs to smother the smell. The dean seemed not to have any reaction to the foul stench that permeated the room.

"Have you had breakfast, Lizzie?"

"No sir, but I'm okay."

"Nonsense," Dean Woodall insisted. "Would you like strawberries and yogurt with some toast?"

"I love strawberries—but I don't know, what you say, yo-gurt?"

"You'll like it—made from milk."

A lady walked in.

"Mrs. Woodall, this is Lizzie, a new student. Would you set another plate?"

Mrs. Woodall was a tall lady with a long dress and high-topped collar. To Lizzie's great surprise, she was a "high yellow" black. She smiled at Lizzie but indicated that she was not hungry. She would bring their breakfast and leave them to school matters. She brought the food with a lighted candle that smelled of vanilla. They ate, he slowly, Lizzie with ravenous disregard.

"Lizzie, here we educate young people, regardless of race. We have some quite young and some who are college students. We take you where you are on the educational scale and teach the best we can."

"Dean, sir, I don't have no money."

"Does not matter. Our school is free. All students work and use their pay for living expenses."

Lilly gasped. "Pay!"

"Yes, pay. You are paid for your work. You have a job based on what you can do to provide some service that the school or other students or the townspeople need."

"I want to try. I'll be good and work hard. I like to work."

"All right, Lizzie, But I need to tell you—it may not last forever. As you may know, there are some states that have slaves, and some who hate slavery. Kentucky is sort of a middle state, and there is talk of a big war. If we have to leave here, we have arranged to go north to a free state where a black person can live in peace. I pray that we can continue in Berea, but I wanted to let you know that this arrangement may not be permanent. You and I may have to run again."

"It's okay. I run good. I want to be free!"

"Just one caution, Lizzie. Freedom means you get to make choices, but it also means that you are responsible for those decisions. Never forget there are two roads to freedom."

"I promise; I'll take the right roads."

"Good. Now let's see about finding you a room, some clothes, and a long bath."

I shared with Maggie my frustration at understanding so little of my study of human relations. I've pored over studies of race relations, human motivation, and the history of man. Maggie and I did a bit more travel than many, and I made trips alone. Altogether, places in Europe, Scandinavia, North and South America, with a smattering of Africa and the Far East were destinations. Still, the simple person I am, it seemed that most people are searching for the same dream, have pretty much the same goals, and act pretty much the same. We all seem to share the positive and negative of human qualities. I do realize that there are so much and so many places that are not a part of my experience. "Maggie, how can I understand myself if I am unable to fathom mankind?"

The vision faded as the moon hid behind low-flying clouds. I went to my bed to dream dreams, none of which were comforting. Why do they invade our sleep if they give no rest?

CHAPTER 10

Word must have gotten around. The courtroom was packed. Judge Longest was on the bench convening the trial while people curved around the outside banisters hoping to get a seat or at least hear rumors from those closest to the closed door. My family, including Summer, were seated in the third row. Their blank faces precluded a perception of hope or hopelessness.

It was quite unusual, but Walter Dunlap arrived after I had been seated. He had no greeting and did not look my way. He seemed inordinately interested in reviewing notes on his yellow pad.

Judge Longest looked directly at our table. "Mr. Dunlap, did you have a motion to present to this court?"

"Yes, Your Honor, I move dismissal of this proceeding without prejudice for the following reasons:

1. The prosecutor has established no evidence of discrimination or racial hatred.

2. The prosecutor has shown no specific intent, motive, or purpose for harming anyone.

3. There is no evidence of pre-planning, anticipated injury, or any prior hostility toward the victim

4. On the other hand, we have shown that defendant was not ac-

quainted with the victim, had no time to determine his race, creed, or color and has no memory of firing the fatal shot."

The judge looked carefully at me.

"Normally, as a judge, I might take such a motion under advisement and carefully weigh the burden of proof and how it relates to the suggested reasons for dismissal. In this instance, it is the individual charged who has requested continuance. While I make no judgment on the reasons presented for dismissal, I am prepared to allow this trial to continue if it is the desire of the defendant to provide testimony. Mr. Warner, would you please stand?"

I stood and said, "Yes, Your Honor."

"Mr. Warner, do you understand the consequences of a decision to testify, that the prosecutor may question you on any subject of record and you will be compelled to answer truthfully under oath? And, that you have discussed the matter with your attorney and you still desire to take the stand in your defense?"

"Yes, Your Honor."

"Then, I am instructing that you be administered the oath and take the stand."

Slowly and with some reluctance, I placed my hand on the leather cover. Not because I was hesitant to swear to tell the truth as I know it, but because of doubts I have acquired over the years about the authenticity or authority of that document. I feel a little hypocritical since I am critical of those who sit or kneel in some church in some country and pay homage to words in some print that they little understand or believe. I know that these words have stood for great good and the vilest of evil. Still, although inspiring both sentiments, brainless faith is anathema to good in my estimation. And so, I compromised my integrity and took a seat.

Walt sat at the table and asked, "For the record, please state your name."

"James T. Warner"

"What is your age, Mr. Warner?"

"Eighty-three."

Walt arose and advanced toward the witness chair. "Do you live alone, Mr. Warner?"

"Yes, for ten years since my wife died."

"Mr. Warner, do you often forget where you left something, tools, glasses, keys?"

"Yes—one time I even found my car keys in the—er—ice box."

"You mean the refrigerator?"

"Yes."

"I noticed you hesitated on that word. Was there a reason for that?"

"Oh, you know, sometimes the right word doesn't come right off, and you substitute another word for it."

"Do you sometimes forget the names of friends or associates, even those you've known for some time?"

"Yes, but I am told that comes with age."

"Is it true that you have poor eyesight, wear glasses?"

"Yes, I have had five operations to repair a detached retina. My vision in the left eye is very poor, and I have corrective lens for the right eye. I drive some in the day in familiar locations but feel uncomfortable to drive at night."

"Mr. Warner, I only want a yes or no answer. When you are alone out on your farm, perhaps when you are unable to sleep, do you talk out loud to your dead wife?"

"Well, yes, but—"

"Yes or no, Mr. Warner!"

"Yes."

"Mr. Warner, is there anyone in the world that you hate?"

"Well no, there are people I don't like, and I do hate what some do, the evil, but I don't just hate anyone."

"Were you acquainted in any way with Artise Bradley Washington?"

"No."

"If you, before all the publicity of this case, were to meet Artise Bradley Washington on the street, would you have recognized him?"

"No."

"Prior to this case, were you aware that Artise Bradley Washington was an African American?"

"No."

"Prior to this case, had you formed any opinion, positive or negative about Artise Bradley Washington?"

"No."

"Mr. Warner, were you aware that your granddaughter was dating an African American?"

"No."

"And, did you on May 3, 2015, know that your granddaughter and a friend would be on the path of your woods walk?"

"No."

"Did you plan or anticipate that you would kill a black person on that walk or at any other time?"

"God. No!"

"And, finally, Mr. Warner, when you slid down that hill by the huge birch tree and apparently observed what might have been interpreted as a rape of your granddaughter, Summer, were you aware of the color of skin or other characteristics of the assumed rapist?"

"I'm sorry, I have been unable to remember. I still don't remember what happened. I remember the boy bleeding and my granddaughter in a hysterical state, but no more."

The U.S. attorney objected to this line of questioning since no witness had been produced to indicate a mental condition. Judge Longest reminded him that a plea for a recess for a psychological examination had been rejected by the prosecution.

"The mental and emotional state of a defendant may be the subject of an examination. Since there are no expert witnesses who have been called, I will strike the answer to the last question and instruct the jury to ignore it. That will not prevent the prosecution the opportunity to question this witness relating to any mental or psychological inquiries touched on by the defense."

Walter Dunbar then asked more inane questions about my family and me.

"Mr. Warner, in what year were you born and where?"

"Central Mississippi, Lena, in 1933."

"Right at the end of the Great Depression?"

"Well, for Mississippi, it was probably at the middle. The economic conditions of Wall Street take a little time to trickle down to our state, and sometimes we are the last to recover from a depression or a recession. At any rate, it was a tough time for a sharecropping family in Mississippi."

"For those of us who have little knowledge of sharecropping, please tell us what that was like."

"In Leake County, there were no plantations, only relatively small land owners who had survived bank foreclosures. There was no machinery, only farm animals during my early years. Land owners, sometimes widows of the first world war, and others who were fortunate enough to have large tracts, needed labor to till the soil. Sharecropping was, I think, an outgrowth of the Civil War, when former slaves were freed. Farming was all they knew, and the former master needed farm labor. So, they worked out a deal. If the laborer had no animals or farm equipment, crops would be grown on halves, the sharecropper receiving a half of what he produced using the landowners' plows and work animals. If the cropper had his own plows and work animals, he would receive three-fourths of what he could produce. Normally, the landowner furnished a shack for the sharecropper and his family. Poor whites made the same arrangements, usually living in shacks similar to those of the black families."

"So, you grew up on a farm in a community that included black citizens?"

"Yes. There were different farms and communities. I believe I changed schools five times. You see, sharecroppers are always trying to improve their lot. If you thought another landowner had better soil, a nicer sharecropper cabin or house, better animals and equipment, or, if you considered him or her more honest or fairer, you would move. We lived on seven different farms, all within two adjacent counties."

"You worked in the fields?"

"Yes. At six, I was carrying water to workers. At eight it was hoeing and picking cotton or harvesting corn or gathering vegetables. I believe I was eight or ten before I had to plow with a mule or horse. There were other chores, helping Daddy saw stove wood and logs for the fireplace with a cross-cut saw, feeding the livestock, and a whole host of other childhood duties."

The prosecutor rose to object. "Your Honor, I'm sure that all are interested in a history of working families. The prosecution is willing to concede that the defendant was a hard-working child in a hard-working family."

"Objection sustained. Mr. Dunbar, would you please get to your point if there is one and let us move on?"

Chastised, Walt turned to a new line of questioning.

That night, I dreamed of those days in the fields. Hours in the sun following a prissy mare or a steady mule behind a turning plow that shed streams of soil like a sausage grinder. Down to the right and back on the left covering plant-killing grass, leaving straight cuts for a middle. In early spring the middle would be spread out with a middle buster to complete a raised bed on which to plant. The sweet smell of soil lifted from sleep, melded with honeysuckle and dewberries waiting at row's end.

Daddy was known as a skilled and reliable log cutter. He was a small man, about five-seven, but put him on the end of an eight-foot crosscut saw, and he was in his element. He would bend his back to a tree he was unable to reach around and never straighten until the tree fell. His sawing partner on the other end, black or white, would be panting and wheezing while Daddy hadn't even broken a sweat. Loggers knew him, and in winter and by crop "laying by" time in summer, they came for him. Usually, it would be three months before the cotton would need picking, and Daddy would saw logs for a sawmill during that time.

When I turned fourteen, during my vacation from school, I would follow him to the sawmill to work there as a strip and slab "toter." Back then, the owner of a sawmill would buy a tract of timber and set up his mill on that property to cut the timber. Saved hauling time and truck expense.

The first thing they did in setting up the mill was to dig a huge pit near the saw at the end of a roller conveyor. At that time the refuse from sawmilling was trash to be eliminated. So a fire was started in the pit to burn it. Long logs were placed perpendicular to the main saw. Oxen were used to drag the newly cut logs to the end near the saw that ran on a track. Men using either cants or "grappling" hooks rolled logs onto the saw platform. A run of the saw would whisp away a side of bark. Workmen turned the log for another swipe. The resulting four-sided timber was set to slice pieces to the desired thickness and pass them to a smaller double saw, dubbed an edger. The pre-set edger sliced the board to width by shaving "outer" strips, and the completed lumber was passed on for stacking. The slab and strip "toter" took these bark by-products and threw them into the pit fire that burned day and night when the mill was in operation. Working by that open fire in the summer heat cemented one's vision of hell as proclaimed by the Baptist preacher on Sunday.

Black and white laborers rode together under canvas in the open back of the labor truck. Up at four, we caught the labor truck about five and got back home at seven that night. I don't remember any confrontations among workers. I do remember taking some ribbing from time to time. Once, we were traveling from Carthage to Clinton, where the sawmill was located in a huge pine forest. After work this day, the truck had stopped in Jackson for gas. During the day, a strip of wood from the edger had been caught in my old jeans and ripped out the crotch. Back then, nobody wore underwear except long johns in the winter. Well, it had been a long, hot, day. We were tired and relaxed in the open back of the truck. Four girls in a red Ford convertible drove up to the gasoline pump behind our truck. They began laughing and pointing, and I began to feel exuberant that they would flirt like that. I just knew that it was me that was attracting all the attention. Actually, it was me. I had forgotten my little fight with the strip in my crotch. I was sitting on the truck bench with my legs apart, exposing my private parts.

Back in court, Walt asked about education. I thought I could just say I graduated from high school, spent two years in junior college and on to the university for a couple of degrees. I know the judge and jury would have thought that sufficient, but Walt insisted on knowing about my family background. He already knew my older half-brother quit school in the eighth grade and the younger brother in the tenth. My two older sisters graduated from high school as did my mother. Daddy never got a chance to even go to grade school and never learned to read or write well.

"Mr. Warner, at that time, did any of your family or relatives ever attend college that you are aware of?"

"I believe that there was one cousin, a lady, may have attended junior college."

"Why did you break that mold—go on to college—end up with a law degree?"

"I don't know. We didn't have electricity, no indoor plumbing. Got our first battery-powered radio when I was eight. No newspapers or magazines—I remember a neighbor woman sharing a bunch of her once-read western story publications, and the local schools had Life magazine and a few books. I was just always interested in reading and learning. I felt there was more out there. Guess I knew there was something better than smelling mule f—excuse me—mules."

Judge Longest interrupted at that point. "Mr. Dunbar, would you please move along? You may place academic records in the file if you like."

"I apologize, Your Honor. If it please the court, I will turn to actions that relate more directly to the charges in this case."

The judge nodded and sank back in his chair for another wink or two.

"Mr. Warner, is it true that you received a commendation from Attorney General Robert Kennedy for assisting U.S. marshals during rioting when the first black student enrolled at the university?"

"Yes."

"Specifically, what did you do to deserve that honor?"

"Don't know if I deserved anything. Spent the night with federal officials in the building that was being attacked. Assisted in providing information for tactical moves, I suppose, and helped to relay communications. Five Ole Miss employees were there that night to witness mob action and the federal response. Two of us were still living until last week. Douglas Houston passed away on the tenth. I think there were either five or six federal officials who were in charge of the action. Don't know if any of them are still living. I'm still kicking."

Noting the scowl on the face of the judge, who frowned like a shriveled prune, Walter moved on to another subject. I continued to see the faces of fallen men and fallen dreams, the one fighting for what he considered "our way of life," the other for the preservation of our union, much like a hundred years before.

CHAPTER 11

For weeks during that memorable September, we were amused by the antics of both the national and state governments. Indeed, campus confrontations between U.S. marshals and Mississippi Governor Ross Barnett were the kind of jolly affairs one might enjoy watching with a brown-bag lunch. A prospective student, James Meredith, would be escorted to campus and summarily turned away by the governor. Most university personnel were convinced that, after a dramatic stand in the schoolhouse door, Mr. Barnett would lower the Confederate flag.

Five minutes after President John Kennedy began his national television address on September 30, 1962, my car eased past the one highway patrol vehicle parked in front of the School of Education building. A mass of humanity, on foot, streamed across the campus entry bridge.

With the assistance of our university chief of police, I slipped past marshals who had encircled the Lyceum building with huge army trucks, and made my way into the building. I was met by four other student affairs personnel who had been called in to assist U.S. justice department officials. Those officials established a control center in the office of the registrar. A single loudspeaker sat by an open telephone to Washington, permitting all in the small area to hear exchanges with Attorney General Robert Kennedy.

News media people and Mississippi Highway Patrol personnel mingled under cover of the "Circle" oak trees with students, farmers, laborers, and the thousands I had passed at the campus entry. The beautiful Circle fronts the original building, the Lyceum. The university was founded in 1844, and this first edifice accommodated all the academic programs and faculty that welcomed the first class in 1848. At the center of campus, the Lyceum represents the history and tradition of higher education in Mississippi. With thirty-five or so canvas-backed monster trucks in a circular path around the building, an aerial image would have portrayed a giant wastebasket. Taunts were thrown at the marshals. It was reported that someone threw a lighted cigarette on a truck's canvas top. Tear gas was fired. Most students and the highway patrol who were brought in for crowd control evaporated, leaving a hardcore mob to battle the federal force.

Memories of incidents, vividly etched in one's mind, have no chronology or time frame, then or now. Sometime early in that hot, humid evening, our group of five student affairs stalwarts disobeyed U.S. marshals and ventured beyond their protective veil into the lovely circle of hundred-year-old trees fronting the building, intent on persuading students to return to their dormitories. It might be noted that in 1962 students paid some attention to university administrators. (I understand that this is no longer the custom.)

Moments after stepping across the street dividing the warring factions, we were engulfed in a sea of flesh, a faceless mob. Not a single student was identified as we became a shield for an attack on the building. Marshals, standing behind the army vehicles, fired. They had warned us what would happen if the building were threatened, even if we happened to be in the way. Tear gas canisters were fired point-blank by the defenders, but our resolve to return to those six white building columns exceeded that of our temporary captors. We made it safely back inside, the safety of the building and its occupants still undecided.

Multiple telephones were ringing.

"London calling—whatever on earth is happening at Old Mississip-pi?"

"Sir, will my daughter be all right?"

"This is Dean Rhea. Would you tell them not to use tear gas near the girl's dormitories?"

Bricks, tons to be used for the construction of a biology building, now became weapons. Yelling—echoing gun blasts—burning automo-biles running toward the building—a giant bulldozer threatening to tear into the building—casualties—murder—unarmed Mississippi National Guard—drone of aircraft—arrival of a contingent of army troops that would ultimately number over 23,000—taking of prisoners; all fade into one long, distorted image.

I do remember distinctly one incident. I had just negotiated a trip to the toilet by stepping over wounded marshals lining hallways. They were bleeding from thrown bricks and rocks, from broken limbs, from punc-ture wounds and one I saw from a gunshot directly through the throat. I was followed back to the control center by a running man I recognized as McShane, the chief marshal.

"Sirs, permission to use our guns?" McShane screamed.

I believe it was John Doar among the officials present who started to speak. But before he was able to respond, a clear Bostonian accent rever-berated around the room.

"Permission denied!"

"But Mr. Kennedy, that mob is using high-powered rifles. We're out of tear gas; the supply truck bringing more has been hijacked."

"Hold your position."

"Sir, permission to use our automatic weapons?"

"Permission denied!"

"But, sir, wounded men lie side by side for 100 feet in two directions—but, sir—"

For the fourth and final time, Robert Kennedy said, "PERMISSION DENIED!"

"But, sir, what are we to do?"

Whether it was reasonable or not, Robert Kennedy replied. "Use your bully clubs."

Eyes red from tear gas irritation, body strained past exhaustion, I stumbled into the brick-piled street just at dawn. I surveyed the debris—glass, smoldering burned-out automobiles, spent gas canisters, blood, and vomit.

I wept.

And the crying continued past the University/Lamar corner in Oxford where two teenagers, silhouetted against the rising sun, slashed at tires on a car driven by an old black man stopped for the traffic light. Two Mississippi Highway Patrol cars, with occupants watching, sat on the apron in front of the Ole Miss Texaco Station, the current site of BancorpSouth Bank. Both the black man and I ran the traffic light, he to whatever that day's measure offered, I to my bed—not to sleep for many more hours, but to contemplate man's inhumanity to man.

Neither Attorney General Kennedy's citation, which arrived a few days later with my name misspelled, nor my great love for so many fine qualities endemic to the South, especially to my native Mississippi, dispelled the bitterness held for the atmosphere that produced the debasing of my Ole Miss.

Robert Kennedy became a hero of mine. Had he not intervened, a massacre would have occurred, further staining the struggle for the rule of law and order. Mistakes were made. The federal authorities chose to rely on negotiations with political entities rather than including the university. The university was completely ignored in planning for a difficult transition.

Among other choices, the riot was augmented by 800 federal marshals bringing Mr. Meredith to the university only a few hours prior to darkness on Sunday after knowledge of so much fiery rhetoric at a crowded Jackson football stadium on Saturday. Governor Barnett had commandeered a half-time microphone, raised his fist in the air, and yelled the words, "Never! Never!"

For those fair-minded Mississippians—and there were some, the pursuit of reconciliation and integration was further damaged by the excessive amount of force involved. Twenty-three to twenty-six thousand active military troops were employed only to test another unrelated strategy, as important as that operation was. We understood that the real question was how fast a large contingent of armed forces could be moved in the event that Russia continued to attempt shipping missiles to Cuba. Apparently, the federal administration used one crisis to prepare for another—a power binge with a fifty-year hangover.

When I lie in my bed with eyes closed, too tired to wake and too tired to sleep, I can see the faces of a tear-crazed mob. They are covered with the smell of battle, tears from the gas, sweat and grime from the exertion. The news media characterized this as a revolt by Ole Miss students. In reality, there were few students involved. Only seven students were among the hundreds who were arrested during the long night, and only three were charged. The three were never prosecuted. But, there were people here from all over the country, some as young as fourteen and as far away as California. I have observed over the years that a number in our society, regardless of the particular cause, wish to be involved if there is a controversy. Naturally, those who formed the mob were primarily from Mississippi and surrounding Southern states.

For what were they fighting—those who had a cause? Rioters knew that James Meredith was ensconced in a dormitory some quarter mile away. There was only a small contingent of marshals for protection at that location. Why was the vengeance-motivated mob not attacking that facility rather than the central administration building of the university?

What drives people to fight? Is it for some slogan such as "our way of life" that no one comprehends? Is it for wealth and power, for territory, for ideas, for fear, for dominance, for religion, for freedom, or for any number of reasons? Surely there were people in this mob who harbored racial prejudice and felt the need to dominate. But why direct that anger and seek to destroy a building surrounded by fellow Americans doing their duty under our democratic form of government?

As I drifted toward a troubled sleep, I thought of the symbolism— This building with its history, revered by many, became the incarnate vision of a state's right to operate independently as opposed to a federal right to protect all its citizens. To the mob, it was "Them telling Us" what we can and can not do.

If I remember my law school course in constitutional law, the issue of a state's right, as opposed to a central governmental authority, has been with us since the beginning of our country. It is no less in contention this very day, despite a civil war that was supposed to reconcile such conflict. That seems to mirror the contention that there was once a "war to end all wars."

From the Declaration of Independence on July 4, 1776, to the Articles of Confederation ratified in 1781, the states pretty much assumed they were independent. As time passed and questions arose among the states, a few men of vision, namely Alexander Hamilton, James Madison, John Marshall, and other visionaries were perceptive enough to realize that a stronger federation was necessary. During the summer of 1787 in Independence Hall, Philadelphia, representatives of the thirteen states gathered and on September 17 adopted the Constitution of these United States. The first ten amendments, a Bill of Rights, were ratified in 1791. This completed a new form of federalism, a unique governing system that provided a framework for democracy. Bitter disagreements and opposite viewpoints have, from the start, threatened that system. Initially, primary issues of strife included the states' rights versus that of the central government. Federalists, represented by men such as John Adams and Alexander Hamilton, sought the support of the commercial classes, people who valued order and stability, security of property, and trading opportunities.

A second group that was by and large in opposition to the new Constitution, the Jeffersonian Republicans, were more attuned to individualistic individuals who sought freedom from authority. Farmers, frontiersmen, debtor classes, planter aristocrats were among those who supported more power to the states.

Names and players may have changed, but the animosity between groups of Americans remain. Parliamentary and other forms of government throughout history reflect the same difficulty in establishing harmony between warring factions. At times, rhetoric has mutated to a philosophical difference where heinous acts are committed by individuals and governments so indoctrinated by hate mongering. Makes one wonder if this is a part of human nature; that violence, even war, is the result of intolerance for the ideas and opinions of others.

The role of the university in the enrollment of James Meredith has never been fully understood. After treating the application for admission routinely, the university was ordered by the political establishment on multiple occasions to withdraw any hint of acceptance. Delay tactics were ordered and in the final stages, Governor Ross Barnett appointed himself university registrar. The constitutionally established Board of Trustees of Institutions of Higher Learning succumbed to pressure and failed to support Ole Miss until they were forced to act by the federal judicial system. Under threat of incarceration for failure to comply with the orders of the Fifth Circuit Court of Appeals, the board finally capitulated.

It took some time to analyze what had happened. The university was fighting to keep accreditation, calm the public and the state legislature, retain students, and adjust to a federal presence on campus.

In the aftermath, there have been many reports from many sources. Although I was on campus daily, I had to go home each night to have television "talking heads" inform me about what was happening. For several weeks, student affairs personnel patrolled the campus after dark. Crowds were asked to go about their business. Those lobbing firecrackers from dormitory windows were chased, identified, and disciplined. Racial slurs were thrown, and some students walked out of classes but, by and large, most went about the business of learning.

While I was patrolling the campus at night, it was not unusual for me to find a member of the state legislature observing how the institution was copulating with the Great Satan, the United States of America. Often the legislator was not only a lawmaker but also a card-carrying member of what was dubbed the Citizens' Council. History has confirmed that the group was little more than the KKK without hoods. They were responsible for many of the atrocities visited on educational personnel who were perceived to have liberal ideas. Faculty were fearful of losing their positions. Many were forced to leave. One of the very best teachers that I have ever encountered in my college career was one of those. The Citizens' Council persuaded the state legislature to have each university employee sign a loyalty oath which, in effect, certified that you were prejudiced against fair and equal treatment for all Americans. On the final day for processing those certifications, I was out of town. There was no follow-up for those who were low-level employees. While I never was critical of those who were forced to sign that declaration, I sometimes wonder if I would have placed my name on that document.

Back in the courtroom, Walter Dunbar seemed to be continuing a conversation from which I had drifted.

"Mr. Warner, would you like me to repeat the question?"

"I lost myself for a moment. I do that sometimes. Yes, I'm sorry. Would you repeat the question?"

"Mr. Warner, I was asking about the integration of the public schools in Oxford."

"Oh, yes—what was the question?"

"My question was, did you have a leadership role in the peaceful implementation of integration in the Oxford Public School system?"

"I don't know about leadership. A great many citizens, civic-minded individuals, school officials, and public servants were instrumental in the public elementary and secondary school integration fight some eight years after the Ole Miss debacle of 1962. People didn't want to re-live that."

"Were you responsible for organizing the Oxford Civic Council, a group whose purpose it was to galvanize public opinion to accept integration without violence?"

"You give me too much credit. I was a part of many who called for law and order. I represented the Rotary Club."

"Were you master of ceremonies at perhaps the largest meeting ever held with parents and citizens of Oxford to prepare for transition from the racially separate system to an integrated one?"

"Yes, I chaired a meeting and introduced speakers, the chancellor of the university—school board members."

"And did that meeting solidify public support for acceptance of change?"

"Well, it was just one action of the civic council. Lots of concerned citizens worked together to accomplish a common goal."

Later, I reflected on those days of public school integration.

After all appeals had been exhausted, the court order to immediately integrate was visited upon the Oxford School Board. It happened mid-year, just before the Christmas holidays. It was imperative that the change occur before school children returned in January. Everyone in Lafayette County wondered how it could be done on such short notice. The case had been in the judicial system for some time, but until the order was handed down, no concrete planning had been accomplished.

Guess it's human nature to put off difficult decisions until the last moment.

Three or four of us who had experienced the rioting at Ole Miss were having coffee the morning after the Oxford Public School decision came down from the Fifth Circuit Court of Appeals. All the discussion centered on how the decision could be acted upon in the specified time frame. It was apparent that many people had reservations about any workable solution. We knew that many citizens had negative views about mixing the races, and many more were just plain scared that violence might occur.

Coffee cooled in the cup, and more was poured. The consensus of the group was that something had to be done to allay fears and convince people that public education had to be preserved. What could we do?

We had to mobilize others. Someone came up with the idea to form an organization composed of representatives, black and white, of various civic organizations in the entire county. With members from the white Rotary, Lions and Jaycees to the Black Men's Social Club to the ladies' sewing circles of both races and all other organized groups; a meeting was called, and we got to work.

The Oxford Civic Council was born. Every representative identified people from their constituency whom the community trusted and might follow. Those leaders were asked to speak to their groups and publicly endorse prepared advertisements. The message was that public education and peaceful transition was essential. As difficult as it was, this initiative resulted in public officials and respected citizens agreeing to lend their name and reputation to the effort.

An extensive public relations campaign for calm was launched.

At the same time, the local school board announced the closing of schools a week early and delayed re-opening four weeks after the holidays. This provided some time for school consolidation, teacher training, personnel adjustments, and a host of other decisions. All teachers were placed into a pool of talent to be assigned to one of the four schools.

In cooperation with city and school officials, the civic council called perhaps the largest group of parents and citizens ever assembled to the Oxford High School. The auditorium was packed, and as many stood outside where loudspeakers had been installed. Chancellor of the university, Dr. Porter Fortune, made an impassioned plea for maintaining public education. After airing alternatives, it was decided that we had twelve grades and four school buildings. It became merely a question of division. Three classes would be assigned to each of the four building locations.

With the advice and counsel of public officials, a call was issued for volunteers. Over a period of six weeks, over 500 carpenters, painters, handymen, "gofers," and others became involved. Two flashpoints seemed prevalent.

The Oxford Training School, formerly an all-black school, would for the first time also have white students. Oxford lumber companies, hardware stores, and other businesses contributed supplies. Doors and windows and fixtures were replaced. The entire school was scrubbed and painted. Floors were polished. It became the one best-maintained school in the system. We wanted it to be a place students wanted to attend.

Another flashpoint of concern was the elementary school for the first three grades. The building had a central office/auditorium/ cafeteria/library arrangement with long wings of classrooms expanding from the center. School officials adopted a "pod" system by tearing through the back walls for the entire length of each wing. Team teachers, one black and one white, could pass unobtrusively between classes to teach subject matter.

The public schools of Oxford re-opened for the spring term without a single incident. The members of the Oxford Civic Council slowly drifted away, their mission accomplished. They and countless others reappeared in commissions, organizations, and committees and as public servants—new citizens of all races dedicated to preserving the quality of life in Oxford.

I was relieved that Walter did not expand his questioning of public school integration. He looked exhausted, and it was the end of the day, so the cross-examination by the prosecution was delayed until the following morning. We discussed how best to prepare for it. Walt had little advice.

"Mr. Warner, we're still in good shape. Just keep your answers short—don't elaborate. At this point, you are wide open for any kind of questioning. Just remember that what you say could jeopardize your freedom."

CHAPTER 12

Lawrence Greenwood approached the witness chair. He stood like stone with plastered hair as if a Roman centurion. He stared at me, and I stared at him as players in a high stakes poker game might chance to see who blinks first. Swiftly turning his back, he looked more like a mythical centaur. His butt protruded from his jacket in a grotesque, elongated shape that suggested a second set of legs that could be dropped at any moment if he needed to take flight. A massive pot belly balanced his profile.

"Mr. Warner, do you consider yourself a racist?"

"I certainly hope not."

"You have been characterized by witnesses as a liberal-minded person with a passion for equality, one who would not discriminate. Where exactly do you think those convictions came from?"

"I suppose they are a product of life experiences."

"And those life experiences began with a family?

"Yes."

"Were your family advocates for minorities?"

"I wouldn't say so."

Larry Greenwood walked away but turned like a wobbly top. "Are you saying that your family had no influence on your growing up to be a champion for minorities?"

"I wouldn't claim to be a champion. I'm more of an average person who sees equality as something to be desired."

"But you are declaring that family ties have little or no positive influence on your moderate views?"

"I'm sure some of what we are is a result of parental influence."

"Is it possible that negative feelings, say prejudice, are projected from generation to generation?"

"Some authorities would argue that, but people can also change."

"Think of your ancestors. Were there any that you feel might have hated, felt superior, or mistreated black people?"

Walter objected to this one. "Your Honor, relevance. How could my client possibly know the thoughts, motivation or action of his ancestors?"

The judge was suddenly alert. He cleared his throat and addressed the prosecutor. "Mr. Greenwood, let me remind you to limit your cross-examination to specifics and avoid speculation. With that warning, I am going to allow the question but please stick to topics for which the witness has reasonable knowledge. Objection overruled."

"Mr. Warner, do I need to repeat the question?"

"No—my knowledge of family genealogy is very limited. My grandfather was apparently abandoned to an orphanage somewhere in south Alabama. He grew up, was a timber man, and had twelve children, one daughter. My father, the youngest, never discussed his father with me. Grandfather died shortly after my father was born in 1900."

"So, you have no knowledge of your family past a grandfather that you never knew?"

"Well, I never pursued my genealogy on my own, but an uncle once told a story about my great grandfather being a Confederate colonel in the

Civil War. That he had a large plantation before the war. He lost the land and left, leaving my grandfather an orphan in a south Alabama home. I don't know that to be true, but that's what my uncle Lewis thought."

"Your great grandfather had a large plantation, fought against the Union? Would you assume that he owned slaves before the war?"

Walter's objection to such conjecture was sustained. Greenwood went on to a different line of questioning. I thought it just as well since there was no way I could verify the stories I had heard about my great-grandfather, Thaddeus T.J. Warner. The eldest of Daddy's ten brothers told those stories. My dad, who was born in 1900, never took stock in their authenticity. He just wouldn't discuss them. Dad was the youngest in the clan and, perhaps, further removed from the reality of the tale. But I went home that night and wondered if, by chance, old Thaddeus has passed some of that malice down through the generations. In my dream, I added particulars, but the essentials of the tale that my Uncle Lewis told flowed through me. My dream lasted the night, and I clearly sneaked a look at Thaddeus T.J. Warner.

Shivering, he looked back through isinglass curtains drawn tight as Indian braids. Still, the wind whipped angles of indigenous canvas across forced aperture. He was dressed appropriately, wearing a satin dickey with black trousers. A waistcoat with a gray frock coat, boots, and wide-brimmed hat shielded him from early morning chill. A fading plantation house lengthened the distance between him and purgatory. The carriage bounced from rut to rut like a swinging door. One tear he knew was viscera, clustered in what normally would be a smile wrinkle on an otherwise smooth face framed in long sideburns. His gut wrenched, his thorax bobbed like a fishing cork, and his heart raced through his chest.

He reasoned that this was best—that to stay would only slip shame into his pocket and elicit retribution on his puritan family. Mother was appalled of course, and Daddy was livid with unforgiving rage. At the age of eighteen years, Thaddeus T.J. Warner had been abandoned—ostracized from polite society. Left with one manservant and a cook happily riding atop—they must be happy. Black people, he thought, are always happy doing anything to avoid work.

So what if she was only fourteen. She was trash. Poor white trash at that. Rubbish to be swept away with a brush broom fashioned by hickory branches. It could have been worse—it could have been that little mulatto stored in cabin number ten by the tobacco patch. Yeah, Daddy would have really been offended then! She was Daddy's prize for habituating an environment filled with straight-laced expectations. At least Bitsy was white and clean for the most part. Wash Henson already had eight snot-nosed offspring. What was another bastard brat to him? Daddy paid him off handsomely. He became an overseer.

It should have gone away. But Bitsy Henson would have none of that. For some reason, she had to show off her rising belly, which was a growing cancer to him. She had never had power over anything, and she was making the most of it. She even started showing up for services at the Tidewater Presbyterian Church and confessed her indiscretion, with names attached, to her Sunday school class. Regardless, she was destined to work in a hot shed stringing tobacco, on sticks, to be stored in a barn to dry. Nothing would change that. If she was lucky, she might get to ride on the back of a loaded wagon to Raleigh where the product would be graded and stacked in a warehouse. She would probably be chewing the stuff by then and have rotten teeth. That's what he wished for her—rotten teeth.

As he passed through Warnersville, he looked neither left nor right. As a vanishing ghost, he must erase even a wisp of cloud that lingered in his head. The schools he attended, the grand houses where he squired the loveliest of maidens, the saloon where he drowned his infatuations, the pool hall and other places of amusement; he banked them all, immediately, without thought of dividend. At the end by the stables, he yelled at his driver to stop. With borrowed gusto and renewed vengeance, he tore down the town sign and pissed on it.

The dash to the rail station would be six hours. The fried chicken Mammy Tea had packed and the flask of bourbon at his hip would last, but he had reservations about the rest of him. He would be sore and disheveled on the platform, but he vowed to keep his head high as he shook the mud of North Carolina from his boots.

An 1853 Patterson, the latest Standard Rogers passenger locomotive lay on the track, puffing its huge pipe, creating a station rhythm attuned to his rapidly rising spirits. At least he would be afforded some of the comforts to which he was accustomed. He supervised the loading of his trunks and saw to it that his two traveling mates were settled in the Negro car. They were screaming their heads off when they were forced into the boxcar, but settled down considerably when they realized there were other darkies occupying shared space. Their cage was a bit smaller, but close enough for conversation with the larger group who, according to the scrawled lettering on a sign, were headed for Natchez, Mississippi. He worried that the housemaid had packed his linen shirts, the new colorful cravats, the formal breeches, and his favorite cutaways and chesterfields. One would think she knew, but he had not specifically mentioned a top hat. Oh, well, they must have at least one quality store in the Deep South.

After Chattanooga and a line change, the less comfortable coach was dragged in turtle-like fashion ever so slowly through Grand Junction, Tennessee, Holly Springs, and on to Oxford. Seven excruciating days, a spate of rain, and uninteresting chatter with fellow travelers. Daddy's West Point buddy, a Professor Bernard, was there to meet him. After restoration of a sense of dignity promulgated by rest and bath, Thaddeus learned his fate. Through Bernard, Daddy had purchased lock, stock, and barrel, a three-hundred-fifty-acre farm not far from Oxford—somewhere between Bay Springs and Abbeville. It was a working farm of twenty-six slaves. With the two house servants who accompanied him, he would have a total of twenty-eight. The farm came with a foreman, who would be helpful in running the place. The crop was cotton instead of tobacco, but then, what's the difference? Professor Bernard indicated that both he and Thaddeus' father felt that a part of his time could be devoted to taking classes at the nearby university.

He spent little time farming, per se. He did take classes at the university, devoting much of his research to the study of seed quality and nutrient requirements of the cotton plant. He experimented with different varieties to increase yield. Without much hands-on application, he trusted management to his overseer; he became one of the most prosperous farmers in Lafayette County.

By the late 1850s, winds of war drifted in transparent clouds to chill the patriotism of 1776 and threaten the unity of the new nation. The resulting schism rode on the back of slavery. Thaddeus was recruited by university students and some faculty to join an organized regiment, the University Greys. Instead, he chose to help organize another army, the Lamar Rifles. It took the name of L.Q.C. Lamar, who at that time was an advocate for secession from the United States. A Mississippi legislator, Lamar is said to have written the document that took the state out of the Union. A slave owner himself and an officer in the Confederate Army, Lamar would later speak for reconciliation. After the war, elected to Congress, he became United States secretary of the interior and later was appointed to the U.S. Supreme Court.

Unfortunately, the fate of Thaddeus T.J. Warner was not to be that bright. Taking his unit of Lamar Rifles and becoming a part of a Missis-

Ken Wooten

sippi regiment along with the University Greys, Thaddeus and the others were commissioned into the Confederate Army in early 1861. They fought in Gettysburg and Sharpsburg and were involved in numerous other skirmishes. He was one of the very few survivors of the conflict. He was captured six months before the war ended and sent to a federal prison in Virginia. Still, with a swagger and braggadocio, he told the prison warden that they should have caught him sooner; it would have saved them both a heap of trouble.

Thaddeus was released when the war ended and returned to Mississippi. Yankees had pillaged his farm; the slaves were gone, and the overseer drunk. He tried for three long years to re-establish a successful plantation. Alas, without funds or free labor, the effort fizzled. In the meantime, he married and sired one son, the mother dying in childbirth. Telling the story, my uncle Lewis had no idea why Thaddeus fled over into south Alabama and left his son on the steps of an orphanage.

Rumor has it that Thaddeus was still looking for free labor. He somehow got to Brazil, where slavery continued to be legal. However, the winds that swept the South with tornado-like consequences silently invaded other parts of the western world. It was not tobacco or cotton. It was coffee that he sought to grow. Thaddeus rounded up a group of former slaves with the promise of work and prosperity on coffee plantations in Brazil. Upon arrival, they discovered that they occupied the same status as they had on the largest estate in the Mississippi Delta.

As the Civil War had approached, benevolent societies arose with the purpose of providing slaves passage back to their African homeland. It was thought that this might avert war. Uncle Lewis considered that maybe Thaddeus bilked some of those "do-gooders" into paying the freight for his slaves to travel to Brazil.

Apparently, Thaddeus did well in Brazil, growing his coffee business and adding more slaves. But things were a-changing. Brazil was the last

161

bastion for slavery. There were abolitionists there too. The legality sat in the legislative proclamation, but enforcement depended upon public attitude. Each political administration, rather than rescinding the law, chose to ignore it. Slaves were abandoning their lives of servitude and fleeing to havens of tolerance. Coffee plantation owners were incensed that local constables refused to hear their complaints and offered no assistance in seeking and returning their human property. Hatred of government, as churning as a boiling pot, grew within the grower community. To Thaddeus, it was a re-enactment of a drama twice played—first by King George and then by the traitor, Abe Lincoln.

For the second time, he organized a regiment—to track down runaways. There were harsh penalties imposed by the group, not only against the slave but also against those who would harbor slaves. Naturally, such vigilante acts caught the attention of the authorities. After a confrontation with the local governor, the group paid a visit to the governor's home at the witching hour. He would not come out. Thaddeus lit the match.

Unfortunately, none escaped the fire.

Uncle Lewis ends his story the same every time. Thaddeus T.J. Warner was never heard from again.

CHAPTER 13

I awoke with some reservations about the Thaddeus Warner story. I was not ready to consider that the action of my great grandfather, even if it were true, would affect my finger on a trigger with a black teenager in my sight.

Making my way to the Lafayette County courthouse I passed the statue of the confederate soldier peering southward. I climbed the three flights of stairs to the courtroom, caught my racing breath, and took a seat to let the old heart settle down before being called again to the witness stand. The prosecutor was armed to continue his cross examination.

Lawrence Greenwood sucked in his gut and fired several questions.

"Mr. Warner, you have been characterized as a model, hard-working child. Did you ever become rebellious, or commit acts of a violent nature?"

"Yes, sir, I guess I was a typical youngster, getting into fights, swiping a few things, lying, harassing my sisters, disobeying my parents, things like that."

Greenwood didn't follow up, but I suppose that I was a little hellion at times and got into my share of trouble. I remember that, at one point, I hated my sisters and had trouble with Papa's orders.

I had just been whipped with a peach tree switch. That was a favorite weapon wielded by a furious Momma. It happened as a result of my reasonable response at age six when my sisters on a Sunday had a visiting female playmate. They wouldn't let me play with them. I sulked in the hayloft of the barn that overlooked an open middle thruway passage between corn crib and stables. I watched as the girls made their way to pass through the opening below and decided to get my revenge. I peed on the tops of their heads.

At about the age of 13, I found myself explaining to Daddy that I just couldn't ask people for things, but he was making me do it. I remember how I was approaching life at the time.

Daddy said, "Just git off the school bus at the fork and walk on down. Tell Mr. Gordon it's been ages since Momma's been anywhere. Git on now."

Breaking into a lope as truck gears grinded down back of the old Taylor place, I knew I could make it to the main road in time to catch that school bus as it made the full circle. Sisters, Joyce Ann and Cheryl, were there by the black jack tree screaming their heads off for me to hurry.

Suddenly, I realized I hated my sisters—a hate that had come slowly but in ever-increasing intensity since Saturday. I slipped into the bedroom after they had gone to bed that night and was up early to avoid them all day Sunday. But this was Monday, and I watched their skinny-assed legs climb into the wood-framed red bus. Most of the school buses were orange-yellow, but Earl Johnson doubled his vehicle as a rolling store during the summer months. You could see where melting ice had rotted the floorboard and could smell coal oil and chicken shit from hens Earl took in as payment for groceries. The bus, with the seats back in, was barn red.

How could Joyce Ann and Cheryl both be doing it? Well, Joyce Ann, maybe. That rooster-legged Cecil Tripp rode her on bicycle to revival back in July, but I had run barefoot along them in the dust most every time. Maybe it happened on that fishing trip when Bobby Tripp was using a handheld air pump to blow up all the girls' dresses.

That didn't explain Cheryl. Cheryl was totally overweight and 100% pimple. No boy had ever looked at her sideways. Still, those sick days came every month, come hell or high water. He heard them talking about it to Momma. And what about Momma? I couldn't believe Momma knew. Maybe she just didn't understand menstruation. Hell, I hadn't understood it until Ross Chambers told me on Saturday.

On top of it all, Daddy had told me I must go begging. He wanted Mr. Gordon's wagon to take Momma to Sandy Hill on Sunday. I had tried to tell him that I felt ashamed asking people for things, but he had decided I should do it because he didn't want to. It was enough to put anybody in a black-ass mood. As the bus turned into the school grounds, I added another to my list of problems. There, old man Oliphant, the principal, had a bunch of boys lined up along the junior high wall.

"Jesus," I whispered—"Je-sus."

Sure enough, with a hook from Oliphant's finger, I was motioned to join the line. There, Bo Lay made circles with his left foot. Junior Cummings had his head back, studying the sky above the American flag. Everybody had the hang-dog look of being caught in somebody else's watermelon patch.

Old man Oliphant looked pissed—extremely pissed. "Boys," he drawled, "this is the most atrocious, most outrageous"—(Mr. Oliphant swore by using big words when he was mad)—"the nastiest and most reprehensible act that has ever occurred at this school. I can't believe that good Christian people in this community produce such heathens. Now, I don't know who did it—yet. But I'm gonna find out and when I do, your little asses have had it. You can give your heart to God 'cause the rest is mine. I want you to think about that."

And, rest assured, some of us were considering the possibility of salvation most seriously.

After forever, Oliphant (we called him elephant butt) continued. "I want a couple of you to clean up that mess and to clean it up immediately."

Naturally, being the last to join the group, I was first to be picked for the chore, joined by Ross Chambers. Scared as I was, I felt lucky to be in it with Ross, who was a year older and knew so much more. Ross was the one to think of asking.

"Mr. Oliphant, what is it you want us to do?"

"You know damn well what I want you to do," Elephant Butt shouted. "Clean that mess out of Miss Cannon's desk drawer!"

It had all started Saturday afternoon. Ross and H.C. Franklin had talked Kenneth Pigg and me into prying open the school cafeteria door. They had picked up crazy Billy Townsend, who watched from a distance. Wild Bill was a high school drop-out who wore women's panties. We never thought of him as queer (that was before people became "gay"— when gay meant happy). Billy said they just felt good. He was a dope-fiend, but nobody held that against him. He had been in the war.

After pilfering a bit and eating pork and beans from cans fractured by a dull butcher knife, we went upstairs to the classrooms.

"Well, I'll be damned," Ross said as he pulled a box of Kotex from English teacher Dixie Cannon's desk. "Who'd a' thought she'd be screwing?"

Everybody else seemed to understand what Ross was talking about, but I ventured a—"What?"

"Why—" Ross chuckled, "everybody knows that a woman don't have to wear these things till she's done it—and this must really be a wild heifer—she has to use the "super kind.""

Nobody wanted to question that superior logic.

H.C. got the idea that it would serve her right if we left Dixie a present. It was Wild Bill who hunkered down and laced the drawer, Ross carefully turning the receptacle to form a circular mountain with a little-elongated tip on top like a machine-dripped ice cream cone.

Walking the four miles home, I was exhilarated with the feeling of having become a part of the gang. I would always remember this fun time. Ross had actually treated me like I fitted in, and Ross knew so much.

And then it hit me—Joyce Ann and Cheryl. I had seen their Kotex box. I began to hate my sisters.

Now, it was Monday, and I followed old Elephant Butt down the hall. Miss Cannon was standing over by an open window, ignoring Ross as he pulled open the desk drawer. Ross gagged a bit but, with me following, carried the drawer from the building.

Down by the creek, we took turns washing the drawer, using a whole bottle of Pine Sol. Placing it in the sun to air and dry out, we lay back on the creek bank. I wasn't accustomed to the camaraderie of such a knowledgeable friend, so I decided to pump Ross about some things that had been bothering me. On a Saturday afternoon when in Lena, kids met in trees back of Riley's store and sometimes played "doctor," but that meant only that we were made differently. I had watched cows and horses and pigs mate, but I didn't know anything about girls.

"Ross," I said, "have you ever had any?"

"Hell yes, lots of times. I'm careful, though—don't want any babies."

"Aw, come on, you can't make babies."

And right there before God and me, Ross demonstrated his manliness.

I remember how low down and inadequate I felt.

By recess time when all the boys gathered behind the gym to smoke, I felt no better. I asked Ned to "gimmie" his nub.

Ned said, When I git through smoking it, it'll be a stub, and I'm gonna chew what's left. Why don't you buy your own tobacco?"

Hell, I hadn't had money for a can of Prince Albert since the crops were laid by.

On the school bus home, I thought about hating my sisters. I really didn't want to, but Ross had to be right. Ross had proved that he knew what he was talking about. Joyce Ann and Cheryl were messing around, and I was obligated to hate them.

I got off the bus at the fork and walked to Mr. Gordon's house. At the back door, Mr. Gordon scowled down at me.

"Mr. Gordon, Daddy said could he borrow," I heard my shrill voice clanking like a hoe in a gravel bed. "We need the wagon on Sunday. We wanna go down to Aunt Cora's in Sand Flat. First time in ages Momma had a holiday."

"And how do you propose to pull that wagon?" Mr. Gordon questioned.

"Well, you know we got Nellie and Butch. Butch is as stable a mule as you'd want."

"And," Mr. Gordon interjected, "Nellie is that sway-backed mare that balks."

"But, if you take a plow line and tie her tail to the single tree, she pulls fine."

Mr. Gordon gave a belly laugh. "Yeah, I seen her doing that, prancing and pawing. How do I be sure she won't throw my wagon in a ditch?"

I remember taking a long look at Mr. Gordon and saying, "Mr. Gordon, I've had a shitty day. Just take your wagon and stick it up yours. Where the sun don't shine!"

After all these years, I seem to remember, in detail, these incidents of growing up poor. It's been a long time since I've thought of such trivia. Maybe such recall is a result of all my reading about how a particular environment affects the development of one's understanding of the world. I wonder about following a leader like Ross and how people react to one who appears to be a knowledgeable, charismatic individual—a terrorist or a preacher or a philosopher. Are there memories hidden in our psyche that push us down one path or another? For better or worse, is humankind subject to a herd instinct that instills a call to act based on past experiences? Does the need to "fit in" govern our thought and action?

Something else to talk to Maggie about.

The voice of the prosecutor cut short such frivolous reverie.

"Mr. Warner, what kind of family life did you experience—what was the attitude of your parents toward minorities; what did they teach you about black people?"

"That's a bunch of questions. Let me think?"

"Your Honor, would you please instruct the witness to answer the question and keep his comments to himself?"

The judge so instructed me, and I promised to withhold comments about the questions.

"Mr. Warner, I asked you to tell us about your immediate family."

"Well, yes sir, it was an ordinary family. All members worked on the farm except my younger brother. He was nine years younger than me. Daddy was pretty much into chicken houses and night watching by that time. Daddy was older and couldn't do so much. Keith did help some with the chickens. My sisters were grown up and married."

"Did your family ever discuss racial matters?"

"I can't say they did. Mom and Dad always referred to blacks as darkies. There were probably 'N' words used, but I don't recall that. Like all

Southern white people, they felt that they were above blacks, but I don't remember hate talk at home. I do recall a discussion about whether Mr. Sears or Mr. Roebuck was black, but no real hate talk."

"You stated that they felt they were above blacks. What did you mean?"

"Well, I guess they felt socially superior. Blacks did jobs that whites might not do, but that wasn't really the case for those of us who were on the low end of the totem pole. You know, even with whites, there was a distinction based on your economic status or your standing in the community."

"The jury might not understand that comment, Mr. Warner—what you mean. Could you give us an example of this status business?"

"Guess I don't know how to put it—to make it plain that we were no different from other people at the time—well, one thing—when Momma and Daddy had a fight—not literally a fight but a difference of opinion, Daddy would say that she treated him worse than the blackest—er—person."

"You almost said another word, Mr. Warner. What was that word?"

"Nigger. He said "nigger." But they were good to the darkies."

"So, would you say your family was prejudiced toward black people?"

"Yes, but not hating prejudice."

"But you say you never discussed family history or prejudice with your father, any acts of violence or feelings towards blacks?"

"It was just a subject you didn't discuss—prejudice that is—you were just born into an environment that was what it was, and there was no reason to talk about it. I did question my father about his parents and ancestors from time to time, but he didn't seem to know much."

Greenwood kept firing inane questions and receiving my perfunctory answers. However, after the day in court, I did have occasion to reflect. That question about family history followed me home. After a bit of iced tea, I relaxed on the side-porch hammock. Not exactly sleeping, I dozed with recollections of growing up.

I left home in 1952 when I finished high school and visited only occasionally thereafter. Daddy had health problems late in life, and I was determined to learn more of the family I inherited. I remember visiting him in the hospital and taking my notebook to jot down whatever family history that he could provide. The last visit was one that I do vividly recall. By that time, I thought of the hospital as a prison, which was the way Dad thought about it also.

It was a modern prison. In a spacious vivarium of plants from around the world, it resembled more an art museum or a university campus. A number of wings radiated from a central core building with a slate granite façade. The buildings and grounds emanated an artificial aura difficult to explain. Perhaps the fact that everything was so perfect, that order was in such evidence, caused the uneasiness I felt. Maybe it was the fact that I knew something about what went on within those walls that made it so foreboding.

It was not an unattractive scene that spread before me, but it seemed cold and unrelenting. Although it had been a mild fall day, I pulled my coat up around my ears as twilight descended. Stalwart camera sentries followed from the parking lot up the broad steps and continued their vigil inside the expanse of glass that included sliding doors at selected intervals.

Inside the entrance, jute rectangles sucked remnants of dust from passing feet. I imagined the coldness of the concrete underneath institutional carpet that lay from gray wall to gray wall in the enormity of a Spartan reception area. Lines of telephone booths, building directories, and the long visitor desk were encased in a sea of metallic. Stainless steel and chrome glistened from chair edges and handrails and elevator fronts. Gleaming blocks of tile stretched along the expanse of corridors in every direction to some point in infinity beyond my line of sight. The very brightness of thousands of fluorescent fixtures suggested an exaggerated brilliance that might at any moment become absolute darkness by contrast. Everything was disarmingly immaculate. I found myself studiously concentrating on doors, hoping to find a fingerprint or some trace of life. Apparently, the throng of fellow visitors touched no object, or the evidence was removed immediately by unseen hands.

Security at this level was amazingly lax. My identification was ascertained and a pass issued without delay. During the process, electronic eyes devoured us, human intruders, flashing computer images to some hidden control center. Security personnel, however, seemed to be showing extraordinary discretion in their inconspicuousness. Alarms were in evidence at ceiling level, and my impression was that instantaneously gates might close, and commando units with automatic weapons would appear.

The elevator stopped only on programmed floors. As it ascended, I noted the increase in uniformed personnel. On the top floor, twenty-one, the maximum security level was located. There, I encountered a beehive of activity befitting an area where the worst of all criminals are housed.

From the reception station to the holding arenas, from operational theaters to employee nooks, the place was a model of antiseptic cleanliness. It was reputed to be a modern prison, but I was unprepared for so much stainless steel. There were no conventional iron bars. It soon became apparent that incarceration at this place relied more upon electronics and psychology than on metal barriers.

After passing the required checkpoints and being issued the appropriate authorization for observation, I was ushered through a maze of passages to the prisoner's cell. Along the way, I passed double cells and those that warehoused multiple numbers, but my prisoner warranted his own private space. The really dangerous criminals had individual cells. My prisoner's cell was small. It had space for a bed, a toilet, one chair and one small metal cabinet. It was decidedly Spartan, but the same cleanliness standard that applied to other parts of the building was exacted here. With heightened reluctance, I entered the small cell to confront the occupant.

He lay in a single bed, lifeless-like and still. Modern restraints were being used to limit his activity. Computers monitored his every movement, and microphones detected every sound. Plastic ropes added to what I surmised to be uncomfortable impediments to freedom. There seemed to be enough tubes attached to detect any thought of escape that he might entertain. Looking at the inert body, I wondered what on earth this man had done to deserve such a deprivation of human liberty. It must have been a terrible crime.

Not knowing how to start, I stepped to the bed and said in an unusually high-pitched voice—"Hi." There was no answer from the bed, so I took the opportunity to observe the prisoner, whose eyes were tightly closed.

God, he didn't look dangerous. He was a little emaciated man and, from his appearance, in the midst of a troubled sleep. His forehead contracted in deep furrows, his face twitched, and there seemed to be a permanent snarl shaping his lips. Even though he couldn't have weighed more than a hundred pounds, I instinctively shivered and averted my gaze—experiencing real fear at that moment, but I was unable to determine exactly why.

Shaken, I sat on the chair by the bed and took the notebook from my coat pocket. The pages were blank. I drew stars and crosses to get control of myself, realizing that the prisoner had made an astonishing impression. My heart was racing, and my hand holding the pen trembled. What had this little man contributed to what I am, my motivation and action, my destiny? I decided to make a list of possible explanations for my feelings, but they seemed to lurk just beyond consciousness, hidden even from me. I threw away the page on which I had scribbled.

Suddenly there was a jerking motion from beneath the sheets, and I jumped to my feet. The little man bolted upright and stared, rather, he glared at me with what appeared to be rage or hate in his eyes. Without any other greeting, I stammered—"Do you need anything?"

He spoke in a low, tired voice. "No."

The jerks that seemed to be confined to the lower torso and legs subsided, and he closed his eyes. Observing him more closely now, I saw the prisoner as no threat. In fact, he looked extremely vulnerable as his breathing became deep but irregular. I took in the whole of him, and my eyes froze at the sight of blood on the sheets. Panic gripped me. I tripped over a waste can in my rush to the door. Wait, I counseled myself. There is no cause for alarm. Just then an attendant appeared through the doorway, casting a suspicious look at me. He made a quick check of the prisoner's bonds and silently left the room.

As the night wore on, I discovered why the cell doors were never locked. Confined as he was, the prisoner could not escape; constantly harassed by personnel who, unannounced, entered and left the room. Periodically he was awakened for questioning, and drugs were administered. I could see that this methodology was an effective design to gather evidence.

My notebook remained blank. The prisoner jerked upright again and again to stare at me. Each time I asked if he needed anything. He answered a resigned, "No."

At midnight, the prisoner roused and said, "I'm going to the bathroom."

I said, "They have you tied up with all this stuff. You really can't get up."

A look of recognition came over his face as he pulled himself back on the bed. "I forgot," he sighed.

Five minutes passed, and then he asked, "Will you bring me a bedpan?"

I found the pear-shaped metal decanter and passed it over to him. The prisoner exerted utmost effort to straddle the object, straining to place it underneath his bottom. In the end, it required my assistance to negotiate the mount. It occurred to me that this must be the most prevalently used and most inhumane form of punishment known to man. Surely some clever scientist could invent an atomizer that would vaporize excrement and solve the problem of incontinence. There might be the introduction of carcinogens; no one would wish to subject people to cancer-producing agents. Still, the economics of technology is winning. It's a matter of balancing risks with expenditures. For now, as difficult and painful as the old bedpan is, it remains.

When I helped to remove the bedpan, I saw *it*. Immediately, I looked at the prisoner's face, but his eyes turned upward as if to ignore *it* altogether. *It* had not happened. *It* was intact. *It* was strong and whole.

Then the prisoner began to talk. His speech was an incomprehensible litany of words strung together. At times it was hardly audible and sometimes rose in torment, alternately lucid and the voice of a madman.

He spoke of *it* following down long rows, the turning plow spading an exact furrow. One minute *it* was racing fox dogs on a moonlit night, the next *it* was tasting the cool waters of Coffee Boat Creek. *It* had kicked hogs, danced jigs, and gone on incredible journeys.

Later, I dozed in the chair, my notebook pages still blank. I awoke to agitated shouts. The prisoner was bouncing up and down on the bed, his covers kicked aside. The stump from his amputated leg pawed the air, oozing bloody liquid through his bandage.

"Do you need anything"? I asked.

"HELL YES," he shouted. "I need a leg!"

It was then I knew his crime, the heinous act that was so unforgivable. He was ninety-four years old. He had lived too long!

In the notebook, I wrote one line. "I'm sorry, Papa—I love you!"

And I fled the hospital room.

Why had it taken so long for me to realize that this was me? The same blood courses through my veins. The genes that dictate so much of me reside here. Like so many poor children, standing on one foot, the other propped on a knee with a hoe handle supporting the balance, I had the same dream. I must be adopted. One day an expensive limousine will drive down that dirt road and re-connect me with my rightful family. I had not thought of that dream for years, but tonight I saw a huge mole on that little man's left shoulder. My fingers automatically went to my left shoulder to caress a huge mole in the exact same spot. What else did my father bequeath to his progeny? Was there passed along a pre-disposition to love or hate—to develop certain habits and tendencies?

These questions were not asked by the prosecutor—I ask myself, and answers lay heavily on a conscience long ignored. I see beauty in the cattail, copper iris, the trumpet vine, and even in every thallus. Do I recognize greed, the pursuit of power, or the desire to dominate? Do I see humanity in every individual?

CHAPTER 14

After a fitful sleep, I drove to the courthouse. A crowd of people waited at the doorway. A young black lady made a motion to hold the door for me. In the middle of this gesture, she hesitated, then retreated down the sidewalk.

This particular morning the jury looked unsettled as if they had, collectively, burned the breakfast bacon. Perhaps they had been caught in the school traffic or overslept, leaving a pleasant dream unfinished. Most likely they were just damned tired of listening to all this crap. However, the prosecutor was alert and quickly attacked in the continuing cross-examination.

"Let us turn to you, Mr. Warner, and your personal experience with prejudice. What is your earliest recollection of any association with an African American?"

"Don't reckon I had any—they were Negros at that time."

There was a twitter of laughter from the audience.

"Mr. Warner, we have no time for cute remarks. Just answer the question."

"Well, I guess it was maybe first grade. We lived on the Lynn Johnson place in a little shotgun house next to black families. I don't specifically recall, but we probably did play marbles together."

"Kids playing together—there are usually disagreements, pushing, fighting. Do you recall any such confrontations?"

"Not at that time that I remember."

"How about a time you do remember?"

"I guess it was when I was about eight or nine. Daddy sent me to Mr. Shaw, the blacksmith, who had his shop on another road a couple of miles across pastures and open land. I took a hill sweep plow point to be sharpened. I got into a tussle with a couple of black boys about my same age."

"What was the tussle about?"

"Oh, you know young boys—calling names and such."

"What happened?"

"Mr. Bill—Mr. Shaw came out with a fire-red poker and threatened to burn the shit out of us if we didn't behave."

This incident I remember just as if it were yesterday. I was glad the prosecutor didn't pursue further. We all had on overalls with knees sticking out like bald spots on a middle-aged head. If one were to look, bare feet covered with dirt and mud would not establish racial identity. One of the black guys was tall and tough looking; the second was a skinny, short guy. Skinny kept asking tough black questions. "Who de white man?"

Tough black would answer, "I am."

Skinny would then say, "Who the nigger?"

Tough black would point to me and say, "He is."

Then or now, I am unable to describe the rage that gurgled up like a pot of boiling syrup. Without rhyme or reason, I attacked the two. There was no thought of "why" or what the consequences might be—just blind madness at the dark. Why would they taunt me, and why does my reaction haunt me to this day? I didn't know those boys, had never seen them before. I can't remember anyone ever telling me that white was good, and black was bad. It seemed that I was innately primed to strike out without having to be instructed. I remember during that day trying to understand my madness at being called a "nigger." Having thought about it a great deal over the years, I am no nearer an answer. It is a straw in a haystack with a number too great to fathom.

The prosecutor is continuing his examination, dredging memories layered as a wedding cake. I am hiding the innards and spreading white icing.

"Mr. Warner, were there other incidents as you were growing up that influenced your attitude toward race relations?"

"Well, there were things we did that kinda set us apart."

"What things?"

"When I was in first grade, my two older sisters and I walked about a quarter mile to the road—our house didn't have a road into it. We walked across a pasture to the Doc Webb place to catch the school bus. On the way, we passed by a Negro house with an old black lady, who often stood by an open window and yelled at us. She would always say, "My, ain't yall lookin' cool now." That was a long time before "cool" became a part of the American vernacular, and it made us laugh. The speech patterns and living conditions were a bit different from our own—although we both had a pot full of miss-pronounced Southern expressions."

"Anything else?"

"About that time, we all went across the field one night to attend a black wedding. Everybody stood outside, and the ceremony was performed on the front porch. There was no electricity back then in our community, so lanterns hung from rafters. The preacher had a long sermon. He yelled a lot and talked some in a breathless foreign language that we couldn't understand. After about an hour of us kids squirming and drawing foot pictures in the dirt yard, the couple was pronounced man and wife. Somebody held a broom at porch level, and both jumped over it into the yard. We laughed and cheered."

"Mr. Warner, could we talk more about recollections that have to do with discrimination?"

"Well, I thought you wanted some cultural differences—but there were other times when even the poor whites went first. Being waited on at the grocery store, going through doors, and the like. I recall that when we were picking cotton, whites got weighed in first and paid first for the pounds that they had picked. Things like that. Different schools—the main difference in my family and the black families was that we were expected to attend every day, and my black playmates would be held out if there was work to be done."

"Anything else?"

"Of course, a thousand things that everyone in this courtroom knows. They sat in the balcony at the picture show, couldn't go in a white café, a white church and, above all, couldn't act 'uppity.'"

"What does that mean?"

"Had to be bowing and scraping, no back talk—courteous and respectful. At the same time, many whites had sort of a paternalistic view of blacks. Maybe it was due to a questioning of their ability to care for themselves, because there were others who took advantage to cheat black folks."

"And for your generation to rape, beat, and lynch!"

There was pandemonium in the courtroom with Walt objecting, the crowd mumbling, and Judge Longest rapping his gavel.

Judge Longest was livid with rage. "Mr. Greenwood, that is entirely out of order. That outburst is to be stricken from the record, and the jury is instructed to ignore that outburst. Oh—and the objection is also sustained."

"I apologize, Your Honor. I meant to ask about the paternalistic remark. Mr. Warner, by the paternalistic view, are you referring to the time when a slave might be administered medicine to keep him or her productive, or do you have a more recent example?"

"I was just referring to general acts of kindness. I know that passing on items of clothing might not seem particularly altruistic, but I have observed members of my generation looking after those in need, offering advice and opportunity."

"Anything else?"

"Well, this is really nothing, but when I was a student at Ole Miss we had an old black man who was the freshman counselor. Having been blind since birth, he was dubbed, 'Blind Jim.' I don't know when he came or how it happened but someone had given him Colonel Rebel suits that he wore with pride and was truly accepted as a mascot for all the athletic teams. It was a matter of pride for a student to escort him to one of the events or merely to be asked by him to take him from one part of the campus to another. Blind Jim always prided himself at never seeing an Ole Miss team lose."

The prosecutor did not question further, but I could have given instances of paternal-like treatment, both when the provider was motivated by a feeling of superiority and by those who sought only to help a fellow man. I remember a family friend, L.G. Barnett, who related a story about one of his employees. L.G. used the dialect of some uneducated black and white men of the '50s and '60s.

It was the year the Mississippi Milk Commission was abolished. To most Oxford residents, action by the state legislature had little significance. It meant everything to L.G. Barnett, partner and plant manager for Jersey Gold Dairy. The commission had stabilized milk prices over the state. Large processors just across the state line in Memphis were required by the commission to maintain prices at local rates if they wanted to do business in Mississippi. Since community processors determined the prices for milk products sold, they were assured of a good portion of the loyal, local market. The arrangement was deemed unconstitutional by the courts, so now small processors had to compete with their larger brothers who could afford to lower prices in order to corner markets.

It was also the year that the Department of Health, Education, and Welfare, through the auspices of the Fifth Circuit Court of Appeals, ruled public schools across the state in non-compliance with Title VI of the Civil Rights Act of 1964. The United States Department of Agriculture, in an unusually pontifical memorandum, stated its intention to serve the poor on a non-discriminatory basis by withholding federal funds for the school lunch program, which provided the only daily hot meal for many of the youngsters in Lafayette County, black and white.

Lincoln W. Washburn had never heard of the Mississippi Milk Commission. Neither was he familiar with the U.S. Department of Health, Education, and Welfare. In fact, except for his weekly paycheck which bore the strange letters, he did not understand the significance of his own name. He had simply always been known as "Red," a quiet, gentle man with huge freckles dotting his dark yellow face. He did possess one additional distinguishing feature. He was known in the black Southern society as a "blue gum." A black man with purplish gums, and in his case surrounded by gold-filled teeth, was at the same time both feared and revered as something very special. Red rather enjoyed it when he overheard a casual acquaintance remark to another, "Don't mess wid dat blue gum—dere's one heap mean nigga."

Actually, he was the very opposite. Red was dominated by supervisors, creditors, and, most of all, by Sister Belle.

Red had first become attracted to Sister Belle about a year after Daisy, bless her soul, died of cancer. Somebody had done went and stole Red's favorite blue-tick hound. Sister Belle, the only qualified resident voodoo woman around Oxford, conjured up the spirits that led Red right to the poke salad-eating thief that had 'im. Red took off like a scalded puppy when the tall, lanky Negro showed his blade. But Red was not one to forget the sorcerous power of Sister Belle.

Dat fat sister sho put a hex on Red. Red admitted as much but laughed and said, "She sho' can make them bedsprings bounce." At any rate, Red and Sister Belle became common-law husband and wife, taking little cognizance of the fact that the state legislature repealed the common-law statute that same year.

Promptly, Red was talked into taking a large loan with the local Friendly Finance Company to purchase a five-year-old but sufficiently long Oldsmobile ninety-eight. Tires, repair bills, and bottles of "white lightnin'" to which Red was especially attracted, contributed to frequent visits to the Friendly Finance Office. Following wage garnishment, his employer, Barnett, bailed him out, co-signing a note at the Bank of Oxford and withholding the payment from Red's check each week.

If there was a special talent that Red Washburn had, it was a propensity for getting the best of his employer, L.G. Barnett. Having the benefit of being forced to learn each little habit and eccentricity of a white boss, Red could, at a glance, discern the propitious time to react exactly as pleased Barnett. He understood the mood and motivation of the man better than Barnett himself. Whenever L.G. turned to speak, Red had already begun a response to the directive he knew was coming. Red could always pass the appropriate comment about the weather, tell the latest joke, or remain silent when he sensed in Barnett a need for quiet repose.

Red took his greatest pleasure in watching Barnett squirm after being led into a conversation about worthy causes for which Red just happened to be collecting.

"Mr. L.G., now I don't know how it is wid you, but we black folks put a heap'uh stock in de hereafter. And de disgrace uv mi fust wife, Daisy, bless her soul, lyin out dere in Mr. Zion, no marker on her grave! Reckon why dey calls dat Mt. Zion? Ain't no real mount'ns nowhere in dis country. Anyway, spose you cud hep me wi a coup'la dollars or git sum uv yer white frins to hep? It wooden mean nutin to you, but aheap to Daisy. Iz knows Ize shu'da done it fore now. God knows Ize try."

Both men, fully realizing that no marble would ever be erected on that particular mound in the Mt. Zion cemetery, would exchange embarrassed glances as Barnett slipped a five-dollar bill into the hands of his friend Red.

Sister Belle just kept on driving that ninety-eight toward Chicago one day. Coincidentally, the edict by the U.S. Department of Agriculture withholding funds for the school lunch program made headlines in the weekly *Oxford Gazette*. Jersey Gold was forced to reduce deliveries to area public schools. Drivers and their helpers (Red was a helper) were brought back into the plant to perform menial busywork until new customers and new routes could be established. A white businessman might work his blacks until they dropped, but laying off workers was considered an extreme measure.

Red had been somewhat of a moocher, picking up a roll or a crisply fried pork chop at school cafeterias as he made the rounds. Suddenly, that source of food supply was no longer available. Ironically, Red had never liked milk products. He did, however, so enjoy that rot-gut licker and began stretching weekends into weekdays. Before anyone at the plant took notice, Red became ill—desperately ill. The diagnosis was alcohol poisoning and malnutrition, the prognosis doubtful.

Miss Betty Spivey, as was her custom, cut through several neighbor yards as she made her way to and from County General Hospital. Even though the aging spinster had nine hours of nursing duty behind her, at six a.m., the stiffly starched white uniform retained its antiseptic freshness. Only the thick-soled white oxfords, turned over at the heels, now wet with morning dew, bore scuff marks of toil. Miss Betty spied L.G. Barnett on the side gallery having his second cup of Louisiana coffee with chicory. Without as much as a howdy, she lashed out at the startled man. He, aware of custom and manners, was momentarily subdued.

"Mr. L.G., you're just gonna hafta do something with that colored boy! He needs somebody to hold him onto the bed. Why, I spent half the night—what with him grabbing at me and hollering and taking on—no, sir—he's strong as any young buck I ever seen—and I'm not going to stand for it."

L.G. watched as Miss Betty's vein-lined legs disappeared through the pecan grove, making her way to the lonely apartment rented from an even older single woman, and Barnett mused the possibility of the vicarious thrill Miss Betty must have received from having a man, even a black man, grabbing for her. He resolved that he would go by the hospital on up in the morning to see if Red needed attention. The shrill jangle of the telephone shattered his speculation about Miss Betty and, indeed made a trip to County General completely unnecessary.

Ms. Tena Bond was a neat, slightly built black school teacher. She sat quietly, poised and confident, across the desk from L.G. Barnett, being the sole beneficiary of a $10,000 life insurance policy purchased some years ago by the recently deceased, Lincoln W. Washburn. Barnett leaned forward, his mind formulating the appropriate way to lead this obviously intelligent young woman to his desired goal.

Ms. Bond spoke first.

"Mr. Barnett, I know why you asked me here. Uncle Red did owe some debts, and I do feel obligated to use a part of this check to satisfy those creditors."

L.G. had been taken by surprise in that he was still thinking about how to impress Ms. Bond with her good fortune, a veritable gold mine dropped in her lap.

She raised her hand as if to stop his embarrassed stammering and repeated softly, "Mr. Barnett, I'll pay the debts."

L.G. did recover, after an awkward silence to inquire, "And what about a tombstone? You know, Red always talked about a proper marker. In fact, he borrowed money from me on several occasions to get a stone for his wife, Daisy."

Again, Ms. Tena Bond was way ahead of him, having removed a previously written check for $400 from her bag.

"Would you take care of that for me, Mr. Barnett?"

"Why, of course," he replied, "of course."

"Thank you, Mr. Barnett."

And she was gone, as unobtrusively as she had come.

Suthern Simms Marble Works was not just the best tombstone dealer in town; it was the only firm dealing with marble works in Oxford. Some weeks later and for twenty-three dollars more than the $400 dollar check would cover, Simms volunteered to go along and help Barnett erect the monument on site. Gentle spring rains had turned red clay on the narrow dirt road to a sticky gumbo. They maneuvered slick spots, void of gravel, en route to the backwoods church and cemetery.

The relatively fresh grave site was not difficult to spot, and the grass-covered mound situated beside it was of no great interest. The older grave did, however, have an aluminum card holder standing upright. One could still read the lettering which had been lovingly traced over and over as it had faded—DAISY.

The two men stood staring, not at the faded card, but directly at the fresh grave adorned with a giant marble edifice upon which, in neatly sculptured rows, were the words: "Rest in peace – Lincoln W. Washburn." A brother, now residing in Detroit, had also been interested in seeing that a proper marker be erected to the memory of Lincoln W. (Red) Washburn.

Simultaneously, both men centered their attention on the most recent creation of the Suthern Simms Marble Works.

"Suthern," Barnett asked, "What can we do with this tombstone?"

"Nothing," Simms replied. "It's already got Red's name on it."

Together, they replaced the aluminum holder with the new piece of granite. Working with chisel and concrete, they obscured, as best they could, the word "Lincoln" and the initial "W."

Crudely, though discernable, the name DAISY glowed in the last rays of evening sun slipping past the wood steeple arched against pine and hardwood branches surrounding Mt. Zion Christ The Rock Apostolic Church.

It was a time before television in Mississippi. Minorities were beginning to show up as sales clerks and out-front restaurant workers. In the '50s, I was young, and all the wonders of the world were opened to me. I had scraped through two years of college and in 1954 arrived, a transfer from junior college, on the campus of the University of Mississippi. I crossed over a bridge to face the campus circle and saw the huge antebellum structure fronted by six tall Ionic Greek columns. For one who had never lived in a family-owned house, this was home.

After I settled into a dormitory room, the first order of business was to find a part-time job, which took me to the office of Dr. George Street, director of placement and financial aid. Little did I know that the position he held would become an office that I would inherit or that he would be my mentor and friend.

"You want a job?"

"Yessir."

"You already have a scholarship. Financial aid is extremely scarce, and we try to parcel it out. The jobs we have go to those needy students who have no scholarship."

"Dr. Street, sir, the scholarship only pays tuition—and I am grateful for that, but I have to have books and food and dorm rent."

"Well, your parents will have to help with that."

"Dr. Street, my parents are sharecroppers. I just had to help them with my summer savings. Well—to tell you the truth, I didn't have to do that. It's just that they had recently got electricity in the Good Hope community, and I bought my mother a Frigidaire. We never had an ice box before."

George Street looked at me for a long time. Abruptly, he jumped up from his desk and said, "Come with me."

We walked from his little World War II office hut over to the university cafeteria. On the way, he shared that Wood Bounds, director of food services, would expect me to prove myself if he were to offer a job.

"Mr. Bounds, this is Jim. He is just off the farm and accustomed to hard work if you can find some."

Mr. Bounds looked over his glasses with a wrinkled brow that looked like a cotton row that had been laid out by a careless plowman.

"Where you from, boy?"

"Graduated Good Hope, near Lena."

"You need a job?"

"Yes, sir, I very much want one."

"I didn't say 'want.'"

"No sir, I meant 'need.'"

"Well, if Dr. Street says you need one, I'll give you a try."

"Thank you, sir."

Mr. Wood Bounds stood and shook hands with the departing George Street.

"Now, boy—what did you say your name was?"

"Jim—Jim Warner, sir."

"Okay, Jim, here's the way we start. If you pass the test I'm about to give, I'll find something for you. After that, you'll get fifty cents per hour worked."

"Yes, sir."

"There is a trailer parked outside at the dock. It's loaded with sugar. Those bags need to be brought in and stacked neatly in the storage room. You can handle hundred-pound sacks, can't you?"

"Can I start right now?"

"Yeah, I'll get Rufus to show you where."

Rufus was a big, black guy who showed me the warehouse and the trailer load of sugar.

"Now don't forget to pile them in straight rows all the way up to the ceiling."

"All the way to the ceiling?"

Rufus had a huge grin. "All the way."

I don't mean to imply that Wood Bounds was a hard man. He was soft, gentle and opinionated, but he was kind to me and advanced my fortune at the cafeteria. Still a student two years later, when he lost a full-time supervisor, I became the upstairs food service boss. In the meantime, I was weekend night watchman and cashier, which provided an opportunity to know the employees, mostly African American. Many of them were bright people who survived an inadequate black public school system to work at menial jobs. There were some who had not had the opportunity to attend school at all.

I remember Lula Mae Billingsly. Lula Mae was a cook in the greasy way vegetables were prepared back then. One day, the grease caught fire while I was in class, and she received blistering burns on her arm and neck. Other workers sat her in a corner with ice on the burns and failed to report the accident to a supervisor. I found her huddled on a hard-backed chair.

"Come on, Lula Mae, I'll take you to the doctor."

A frightened look spread on her face. "No, Mr. Jim. It ain't bad. I'll be fine."

"Don't be silly. That's a bad burn, and it needs attention."

She turned from me and in a whisper said, "Jonah won't let me!"

"What you mean, Jonah won't let you?"

"My husband, Jonah, he won't let me. He'll fix me up. He'll be mad if I go to a doctor."

She kept insisting, so I put her in a car and took her home, stopping at the drug store for Unguentine. They lived west of town in a broken-down house trailer that had in its yard a rusted truck perched on blocks, staring forlornly toward the dirt road. Lula Mae was back at work next day, no Unguentine, no bandage, but a blood-red paint on her oozing burned surfaces—Oxblood shoe polish.

Mr. Bounds had Rufus and me force a crying and begging Lula Mae into a van for transport to the emergency room.

"But," she cried, "He'll kill me."

The sheriff made sure that Jonah didn't kill her for a week. On Friday, payday, Lula Mae spent all of her pay to bail Jonah out of jail.

The prosecutor was staring at me. The courtroom was silent.

"I'm sorry, Mr. Greenwood, I was thinking somewhere else. What was your question?"

"Were whites restricted from entering black establishments back then?"

"Not unless they thought that it would ruin their reputation. At about fourteen, Bobby Coleman and I would sneak across the GM&O Railroad tracks to a Negro juke joint to listen to their music. On occasion, we might get a sip of the white lightning they drank. They could have thrown us out, but they didn't. Probably didn't want to make a fuss."

Greenwood had ridden that horse about as far as it would go, so he gave it up to Walt for cross-examination.

Walt asked a question that I had to consider a bit before answering.

"Mr. Warner, you have been questioned about childhood experiences with minorities. Can you recall the one personal experience growing up that has had the most profound influence on what you have become relative to your understanding of race relations?"

"I guess it was when I was about eight or nine; I observed the arrest of some black people."

"What happened?"

"They were beaten for no reason and put in jail."

"How did that make you feel?"

"It opened my eyes to how people are treated when they break with tradition and transgress societal expectations."

"Mr. Warner, did you discuss your feelings about the beatings?"

"No—but while I was walking home from Ludlow where this happened, I met Willie, a black boy I knew. I told Willie about it, and Willie decided he didn't want to go to Ludlow after all. He turned around and walked with me beyond the three miles to where I lived and on another mile to his home. After that, I heard other people talk about the incident, but I had nothing to say."

Walt had no reason to pursue that story but the day is stamped on my memory in carbon copies lined in single file. After a few years, I did write a little story that is tucked away in my dresser drawer. I never showed the story to anyone. I even used "he" instead of "I," perhaps to deny authorship in the event it ever surfaced. For some reason, I could not claim ownership. I still wonder why.

He seen it all, seen it in its entirety, seen it better than Harley Tripp or Cecil Goings just rounding Gene Anderson's store and filling station. He seen it, felt it, and heard it just as good as all the grown men standing in the street. Just as good as Daddy, who was now sending him home so as him not to hear the talk and so as not to see and hear whatever else might go on. He heard good enough when there was a general mumble and when mor'n one had remarked that, "Harvey warn't gonna' take no smart alecking of'en no nigger."

He was now retracing his steps, but he could not recollect going from whence he was now coming. He was on that road again toward home watching puffs of dust preceding each step as if it knew some primordial secret to anticipate the approaching tread.

But he could remember the mules and wagon, the old uncle and his woman on a spring seat and the son, a boy as black as the blackest night—blackner'n the tar we chewed when we could find it by the GM&O train track. The tall black boy was standing erect in the back of the wagon, leaning slightly to grip the seat.

Everybody knowed as good as could that Uncle had sold a bale of cotton, bought some flour and fatback and some other provisions that included a pint of white lightnin', which had to be drunk behind the gin, outta sight of law and wife.

Uncle stood in the wagon as steady as you please. He tapped the mule's hind-end with the lines, took off his dusty black hat and bowed from the waist to the crowd of whites standing around or perched on benches circling the water oak tree in the middle of the dirt street, halfway between Lee's Drygoods-General Merchandise and Sessums' Grocery.

Constable Harvey Comfort had the bridle of the nearest mule in his grasp before a leisurely trot had been struck, and he flung himself toward the old man, who was still bowing and smiling. Mr. Harvey had to stand on a spoke to reach the object of his agitation, a quick jerk landing both men in the street. Fuming and "cussin'," Mr. Harvey jumped to his feet, the old man struggling to pull up his pants that had dropped to his ankles. Like a black streak in slow motion, the young man cleared the side of the wagon frames to land between Mr. Harvey and the old man, the latter wearing a bemused, almost disinterested, expression.

"Mr. Harvey, please don't hurt Papa," the plea echoed up and down the now quiet dirt street, making its way through the store windows, around the circle of men in the shade, reverberating back again as a challenge. A tree root left by a road grader shaving bumps from the ground seemed to fly up and over the constable's shoulder. But all saw the hand that grasped it and brought it down. Down it came, chalky and white, to meet hair and skull and face. The boy fell to his knees, back straight, his bloodied head erect, dust mingling with dark red streaks flowing down his black-skinned neck to form bulbous patches glistening in the sunlight—breaking to run anew.

He was there long enough to see the two, father and son, thrown into the back of a World War II jeep to be carried off to jail in Forest, the county seat. He was there long enough to be put on the road home and to remember and to ask why and to forget only to remember again and to grow and to question—to question why a year later, Harvey Comfort was found shot to death, deep in the swamps of the Flatwoods. They said Mr. Harvey was bad to take off after folks gathering a little meat outta season, and maybe some hunter most likely mistook Mr. Harvey for a deer.

Chapter 15

Walt moved on from those questions related to my family and the formative years.

"Mr. Warner, were there incidents that occurred after you grew up and left home that contributed to attitudinal changes in your perception of race relations?"

"Yes, a great many."

"Would you care to relate a few?"

"Well, I went away to junior college and began to broaden my knowledge of the world and to develop an appreciation for different cultures."

"Anything in particular that might have tended to promote what could be called liberal views?"

Larry Greenwood objected. "Your Honor, the prosecution stipulates the value of a college education. Whether it changes fundamental beliefs held by individual students is a matter of conjecture. At any rate, it has no direct relevance to the charge lodged against this defendant."

Walt maintained that education spoke to the state of mind of an individual.

The judge sustained the objection but delayed further testimony until the next day.

For the first time in weeks, my lawyer seemed more relaxed and confident. As the courtroom emptied, he turned to look at me.

"Mr. Warner, I apologize. Your testimony is going better than expected. Let's get together and talk a little strategy—anticipate what we can present that would leave Greenwood with no chance for rebuttal."

I said, "Sure," but I was still thinking of how educational experiences fashioned whatever I have become.

Stela Newsome taught literature, not just the words or rhyme, or metrical composition, but the emotion and meaning. She brought Shakespeare to life and spread the beauty of recognized verse and stories to the mostly country kids who attend two-year colleges. With enthusiasm and passion, she wound her tongue around history and culture. One couldn't help sharing world values and respecting the contributions of many races and peoples very different from our assembled classmates. She opened the world. She was a teacher!

After a year at the community college, I sold Bibles, a summer job that took me through more than six additional years of higher education, including law school. The first summer in Clinton, North Carolina, shattered some of my conviction for that written word and left me to consider the ordered world from which I sprang. I had many conversations with many people, some of whom were convinced that I was going to hell for not agreeing with them. Even the snake handling group was offended when I declined to visit their church service.

When I was visiting in the home of a potential customer, my perception of religious literature was challenged by a furious indictment for adherents of the "good book," who practiced genocide against the minority race. I can still hear him shouting, "We don't want your white women.

We have beautiful black women of our own." Whether that was a racist statement or not, I began to see an attitudinal change that later would inflame the Civil Rights movement.

Back on the university campus, it was a clear summer morning in 1955. Ted Walsh, my Nashville sales director, related the news of a young black boy being pulled from a watery Tallahatchie River grave not that far from campus. My first reaction was that he should have known better than to flirt with a white woman. Immediately, I was ashamed. Why on earth would I say that? It was an utterly abhorrent and uncaring remark. I quickly apologized to Ted, but my embarrassment and remembrance of that statement remain to this day. To think of a fourteen-year-old kid being beaten, having an eye gouged out, shot, tied to a seventy-five-pound cotton gin part, and thrown into a river is an image not easily erased.

A couple of years later, I began to collect stories from "old timers" who would talk of past atrocities. One claimed to have, as late as the 1920s, witnessed a black man burned at the stake in New Albany, a town about thirty miles from Oxford. I don't know the authenticity of the story, but he swore to seeing it with his own eyes. Again, the horrific act was the result of a white female charging that the victim had made sexual advances.

I assessed more credence to unforgettable visits in the 1950s with a ninety-year-old resident of Oxford that occurred in the late '50s. Ike Ramsey had been sheriff of Lafayette County during the Great Depression and now spent much of his time during nice weather sitting on a bench under a Lafayette County courthouse tree, swapping stories with retirees and loafers. He was a colorful character with a red face and a considerable pot belly. His eyes twinkled with a hidden smile that failed to reveal a lifetime of dedication to law and order. He was not one to tolerate pen and paper, but he was addicted to story-telling. Since I was an aspiring young attorney, he felt an obligation to educate me in the vagaries of human nature. We sat, and he talked in a slow, husky voice that demonstrated strength of character with a hint of whimsy. Since I couldn't write anything down at the time, I committed to memory as best I could. Although I am at a loss to reiterate exactly, I am reporting my interpretation of his recounting.

It was a hot, sultry night—but I'm getting ahead of myself. Rather, it was a hot 1936 autumn day about seven miles east of Oxford on the old New Albany road near the Bay Springs community. Young lovers, incompatible though they were by heritage, lineage, tradition, and community mores, had considered their morbid differences and, nonetheless, discovered an uncontrollable physical attraction. The available haystack turned out to be an inhospitable place since the opposite side from where the straw flattened was occupied by a sleeping farm boy, who awoke and sounded a shrill alarm reaching the farmhouse occupied by father and brother of the female participant.

Through late afternoon and early evening, the tracking proceeded, father and son soliciting soldiers, dogs, horses, and guns along the way. Through sloughs and briar patches, alternately bogs and dust, they passed beyond a thicket to a cabin door. Pine lighter knots lit, guns ready and dogs barking, they called for the lone occupant to show himself. From inside came warnings to "go away," but the son with appropriate epitaphs urged the father to do his duty. A shotgun blast through the locked door ripped the outer stomach wall of the father. The door was shattered, a young man dragged and tied to a huge persimmon tree. With the victim surrounded by dry sticks and boards, not to mention seasoned stove wood, the son lit a match.

Attention was then paid the father who lay with entrails spilling onto the dirt. An ambulance was summoned from Oxford to transport the dying man, young son riding in back to give solace. The ambulance roared at break-neck speed over the dusty gravel road, barely slowing for the right turn onto Highway 30. Alas, the back door did not make the ninety-degree pivot and opened wide. An unsecured patient cart rolled, taking both the father and son to their doomed destiny with asphalt.

Sometimes, I question the truth of that story since Sheriff Ramsey also told ghost stories about the Bay Springs area. One had some reference to the tale just related. The springs consist of a series of spring-fed pools that cascade down from surrounding hills. At one time they were used to grow minnows for avid fishermen. Today, they serve as a biological field station for scientific experimentation. Surrounded by forests of huge hardwoods, little light is available at night to obliterate the ghostly shadows cast upon flowing underground water that seeps to the surface.

A young university student in a red convertible was returning from a romantic frolic with a young lady who lived in the Bay Springs community. He had parked in her front yard and enjoyed a "beerful" evening. Traveling on the road leading back to campus, he braked at the bottom of a steep hill where springs ford the road. If he had only noticed earlier—the huge St. Bernard that lay on the porch while he consumed a dozen drinks decided to sleep on the back seat of the convertible. As the car moved forward, the dog sat up to enjoy a cool breeze. When the automobile braked suddenly, the dog fell forward, literally surrounding the young driver. Having heard stories of ghostly creatures from university professors who play in the springs with fish and frog, he envisioned a father trudging along with an arm full of entrails, a skinless son following and a headless body engulfed in flames to the rear. Alas, stepping on the gas was a bad decision since the convertible dove headlong into the depths of Bay Springs Lake. Now, they say there are four spirits that skulk Bay Springs, wailing and shrieking—just waiting for others to join them.

Walter Dunbar caught me plying water to geraniums wilting in the blistering summer sun.

"Mr. Warner, I wanted to talk about what's happening and reassure you that your case is different. The newspapers are full of that trial in Jackson and the verdicts for ten young people with penalties handed down for hate crimes."

"Yes, I've been keeping up with that."

"Good. Our case is different. Your motivation was different. You had no hate for the victim, no malice in your heart. All those things affected the harsh sentencing you've been hearing about. Keep doing what you're doing and don't equate jail terms visited on those people in Jackson and let it upset you."

"Walt, I've told you before. I'm not concerned with what happens to me, but let me ask you a question. How do you know what motivated me to fire that weapon? Was the hate, recognizable or not, just a matter of degree as compared to the Jackson case? Was there malice planted in me at birth that I failed to control? With all my so-called good deeds, did I harbor resentment for a teenager because he was black? And how will things ever change if no one is held responsible?"

"Mr. Warner, we've already been over this dozens of times. If you insist on committing suicide, so be it, but wait until after the trial is over. Let's not jeopardize or compromise thousands of cases that will be coming in the future where innocent people accidently create tragedy. The Jackson case is just one in which people are held responsible for blatant acts spurred by hate."

"Yes—yes Walt, I know. I wonder how many covert acts occur for which there is no justice?"

"There's no use talking to you, Mr. Warner! There is no perfect world."

After Walt left, I tried to get into the heads of the ten Jackson-area young people now connected with the story of James Craig Anderson.

According to media reports and trial records, at 5:00 a.m. on June 11, 2011, a forty-nine-year-old black man, James Craig Anderson, was in a motel parking lot attempting to get into his locked vehicle. Two car loads of young white people, ages between eighteen and twenty-four, arrived. Anderson was beaten, robbed, and deliberately run over by the driver of one of the vehicles.

While I was not acquainted with the perpetrators, I grew up with people who held the same views as have been attributed to what was labeled as a conspiracy to deprive minorities of their civil rights. Although it is difficult to imagine such cruelty in the twenty-first century, current happenings around the world attest to unbelievable inhumane acts by some still classified as human. My own search for personal characteristics that motivate action toward a young black man demands that I examine underlying causes for such hate. As I contemplated Walt's remark about an imperfect world, I put the old lounger in the prone position and imagined the world of kids who fail the test of decency.

My name is JoJo. I'm free, white, and almost twenty-one. Well, maybe not completely free. I work on the line at a Jap auto assembly plant. My supervisor is a nigger woman that ain't smart enough to pour piss out of a boot. And here she is, one of them African Americans that got her job because she's black. Don't know but sleeping with a big boss may have helped. Men along my line got to be 50-50 color-wise, although some Chinks are thrown in with the blacks. Wetbacks are everywhere. Don't know how they count them. They all vote Democratic and most live with black women. Don't get married because that would cut off the food stamps, health care, and welfare checks. I want to puke when I have to pay taxes to support such crap.

Can't wait till four o'clock to wheel outta this shit hole. Don't know how I got here in the first place. I hate work but gotta have my Budweiser. Got my taste for the beer when I was about knee-high. Don't touch the hard stuff my Momma drank, but I share her penchant for weed.

Daddy left home when I was seven. Substitute daddies came and went. School was a bore, and I started as a grocery stock boy after the tenth grade. Just as well. Them football pricks were always on my butt. Those big blacks were treated like kings and got into the pants of white cheerleaders. Made me want to take an AK-47 and mow them all down. Teachers were afraid of them and gave them the grades they needed for college.

Well, that's O.K. Got my crowd. There's Fang and Tommy and Bo and Jimmy and Bart and Long John. There's usually four or five gals that hang with us. We meet at Gus' place on Wednesday and on weekends. Gus hates blacks and foreigners. Has to serve 'em, but they're always served last and for more money. Gus always turns up the Fox network when one comes in. They get the idea and don't come back.

Most customers sit at the bar, but our crowd generally pushes a couple of tables together. One night, after a few beers, Fang pulled out a slingshot he had made. He had taken the fork of a small tree branch, tied strips of inner tube to the prongs, and attached the tongue of an old shoe to the loose rubber ends.

"How y'all like my new weapon?" Fang asked.

"I prefer my nine millimeter," Bo said.

"I'll stick with my shotgun and snub 38," added Tommy.

A discussion ensued as to the usefulness of particular weapons to kill birds and deer and any bastard that cares to mess with us.

"And what about niggers?" Bart wanted to know.

"Buckshot!" cried one of the girls.

Everyone turned to her.

"Buck—Shot," she repeated.

The immediate laughter filled the room, causing even Gus to remark, "Damn, that must have been a good one."

Jimmy chided the girl, Laurie, having heard a rumor that she sometimes dates outside our circle. "Buck Shot—wouldn't surprise me if you were partial to a black buck. They've put out that shit about having bigger pricks."

Laurie merely sunk into her chair and said, "I'm happy."

"Hey," Fang suggested, "let's go outside and test this booger on a bottle—see who is best with a rubber drubber."

"I've got a better idea," Long John drawled. "Let's go out and practice on a few 'Sambos.'"

With one girl who would go in each jump seat, a pickup and an open Jeep were pointed toward a black neighborhood. Two guys in the back were armed with small rocks for the slingshot, taking alternate turns to compete for a confirmed hit. The only target found was a teen riding a bike. We laughed and clapped when the bike veered off the narrow street into a ditch. Not wanting to get caught, we were back on the road to Gus' with tales of valor. As with any sport, word spread, and additional people became players, the ammunition graduating to larger stones and bottles.

It was a typical night of drinking and playing. Toward the beginning of a new day, the supply of beer was exhausted, and Gus was closing. Driving to find more beer, we spied a black man in a motel parking lot trying to get into his car.

"Stop," Fang yelled, "let's have some fun."

"JoJo, call the others," Joanie said.

We just kinda stood around until the others came. Fang was bantering some with the black dude.

"What'cha doing, boy?" Fang asked.

This guy had a straightened coat hanger in his hand with the hook end bent to slide under window glass to catch the door latch. He stood up and looked at Fang and then at the little crowd that had gathered. The Jeep load had arrived by that time. He ignored the question and went back to work on the window.

"I asked you a question, boy," Fang said.

The black man continued his efforts to reach a door latch that eluded the curved coat hanger.

"Bet you're trying to steal this car. Ain't ya?"

The man turned from his work. "Look, I don't want any trouble. I locked my key in the car, and I'm just trying to get home."

"A likely story," Fang said.

"It's true—now you young people just leave me alone!"

Long John spoke up. "Who do you think you are, nigger—telling us what to do?"

Fang came closer and slapped the man. The victim grabbed Fang and wrestled him to the ground. Bart and Jimmy pulled the enraged man off, and Fang landed a face blow from his knee stance. Red blood gushed from the black nose that evidently had been crushed. The three whites kept hitting and kicking the downed man, who made not a sound.

"Don't that hurt, nigger?" yelled Fang, breathing hard.

The victim merely curled up into a fetal ball while others took turns landing body blows with their feet.

"That's enough," Ruthie yelled. "We taught the black bastard a lesson. Don't want to kill him!"

With a final kick, Bart jumped into his Jeep and, with his riders hanging on for dear life, scratched off the lot.

As we entered the pick-up, Joanie looked at me.

"JoJo, are you a man or what? You just stood there and let the others do all the work! I don't know about you!"

I sat staring at the lot, watching as the black nigger struggled to his feet, staggering along in the direction of the motel office. I gunned the F-150. The tires spun out of control with the black man in my headlights. For good measure, I switched to reverse and backed over the body hearing what I thought was the crush of bone.

As we spun off, Joanie moved closer and whispered, "You're the man!"

And we were on the highway that was just awakening to a new day.

I sat upright in the lounger, shaking off a night chill, and began to stretch tired old muscles. It's a pity that everything that was resilient when I was younger has now become stiff. As old age sets in, everything that was stiff becomes useless. Negating the doctor's admonition to get plenty of sleep, I put on a pot of coffee. If I'm going to be thinking all these thoughts, I might at least be awake. Settling back against a cushion, I tried to assess some of the lessons learned from an incident where a group of young white people would attack an innocent black man whom they didn't even know.

Oh, there was the public reaction. Ten people in the actual case that inspired my dream received four- to eighteen-year jail sentences by the state court. The driver of the truck was convicted of murder, and both he and another were sentenced for "hate" crimes. Counting a conviction of murder in both the state and federal proceedings, the driver of the truck was sentenced to two life terms. It seems to me that enforcing two life terms might prove difficult, but such sentencing for a particularly hei-nous crime seems to be acceptable in our society.

Aside from the fact that hate is a learned condition, legislated into our blood like drugs or cancer, it seems that putting a bunch of hate to-gether creates a new dynamic. There appears to be something about the herd instinct and the length an individual might go to be a part of the crowd.

Other creatures seem to have the same predilection. From my farm days, I remember how baby chickens acted with no advantage of environ-mental instruction. If one in the brood were different in color, handicap or had a scrap of something that clung to its feathers, that chick was sub-ject to ferocious pecking. Once the blood showed, all the others would attack. They didn't let up until the victim died. I wonder if that term, "pecking order" came from the fact that chicks take turns?

CHAPTER 16

While in law school at Ole Miss, a class in constitutional law illustrated consequences of a "pecking" order through the legislative and judicial process. While I am unable to recall all the intricacies of the case, a Revolutionary War veteran who owned 5,000 acres of land and 300 slaves in Jefferson County, Mississippi, called his daughter into his Prospect Hills study. I am imagining what transpired.

"Brenda Faye, you are aware that I started the Mississippi Colonization Society a few years ago?"

"Yes, Father."

"And, do you know the purposes of that society?"

"I have read that the national group wants to send our slaves back to Africa."

"Brenda Faye, do you understand why?"

"Father, I cannot understand why they would wish to go. Most of them were born in America."

"I had not thought of that. Perhaps they should be given a choice, to go or stay. Brenda Faye, there are drumbeats all over the country to free slaves. In new territories, there are fights to reject new slave states. There is a divisive feel in our country that portends the establishment of a separate country. Northern states will fight to keep the states united. That means war! If slaves are just freed, they would threaten the stability of our country, especially the South."

"But Father, I read in the papers that the Mississippi State Legislature introduced a law that would prevent letting slaves go, even though they are the property of one who wishes to free them. If passed, the law, I think it's called manumission, would not allow an owner to send his slaves to one of those free states for repatriation."

"I see you've been keeping up with this situation."

"Since you contributed a lot of money to that Negro college in Norman."

"Brenda Faye, don't you see that if there is emancipation, these people will need to be educated? That doesn't happen overnight. That is why sending most to Africa would solve the growing problem of slavery. Our country could be reunited, and all could live free."

"What about Prospect Hills? Where would the labor come from? What about me?"

"The will provides for you as long as you live."

"Will?"

"The will I am proposing. Prospect Hills production could be cut in half, and we could still live in splendor. Those who decide to stay as free men and women would be paid for their services. A bonus equal to passageway for those who go would guarantee loyalty from those who stay."

"Father, I was an obedient child and in adulthood have always respected your judgement. And I have loved you as I should have. Please now forgive me for I must tell you that you have lost your mind. The rest of the family will oppose this scheme to the death."

And that they did. The planter filed his will, leaving Brenda Faye a life estate with, upon her death, the plan to repatriate slaves to Monrovia, later to become a part of Liberia. The planter died in 1836, Brenda in 1838. In the meantime, a grandson with the support of the rest of the family took the matter to Mississippi courts with the sensible argument that slaves were chattels with no rights to inheritance. There were questions relating to the organization in Ohio providing for the transfer, that it had violated the Manumission Act. Repeated decisions and appeals were forthcoming over more than ten years when the Mississippi Supreme Court ruled that the will was valid. A little late for Prospect Hills. Frustrated slaves burned the mansion, and a six-year-old child died in the fire. Twelve slaves were lynched. Land was sold to provide the funds promised in the will.

Unfortunately, that was not the end of the story. About one-half of the Prospect Hills slaves migrated to Monrovia with funds provided by the will. They joined many others sponsored by colonization societies throughout the United States. Some carried with them the learned ways of their former captors, enslaving indigenous tribes and amassing huge fortunes and large homes. Some years ago, Maggie and I had an opportunity to visit Africa, where we found there was still dissension between original tribesmen and the "newcomers." Today, it seems that the disparity in social and economic opportunities between peoples of the two groups are a cause for concern. The pecking order is visible.

Many of the African countries are fraught with war and the waste of resources that could lift them out of poverty and save the most important resource, their people. I wonder about the distribution of wealth in my own country and whether the disparity can long be sustained.

It seems to me the pecking order, the desire for one group to need a feeling of superiority or power over others, is rampant in our society.

Even if the overt action is that of a few or even one, others stand by and provide no intervention.

W hen I was in the first three grades, Ludlow was my school. All three grades were in the same classroom. The room faced a small open auditorium; the office of the principal occupying the anchor spot at the front entrance. The community had one service station, one grocery, one dry goods store, one school, and two churches. None of the entities had indoor plumbing. I remember the boys' outhouse, located down the hill at the back of the school building. The administration was quite strict about not permitting even the youngest children admission to that facility except at recess and during the lunch period. Since a child must go through the small auditorium and past the office, few students even thought of going at any other time because the principal was prone to paddle any who were caught outside a classroom during class periods. That principal, Mr. Neal, was furnished a little house on the school property as a part of his salary.

One morning my school bus had arrived early, before the 8:00 bell. I was playing outside with friends. Mrs. McDonald, the cafeteria cook, called from her doorway located at the side of the gym.

"Hey, James, come here."

"Yes'um."

"Mr. Neal forgot to leave his slop buckets. Go on down and get 'em."

"Yes'um."

I was aware that Mr. Neal had his hog pen back of the house with two good-sized shoats always ready to be fed. One of the perks that Mr. Neal enjoyed was to get scraps from the lunchroom to feed his hogs. Just as I rounded the back of the fence looking for the five-gallon buckets, Mr.

Neal stormed out of the house headed for the school.

"Boy, what are you doing out here?"

I was so frightened that I was unable to answer. Whereupon he picked up a tree branch and switched my little tail good. That's the kind of man Mr. Neal was. He had no time to stop and listen to explanations.

The older boys knew that Mr. Neal knew only one form of discipline, and they took full advantage. At recess, we little fellows would hold our pee until Mr. Neal put his finger on the bell and then with break-neck speed run for the outhouse. The reason for this behavior had to do with the older boys who, if they caught a kid in the outhouse, would turn us up by the heels and hold us over the open toilet threatening to drop us in the hole that had been dug underneath to contain excrement. Everyone knew that Mr. Neal kept his finger on the bell for two full minutes and that everyone was expected to be inside the school building by the time the button was released. It wasn't that we didn't have options. We could choose to be held upside down over an outhouse hole, risk a paddle spanking, or pee in our pants.

Surviving those hazards, one cold January day, I was in Mrs. Mayfield's fourth-grade class, and I had a terrible stomach virus. Mrs. Mayfield understood my dilemma and gave me permission to go to the outhouse during class hours, but every time I stuck my head out in the hall, Mr. Neal was there. I didn't make it until recess and, thereupon, proceeded to leave school and walk the five miles home. There was ice everywhere, but the road was clear. I had to go by Mary Jo Nutt's house about half the distance to mine. She had stayed home from school for some reason and was in the front yard next to the road.

"Hey. Why you walking so funny?"

"Hey. None of your business."

Nonetheless, I was in love with Mary Jo Nutt and terrified that I had lost her forever. Well, I guess I did.

I understand that bullying takes a different form now. I don't know whether young people are more sensitive or if the pressures are greater because of the multiplicity of social media. In my day, bullying was common, primitive, and expected. It was vulgar and unnecessary but less violent, I suspect. There don't seem to be instances of death recorded, as is the case today. There were this anxiety and fear that existed as a part of my generation. I'm not sure that we handled it better or if the trend toward protection from all bullying is the appropriate response. Are we more or less strong having faced that tendency for the strong to oppress the weak? Can we separate simple bullying as a fault of human nature as opposed to violent criminality? Is there a way to teach "goodwill" toward all? Is conscience learned or inherited? A simple old man can only ponder. I did dream of a young girl named Deborah.

Deborah Delaney was not the most popular girl at Branson High. Indeed, she was not the most attractive, nor was she solicited for enrollment in sought social circles. A junior, she had moved to Higginsville two years before and had not been able to find many new friends. A good student, she concentrated on her studies.

Gary Pickens was the most handsome of the senior-class boys. He was captain of the basketball team and the heartthrob of a team of girls who spent most of their time positioning themselves so as to attract Gary Pickens. Gary was not first-team in football, but he did everything he could to seek friendship with the star players.

The book was the story of Anne Frank. Deborah sat on school steps in the warm spring sun, half reading and half watching little cliques of socially active girls preening for matching groups of boys. The male group of boys with lettered jackets were laughing and goading one Gary Pickens, for what reason Deborah could not fathom. Finally, Gary sauntered over to where she sat.

"Yo, Debbie."

"Hi, Gary."

"What'cha reading?"

"Getting a little inspiration, 'Anne Frank.'"

"On Friday? I would think you would be lining up a fun weekend."

"Afraid not. Next week is exam week."

"Yeah, I know. I was just wondering—I've got to pull up math grades to stay on the basketball team—I was wondering if you might consider helping me some?"

"But, I'm just a junior."

"Yeah, but this is algebra that I failed in the ninth. You're probably in calculus by now."

For a fleeting moment, Deborah puzzled over why she would be asked to tutor a sophisticated senior. The fact that he was the best-looking guy on campus and was asking a "plain Jane" to spend time with him was exciting even beyond the blush she was attempting to suppress.

"When were you thinking? The public library is open each day after school."

"Well, this is Friday, and I'd like to get started right away. Tell you what—I know it's date night, but are you possibly free tomorrow night?"

She paused, not wanting him to think that she had no Saturday night plans. Finally she said, "I guess I could cancel—you could come by my house any time Saturday, and we'll see if afternoon or evenings would work out."

"I have to work all day Saturday. But, I do need to get started as soon as possible, and I don't want to bother your family."

"I'm—I'm sorry," she stumbled over the words. "I'm sorry it didn't work out."

"Say, I have an idea. My parents have a guest house. We could use it anytime and not be interrupted. It's right next door to our place. We could have pizza while we work tomorrow night—that is, unless you don't trust me."

"Oh, it's not that I don't trust you—I was just wondering if it would be a good idea. Not that it's a date or anything—people do gossip."

"Had not thought about that. Say, we could make it a work/date and have early dinner out somewhere before we start. Then if anyone took notice we would just be on a date. Or, better still, we could order out that pizza."

Deborah almost choked. A date with the most popular guy in school! Maybe it would develop into something more. They would be working side by side—perhaps innocently touching from time to time. The thought made her shudder as perspiration tracked along her spine. Still, she was hesitant. After all, she was "Plain Jane," and he was "Mr. Everything." Maybe she could take off her glasses and let long, lovely tresses fall upon her shoulder. Only problem—she didn't wear glasses and had short, frizzy hair. She did have a fair body and good boobs. Maybe after she left her house, she could open a button or two.

"I don't know, Gary," she said hesitantly. "I'll talk with my mother."

He showed every evidence of being hurt—offended. Inwardly, he sensed her indecisiveness.

"No, don't do that. If you don't trust me, let's just forget it."

"It's not that. It's just—it's just that when I go out at night, my mother wants to know where I'm going and with whom."

"Can't you tell her you're going down to the malt shop with a friend and you might hang out somewhere?"

"I guess so, but why would you care if she knew we were studying?"

"Well, if you insist, I don't want anyone to know."

Deborah was devastated. He didn't want anyone to know! He was ashamed of her—to be seen with her!

"Let me explain, Debbie," He was speaking through tears welling up in her innocent eyes. "You see, I don't want to admit this, but I am ashamed at having to need help. I think I can get the material, but I've played around this semester and can't graduate without this course. My dad has pulled strings to get me into his alma mater, but I can't go without a high school diploma. It's as simple as that."

Saturday was the longest day of her life. Leisurely bath and make-up became a tortured effort to meet impossible standards subject to critical observation. Six outfits were selected and rejected. She finally settled on a soft cotton sweater and a plaid skirt. She literally skipped to the malt shop meeting.

Ensconced in a baby-blue Jag convertible, she sat back straight, the happiest girl in the world.

The guest house held a spot down a gravel drive some distance beyond street homes in a modest neighborhood. Gary showed her the place stuffed with what appeared to be salvage furniture. She was about to ask about his algebra textbook when young men began arriving with pizza and beer.

Gary noticed the fear in her eyes and patted her hand. "Don't be upset. My friends will be leaving as soon as they have had a drink and a little pizza. Deb, you're a lady. I know you want your beer in a glass, so I'll just go and fix you one."

Sipping the drink while making small talk with three of the larger footballers she recognized from school, Debora began to feel dizzy. That was her last remembrance until she awoke on her front lawn, sweaty, dirty, bloody, and pained beyond endurance. Wait, in her stupor, she did remember a face close to her ear, someone whispering. Yes, she did remember. Through the haze, she could see, not the handsome Gary, but a contorted version with wild eyes and half a face. The half-face was speaking through a long megaphone—yes, it was a megaphone grown to her ear. She wondered about that and what it meant but tried to concentrate on the pulsating voice ringing the spirals of the instrument. What was it saying? As booming volumes rolled in tiny syncopated sound bites, she heard repeated words synonymous with parrot chatter. "Debbie, I'm sorry. I never thought. I didn't mean to. I wanted to please them. They made me do it."

Over and over the words resounded, becoming fainter and fainter, trailing into oblivion. Fortunately, her mother and the new boyfriend had gone out that night, so she dragged herself into her bedroom with an intense hurt beyond her experience—more intense pain than she had ever felt—until two days later when pictures were posted on Facebook!

Maybe I'm just an old fogy, but I wonder about this "hate crime" classification system. It seems to me that if I hate a Jewish person, I have engaged in some sort of reflection as to why. Perhaps it was a learned response, political reaction, or even a stacking of a set of chromosomes. But at least there was a reasoning or belief whether the conclusion was reasonable or not. In the case of rape, it seems that the perpetrator has absolutely no regard, positively or negatively, for the victim. To me, a total disassociation of the act from the object of the action is more reprehensible than the process of learning to hate. The latter, at least, requires some decision-making. The argument might be made that a rapist hates the opposite sex for some psychologically understood reason, but that does not explain same sex rape which, I understand, is entirely possible. The victim still remains an object, never to be confused with flesh and blood.

I have had opportunity to observe pressure by an authoritarian figure to influence those under his or her control. One instance that I recall involved an employee who just happened to be vulnerable in a relationship with her supervisor, who had his own reasons for being aggressive. Although not rising to the level of prejudice, it does suggest the human trait of dominance and control—perhaps the basic ingredient of a feeling of superiority that seems to produce prejudice.

Sally sat in the secretarial pool, the third desk in the aisle of six.

"Hey, Gina, have you seen the Hawkins file?"

"Naw," Gina grunted, studying a cuticle on her middle finger.

"Well, girl, you could help me find it."

Gina shifted her buns and asked, "Why?"

"Because," Sally retorted.

"Because why"? Gina persisted.

"Because, Jenkins is gonna have my ass if we don't get that entered."

Gina looked thoughtful for a moment and asked, "Why just your ass?"

"Gina!" Sally pretended to be offended.

"Well," added Gina, "I wouldn't mind him having mine."

"You're impossible," Sally shrieked.

"You can play that game, but I've seen how he leers at you," Gina laughed.

Sally threw up her hands and went up front to search for the file.

Gina watched Sally's long legs, thin waist, and firm body, crowned by medium-length red hair. Shit, Gina thought to herself. I'm bigger up front, divorced, and blonde. Why don't blondes have more fun anymore?

Returning with an armload of paper, Sally shook her head at Gina. She was halfway through entering the Hawkins contract number when

Gina interrupted.

"What's your husband like?"

Keeping her eyes on the computer screen, Sally mumbled, "okay."

"What do you mean, 'okay'?" Gina questioned.

"I mean he's okay—he's nice—he's okay."

"But not prime rib," Gina pressed.

"Gina, I'll swear—you're the craziest crazy I've ever worked with."

"Not really prime rib, though?"

"In a million years, I'll never be able to understand you, Gina."

"Now Jenkins—that's prime rib." Gina rounded her lips and pushed out the words.

"I'm sure I don't know what you're talking about." Sally turned her back to Gina.

"Shit," Gina moaned as she went for a second cup of coffee.

The intercom buzzed, and Sally picked up.

"Ms. Craft, would you bring in the Hawkins hard copy?"

"Right away, Mr. Jenkins."

Sally felt Gina watching her from the coffee pot. Without a glance in that direction, she quickly made her way to the office of the second vice president.

Hal Jenkins rose with a phone at his ear and motioned her to sit. Sally quietly studied the room, the beige carpet and flowered tapestry wall hanging. The desk was not as neat as the man behind it. Sally liked orderliness in everything, but particularly in dress. Hal Jenkins passed her inspection. She judged Jenkins to be about eight years older than she, maybe forty-eight. But who can tell, she asked herself. Men always appear younger than they are—it's not fair.

"Why, Ms. Craft, how nice you look this morning."

Sally mumbled a thank you, but did not blush.

"No, really. You're quite attractive."

This time Sally did feel the blood rise in her cheeks. A silence hung like the brocade in the drapery. Hal cleared his throat. Sally sat.

"Well," Hal finally said. "This Hawkins thing means a lot to the firm. We don't have anything signed, just some promises. I need someone to help me keep on top—to be knowledgeable about the negotiations."

Sally did not say anything.

Hal continued. "I was wondering if you would work with me on this."

Sally nodded but still did not speak.

"It might mean working overtime a bit. Of course, you'll get paid for the extra hours. Is that a problem for you—the overtime, I mean, not the money?" And he smiled at her.

She heard herself say, "I'd like that very much—what I mean is the overtime will be no problem."

"Thank you. I knew you'd be agreeable," Hal stammered, embarrassed for some reason he could not understand.

She stood in the doorway and for the first time during the conversation, smiled back at him.

What the hell is wrong with me, Hal thought. Why do I feel guilty? I do need help, and Sally Craft is the best damn secretary in the pool. She works hard and deserves a break. Probably needs the extra money too. I'm surely not looking for anything more than an intelligent person to do some extra work. I surely don't want an affair, especially with someone in the office!

Sally ignored the catty looks Gina gave her when she got back to her desk. Gina smiled knowingly, like she was keeping a big secret. She did not mention Hal Jenkins for the rest of the day.

It was only 5:30 when Sally left work, but darkness filled the cold November evening. Fog hung from overpasses like a shroud of Spanish moss. She was on her way home. Home was Biff, and she knew he would be there. Not that his presence meant anything—it no longer mattered. Nothing really mattered.

Parking on the street, she sat in the car for a while watching the flicker of a candle in her bedroom window. Wearily, she left the car, inched by a Chevy Blazer in the carport, and entered through the kitchen door. Finding the light switch, she saw empty beer cans from a six-pack stacked on the counter, four on the bottom and two on top like a practice target.

Biff called, and Sally walked resignedly to the bedroom door. As she knew from experience, there would be more beer cans, and Biff would be cringing in the middle of their king-size bed.

He had a gun to his head. Curiously, she had forgotten what caliber it was or even what it looked like. She barely noticed it now in the yellow light.

"This time I'm gonna do it Sally," Biff blubbered.

"Yea, Biff, I know."

"I'm really gonna do it," yelled Biff.

She left him sucking the pistol barrel, crying like a baby.

It was a scene so often repeated that it evoked no emotion. It was to be tolerated like the grocery list stuck to the refrigerator door, a reminder that some things are used up.

For a long time, she had told herself that Vietnam made Biff that way. But one day she ran in the park and could not get free from it. The stranger appeared from nowhere, grabbed her arms, and twisted her to the ground. She lay on her back, a knife at her throat, and counted to one hundred. As she lay hurting, Sally thought of Biff and suddenly realized that Vietnam wasn't to blame—it just gave him an excuse. Afterward, she understood and did not tell Biff or anyone about what had happened in the park.

Sitting alone in the darkened kitchen, she remembered the violence in Biff. At nineteen, when he brawled at Crowley's Bar, Sally's fear was exceeded only by her heightened excitement. Strangely drawn to the wildness in Biff, she married without thought. A single day after the wedding, Biff shipped out for Southeast Asia.

Returning to the reality of the moment, Sally scrubbed the counters and washed dishes. With the toilet spotless and clothes folded, she sat again until eleven. God, she pleaded, let him be asleep!

Silently, she made her way to the bedroom, undressed, and slipped into bed. She held her breath for as long as she could and then began to relax. Just as she was drifting off to sleep, Biff rolled over on top of her. Sally counted to one hundred.

Hal Jenkins got home after seven. "I'm sorry, Vie," he apologized.

"It's cold." Vie said, her eyes never leaving the television.

Cold lasagna is cold lasagna, Hal thought.

When he returned from the kitchen, Vie had stretched herself on the couch. Hal sat and placed her head in his lap.

"Say, Vie; there's a great play on the public station. Why don't we have a glass of wine and watch?"

"What play?"

"Tennessee Williams' *Glass Menagerie.*"

"You mean that sex pervert?"

"Well, I don't know about that. The T.V. Guide says this is a great presentation. Why don't we watch it together?"

Vie grunted and went for a bottle and two glasses.

The character in the play, Tom Wingfield, was in the middle of his first soliloquy. "But I am the opposite of a stage magician. He gives you illusion that has the appearance of truth. I give you truth in the pleasant disguise of illusion."

Vie was snoring.

The play depicted a family abandoned by the father. The son, Tom was trapped with an overbearing mother and a crippled sister. Hal watched Tom blending with a stark set depicting a trashy tenement in St. Louis. Even the disruptive "support your public television" sequences did not spoil the mood for Hal. Tom was Hal, and Hal was Tom. It was Hal, torn between responsibility and living. By the final "Blow out your candles, Laura," Hal felt the hot tears on his cheek. He tried to wake Vie to explain how he felt—but the wine was gone.

After two weeks working together two nights a week, it was still Ms. Craft and Mr. Jenkins. He ordered sandwiches in, and they worked until nine. During the third week, Hal suggested that they run out to the corner "greasy spoon" for a bite.

Salting his hamburger, Hal said, "Boy, I'll bet you're sorry you ever got mixed up in this project."

"No, I need it."

"You could be doing all sorts of interesting things."

"Yeah," Sally said flatly.

"Don't you get tired of the rat race?" Hal asked. "Wouldn't you sometimes just like to leave it all behind and go to some tropical paradise?"

Sally looked puzzled. "I guess I never thought about it."

Hal put on a professional face. "I was reading about a little island in the Caribbean, Bart. You know, ole Chris Columbus named that island. Called it Saint Bartholomew after his brother. Most people just say Bart these days."

"What would you do there?" asked Sally.

"Oh, just lie on the beach, swim, snorkel. The temperature is about eighty degrees year round. Lots of blue sky and beautiful flowers. One time I wrote a little poem about it. Just dreaming, you know. I think that I can remember how it went. Just in case, I tucked a copy in my briefcase.

I titled it 'Flight.' Would you want to read it?"

"Yes, I'd like that," Sally said.

Here we are, lovers over the city, a Chagall image
Superimposed above buildings and houses and barns,
With a tentacled Cathedral, spreading its arms
Along boundaries of fences all measured and stark.

Come fly my love beyond the harbored morass,
Set sail to float free the moorings we know,
To rise slowly skyward with the listing breeze
That ruffles your skirt and kisses our cheeks.

The new moon cusp beckons with slender fingers,
Caressing your body so light in my arms.
How little you weigh, abandoned by gravity,
Exposed and innocent as on the first day.

Lie back on the feathered bank of a cloud.
Look, there is no convention in how it rises
To meet the moment and change its shape,
Wrapping itself about you as I long to do.

Why not push all space from between us,
Let our bodies touch, fill all the proximities,
Holding the clock hands, stopping the circle
Until tiny electric strings cover the heavens.

"That's nice," said Sally. "Where ever did you come up with all that?"

"Well, there was this painting I saw at an art gallery. It was painted by an artist named Chagall. There was this couple just flying in the air over a town. I guess it represented freedom to me."

Hal's knee touched hers and lingered, sending magnetic charges through both their bodies. The moment passed, and knees withdrew. Hal suggested they call it a day.

"Yeah," Sally spoke from far away. "I'd better be getting home."

"You have a family?" Hal spoke as if just discovering something new.

"Yes, just a husband. How about you?"

Hal nodded. "The kids are gone. Vie and I are all alone."

Sally stood. "Well, I'll see you tomorrow."

On Friday, Sally told him. "I just don't know."

Hal responded, "It is an outstanding traveling art show that has never been to the museum before. Some of the world's finest paintings. It's not like a date or anything. It's just two friends enjoying something beautiful together on a Saturday afternoon. With Vie out of town, I just thought you might like to go. Bring your husband if you like. I just want company. It's no big deal."

"No," Sally said, "Biff wouldn't go."

She was inside the building when he arrived. They met, smiled, and walked separately. They did not speak, although they were sometimes together admiring the same painting. They circled and found each other again.

Glancing about to make sure he was among strangers, Hal whispered. "Want to get some coffee?"

Sally followed him to the snack bar.

Hal managed to spill from the Styrofoam coffee cup getting a brown stain down the front of his pants. Instinctively, Sally reached to dab it with a water-soaked napkin but then thought better of the idea. Hal tipped the cup again, losing half the contents on the table.

He broke the silence. "How did you like the exhibition?"

"It was great!"

After another long pause, Sally asked. "Which painting did you like best?"

Hal thought a minute before answering. "I think it was the one by the Belgian artist—I think Delvaux—yes, Paul Delvaux."

"Which one was that?"

Hal wrinkled his brow. "It was called 'Village of the Mermaids.'" There were all these women sitting by their doors dressed in dark robes and a man going down the street toward a beach in the distance."

Sally laughed. "What's that got to do with Mermaids?"

"Ah ha," Hal responded. "You didn't read the little blurb by the painting. It stated that the artist was inspired to paint that scene because of a dream. He dreamed that he was the man passing down that street, and when he got to the beach, all the women in black robes were already there, but they had turned into mermaids."

"That's weird," offered Sally.

"I guess so. Which was your favorite?"

Sally blushed. "I can't pronounce it." She pointed to the description in the printed program.

"Oh, you mean the Lautrec—"Le Moulin de la Galette"—the one that shows people dancing and some sitting and looking?"

"Yes," said Sally. "And one man, an onlooker, gazing at nothing, so sad and lonely in that crowd."

Hal explained. "You know, that scene is from a Paris cabaret. In fact, Renoir painted the same place about ten years before when it was more prosperous and all the beautiful people went there. By the time Henri de Toulouse-Lautrec painted it, it was kind of seedy."

"All I saw was loneliness," returned Sally.

Hal continued his lecture. "You know, that place must have made a comeback because it's supposed to be the forerunner of the famous Moulin Rouge. But now, I understand that even the Moulin Rouge can't make it anymore. Too many string bikinis and nude beaches."

"Loneliness," repeated Sally.

Hal ignored the comment and drank cold coffee left in his cup.

Sally could see figures in the gallery with upturned heads, stalking the art, seeking to satisfy some human need. She also felt gnawing hunger inside. Loneliness surged up within her. She looked at Hal and saw Biff. But now she knew that she deserved more—more than being a crutch, more than a flight of fantasy.

Hal's voice and the fact that his knee was again touching hers interrupted her thought.

"I've been watching you. You're puckering your mouth, and your lips move as if you're talking to yourself."

Sally smiled. "I just counted to one hundred."

She stood at the table before he was able to rise.

"Please excuse me, Mr. Jenkins, I've got to go. I'm sorry. I won't be able to work late anymore."

The Sally/Jenkins encounter makes one wonder the real distinction between a discriminatory feeling and a deliberate action taken merely to satisfy one's own need to dominate. We may use advantages in wealth, position, education, social, or political standing, attractiveness or other personal qualities to devalue another individual and exert control. There is a tendency to justify such action through convincing ourselves that we deserve a more satisfying position in society because of some real or imagined circumstance. A sense of assumed privilege often is manifested in action that ignores the feelings and expectations of others. Do we fear rejection and wish to prove ourselves, or is it merely a sense that we are missing an experience that others enjoy? Are the victims merely compliant, or do they fear retribution for failing to go along? Is using our fellow man unfairly for our own gratification a crime?

I thought long and hard about this apparent need to seek approval of others and the peer-pressure factor in "going along." Was my action for which I'm charged a result of a lifetime of ignoring racist talk that I privately abhorred? What about those racist jokes that I sometimes thought funny and, if not, kept my peace? In my younger days, I even shared stories in jest that reflected on the language, customs, or short-comings of a minority. With the advent of social correctness, I have tried not to do that, but sometimes I have to admit that I regret the passing of a good-humored ethnic joke. On occasion, I have caught myself beginning such a story and changing a reference to race, religion, etc., finding it falling flat without the, admittedly, learned discriminatory reference.

My law class of more than fifty years ago has no such reticence. For the last thirty years or so, about fifteen or twenty of us, together with wives or lovers, have gathered twice each year to remember our college years. Maggie used to cook for them and enjoy the good parts of our visit, which were many. It may have been difficult for her to remain less than hostile when racially based conversations ensued since she was a Yankee from northern Illinois.

Now, here I go again, assuming that Yankees are less prejudiced than those of us who have spent more years in the South. I guess it was peer pressure that caused us both to bite our tongues and totally love the many positive moments with those guys.

I am told that adherence to peer pressure declines with age but am not convinced of that fact. All ages may be subject to be driven or subjected to peer pressure. A friend who is a counselor at the local high school and deals with adolescents assures me that it is especially rampant in that age group. In my study, most of the definitions of peer pressure deal with the exertion of influence to change attitudes, values, or behavior so that one conforms to a group dynamic. Social cliques, organizations, sports, religion, and numerous other entities are included in molding participants into a cohesive unit.

Peer pressure can be good or bad. It might encourage one to become a better student, volunteer for positive endeavors, excel in sports or in any number of competitive events. Competition can be positive, but it can also promote taking risks to be popular, engaging in bad behavior, using tobacco, alcohol, drugs, and the like.

CHAPTER 17

I got to thinking more about peer pressure. Charismatic people seem to use it to achieve group adherence to all kinds of behavior. But when I read about those who are listed as charismatic, they can have different styles of leadership. I don't know much about leadership, but it has to mean that anyone who can find followers is a leader. Charisma must be in the eyes of the beholder if a leader has to have a healthy dose of it. It appears that the leaders for good have characteristics similar to the characteristics of those who are destructive. Money, titles, privilege, personality, even good looks, have little to do with leadership. Random House Dictionary defines charisma as "the special quality that gives an individual influence or authority over large numbers of people." Others see it as a rare personal quality one uses to engender devotion and enthusiasm. I guess we can also use that definition for good as well as destructive charisma.

To me, there are many commonalities among these charismatic leaders. For good or evil, they have commitment, work ethic, analytical ability, and an understanding of human dynamics and interaction. They, depending on their purpose, can share praise or withhold gratifying recognition to achieve compliance.

It is difficult for me to think of bad leaders as charismatic, but they must have followers. It is also hard to understand how they, even with their atrocities, have influenced people over the centuries. Did their actions color the cloth of mankind with lasting stains that reach a wooded area of my beloved Wyldewoode?

Various recorders of history have classified what society has judged to be bad leaders. Narcissism is an accepted character fault in many. If I understand the word, it comes from a story in Greek mythology concerning an attractive young man who had never seen his own reflection. One day he was thirsty and took a drink from a lake. Upon seeing his image, he fell in love with himself. He couldn't abandon that reflection, so, he fell into the lake and drowned. That doesn't square with the fact that most historical bad eggs avoid that end. Still, a bad or good leader appears to have a healthy self-respect.

Bad leaders are said to be arrogant, self-centered, self-absorbed, prideful, competitive, and lack empathy. They exaggerate talents and accomplishments, perceive themselves as superior, crave power, and are abusive. They don't seem to learn from their mistakes, break rules, are prone to corruption, take risks, resist changing tactics, and fail to learn from mistakes. Bad leaders can be personally or socially motivated. Leadership may be based upon a need to satisfy self or the dedication to some cause.

We tend to judge good or bad leaders by their overt actions. Attila the Hun murdered his brother to gain power, was ruthless in killing and persecuting those whose territory he sought. Augustus had his opponents assassinated and manipulated family relations for political purposes. Vlad the Impaler, a Romanian ruler, is said to have impaled enemies with such blood-thirsty methods as to be called Dracula. Under Ivan the Terrible, some sixty thousand people are said to have died. Genghis Khan is known for brutality in establishing the mogul empire by attacking his neighbors. Stalin sent millions to gulags, executed and tortured non-followers. Mao Zedong is said to have killed thirty million people. Idi Amin relied upon chopping up enemies. Hitler oversaw Fascist policies in exterminating six million Jews and numerous Polish citizens. Pol Pot, leader of the Khmer Rouge, killed four thousand innocent civilians.

And the list goes on, not including those like Karl Marx, Machiavelli, Bin Laden, and those, beyond count, who may have inspired human sacrifice.

Some cult leaders strike me as different from those motivated by social or political gain. It's not so much just garnering support, developing team players, demonstrating salesmanship, demanding obedience, or merely demonstrating psychological superiority. To exert total mind and physical control over large groups of otherwise fairly reasonable people, one must possess special hypnotic powers. I suppose some victims may have a predisposition to dependency, but those who escape a cult influence seem unable to explain how they were so brainwashed.

From what I have read, cult leaders have a genuine inability to connect with reality and have no empathy. They demand loyalty and respect while failing to recognize that others might desire the same. They exert control by lying and withholding information. They seek conformity, establishing a new belief system. Perhaps they can be contrasted with Adolph Hitler, even though belief systems were challenged in his rise to power. Unstable, paranoid, Hitler was able to instill hope and affection bordering on idolatry. He masked truth couched in love of country to an irrational degree. I have always marveled that he could peddle a superior-race doctrine while personally possessing none of those physical characteristics. Still, his appeal was to patriotism and the need of a vast number of citizens for stability. Perhaps he was more of a salesman for that which the nation wanted to believe. A cult leader is indeed a promoter, but his or her product is a figment of the imagination of the leader. The follower has no choice in the belief system propagated.

My studies over these last eighteen months lead me to believe that cults are generally based on ideology—some political, some religious, some commercial, and some of a spiritual nature inspired by the leader. I talked it out with Maggie until after my usual bedtime. When sleep came, a dream scenario provided details if not much understanding of one so gifted in manipulating people.

Jimmy Jones, in my estimation, combined his own spirituality with religion and madness to induce a mass murder-suicide of over 900 people in Johnstown, Guyana, in 1978. Although I am unable to fathom how so many could have been so inspired, I have to accept that such extreme measures are adopted by a cult leader. I can picture some of the history and actions that must have occurred.

He sat on the floor of the three-room shack void of indoor plumbing and watched a drunken father struggle into an unmade bed. He lay there where he had been beaten with a leather strap that produced no resistance and no tears. His mother gathered the five-year-old into her arms.

"There, there, Jimmy, you're okay—you're special—very special! You're the savior, the Messiah, and you will save him, save us all.

"But, Jimmy, you are only ten. Your teacher tells me that you're reading stuff far advanced for your age."

"Don't worry, Momma. I am a Christian—love Jesus."

"But these thick books—Marx and Stalin and MAO—I can't pronounce the last name?"

"They are great men, along with Jesus and Gandhi."

"Com'on, we need someone to complete the team. What's that crap you're reading, anyway?"

"It's the Bible. I love God and Jesus. I don't have time for a stupid ballgame."

"Weirdo!"

"Momma, I'm fourteen now. When do you think I'll die?"

"What a crazy question! You'll live to an old age—in fact, you are special. You will never die."

"Hey, boy, I know you're grown and starting college, but I want to know about you messing around with this Communist shit. The FBI come here last week and asked if your Momma and me were Communists."

"What did you tell them, Daddy?"

"I said, hell, no. I fought in the big war."

"Good. They've been harassing me for going to some of the rallies."

"Well, stay away from those people. Neighbors are talking, and besides, it's un-American."

"I went to hear Eleanor Roosevelt speak. Want me to stay away from her?"

"Just stay away from all those shitheads. Have some real heroes, Nathan Bedford Forrest, for example."

"You mean that Mississippi son of a bitch that started the Ku Klux Klan?"

"Yeah, and if you would stop prissin' around as a liberal and help keep them black bastards in check, we'd all be better off."

"Son, don't you want to tone it down a bit?"

"But, Momma, my Methodist church refused to admit black people. I'll just start my own church! It will be interracial."

"Jimmy, you've got to start thinking about making a living."

"Momma, I went to a Pentecostal healing service last week and saw them raking in a ton of money. I could do that."

"Jim Jones, spiritual leader of the Peoples Temple Christian Church of the Full Gospel, to see Mr. Kartiganer."

"Well, Reverend Jones, so good to meet you. I've heard so much about the Peoples Temple and the huge crowds you're attracting."

"People are flocking to hear the true word of God, and I am only the vessel to share the good news with them."

"Good! Good. I was wondering if this network might provide a way for you to reach even more people. You would, of course, have a station on which to preach, but we would like you to become a permanent commentator in our religious segment."

"Nothing would please me more, Mr. Kartiganer."

"There is one problem."

"What's that?"

"I understand that you are a member of the Communist party. With the many 'witch hunts' in Congress, we can have none of that."

"Absolutely no problem. I have been led away from that false prophecy and found the true light."

"Well, that is good news! Let's look at a contract."

"Mr. Jones, your unconventional remarks on the religious segment and the unfortunate tenor of your printed sermons and radio addresses leave me no choice. I'm afraid that we must cancel our agreements."

"This is a shock, Mr. Kartiganer. Is it the integration of my congregation, my fight for civil rights, the suspicion that I harbor socialistic ideals? What is your problem?"

"Your militancy, Mr. Jones, and what many feel is an insanity creeping into your work."

"I know it's because I have joined the NAACP and other black movements and the fact that I show humility by volunteering to empty bed pans at the charity hospital that has your bowels in an uproar. Take your lousy network. I'll show you what a Messiah can do."

"Ladies and gentlemen. Thank you for attending this rally along with thousands of your closest San Francisco friends. But now, let me introduce the person you came here to hear, the governor of the great state of California."

"Thank you so much, Jim. As most of you know, Jim Jones is one of the top evangelists in our entire country. He is spiritual advisor to those at the very height of administrative authority in Washington, and we are indebted to him for his superior leadership."

"Jimmy, we moved the church to several locations. Our faithful follow, but people are being persecuted, and some are deserting us."

"Morris, my man, don't you think I know? It's the damn F.B.I., the newspapers, and the hypocrites that lead the corrupt religious organizations and have no idea of world affairs. The press accuses me of emotional and sexual abuse. They say I have sex with followers, both men and women, and even with my own mother. The segregationists have painted swastikas on the church, left dynamite in the coal pile, and thrown a dead cat at the house."

"Remember, Holy One; the swastika was your idea."

"Yes, yes, but none of them realize that Armageddon is upon us. The whole world is against us. Don't they know that Christianity is a myth, the Bible a tool to repress women and minorities? Don't they know that it is a sin to be capitalistic, racist, and Fascist; that Communistic socialism is the only answer? Can't they see me—a divine reincarnation of Gandhi, Jesus, and Buddha? I am their savior, savior from the nihilistic ravages of nuclear war. Traditional religion is only an opiate. There is no heaven or hell. We must establish our own paradise. Morris, I know there will be war. I've made a study of the safest place to be when a bomb explodes. We've got to move once more—to Brazil—or better still, Guyana, where we can live in peace in a socialist paradise."

"Yes, you're right master. First, let's take your pills."

"Friends, we have had some problems here in Jonestown, all because those of little faith and commitment have abandoned us. The infidels have fomented a protest in Washington and the corrupt powers there are sending a congressional delegation to investigate what could be our heaven on earth. One day, we may have to seek other shores. We have discussed many times 'Translation' to another planet to live in peace and comfort. We shall see if this Washington delegation is intent on harassing us—preventing us our right to live as we please. In the meantime, show these visitors our loving relationship, our happiness, and our courtesy."

"Men, they have abused their power—stuck their noses into places that are none of their business—questioned our way of life, our shared knowledge of good and evil. They have left the compound and will be at the airport preparing to take their lies back to the United States. Your savior admonishes you to not let this happen."

"Morris, call for an assembly in the Temple, every man, woman, and child."

"Yes, Master."

"My people, I must tell you that our time here has been compromised. The delegation that we have, today, treated so kindly has betrayed us. They were going to leave here to spread lies throughout America. Divine intervention has prevailed, and they are dead. We will be blamed. You all know what that means. The U.S. government will be relentless in tracking us down. There will be parachutes blinding the sun to bring murder and torture to our people, even our babies. They will spare no one. If we believe in ourselves—if we believe in one another—we can avoid that. We can transport ourselves to another planet where only peace and harmony will reign. I have told you many times how Transportation works. We will all drink the magic potion and drift into a peaceful sleep. All true believers must participate; others will be destroyed. Kool-Aid has been prepared in churn batches. Parents will administer a cup to their children. Any over the age of eighteen will take a cup and drink. All will lie down and embrace loved ones. When we awake, we will be in paradise. As your Messiah, I command that you do this."

"Well, Morris, a few escaped to damnation, but others are drifting off. Your turn for the cup."

"Yes, Master."

"Good and faithful servant, Morris. I have taken enough of your little pills to do the trick, but I prefer to go a bit faster."

The pistol reacted with a resounding bang.

That may not be the way that scenario happened, but the magnetic personality of a madman combined with the pressure of peers to go along resulted in the death of over nine hundred people.

When I awoke from this dream, I was wondering if one might be influenced to do crazy things without the presence of charismatic leaders. Is there a set of societal peer pressures that might precipitate uncontrolled action? Would that hidden machismo peer culture demand that I not let a black person defile my granddaughter?

CHAPTER 18

Naturally, I think of charismatic leaders such as Churchill, Roosevelt, Gandhi, John Kennedy, Martin Luther King, and countless others as positive leaders. We see in them some of the same markers of character as those of the ones characterized as negative leaders. We tend to see them as forceful, full of confidence, little inner doubt, seekers of respect, aggressive, responsible, visionary, trustworthy, curious, inspiring, action-oriented, promoting a belief system, taking risks, competitive, socially or personally motivated. They also possess other characteristics that overshadow some of the good they might exemplify. They are just human with all the foibles that hassle the rest of us, but they possess the unique ability to lead in a positive direction.

I return to a Greek mythology example for guidance. It is the story of Icarus, who so wanted to fly. His father, Daedalus, made Icarus wings of the finest feathers and waxed them sufficiently with the very best of product. From the top of a mountain, Daedalus gave his son two pieces of advice. First, he advised not to fly too high and secondly, not to fly too low. Fly too high, and the sun melts the wax. To me, that means that a real leader aspires to the highest ideal but overcomes human hubris. One may not be in love with himself. He or she must consider others. Don't fly too low, for obstacles get in the way. One must compete in the fray of life.

Dropping out and expecting someone else to do the job is not an option.

That's a bit much too much philosophy for an old man to handle, so I'll just scratch my butt and go back to bed.

But the darker shades of night prevailed as I dreamed of misguided leaders and their trusting followers.

Yes, my name is Charlie Manson, a synonym for Jesus Christ—not just a comparative-like meaning or like name, but a living, breathing reincarnation. My mother was sixteen years old and unmarried when I was born. Rumors my father was an African American cook are damned lies. No black blood flows in these old veins. I acquired stepfathers while my mother leaned toward alcoholism and abandoned me to reform schools. They couldn't hold Jesus, so I broke out to help myself to cars and shared billfolds of rich pigs. So what if I never learned to read well and purposely failed a few I.Q. tests? When, as a teenager, I was accused of sodomizing a reform school partner, I was smart enough to escape and avoid going back. Getting married and working part-time menial jobs was not so smart. Nor was getting arrested for stealing like a small-time crook. Jail time, however, was instructive. I learned to play the steel guitar. Helped me to get into the Hollywood scene and to pick up women. Even got to play Jesus in one movie. They never suspected that they were dealing with the real kahuna. Collected about 18 girls and a few loyal men. We formed a family and found gullible people to let us live in buildings or on ranches outside general public scrutiny. Had to let some of the slobs sleep with some of my girls, but it was a small price to pay. I kept my girls in line with my enormous manhood. Became a special kind of Scientologist, with drugs and vision. I knew that Satan and Christ would hook up in the end, and we would rule the world and judge mankind.

From time to time, an unworldly voice would speak to me, and I taught the family. We were the reincarnation of early Christians, and all others are black Romans intent on destroying us. This would come as a gigantic struggle between our own and those black Romans. Racial tensions were growing, and the rich pigs were going to lose their asses. Blacks are to rebel just as the Beatles predict. Our spirituality is derived from these prophets that speak to us in song. They speak of "Helter-Skelter" when Armageddon reins. I knew that I must hasten the fight, for a holy vision kept returning.

I envisioned the black placing me on the cross and felt the nail spikes driven into my hands and feet. Yes, we must foment revolution. The black face of the Devil must be smashed. And all the while, the Beatles sang!

The plan was simple. Kill a few rich pigs who crossed us and blame it on the Black Panthers. I found it amusing to teach the family how to shoot and slash. The women of the clan became especially efficient in this role. In the summer of '64, we became a regular army of extermination. In ones and twos and in fives, victims were selected. It was exhilarating to write "pig" in fresh blood. I insisted that each female take a turn at stabbing for a source of red.

Naturally, there were traitors, and a mistake was made in including a movie star in our little kettle of fish. The pigs got us, locked us up like animals. Some, like me, were sentenced to death, but the weak-kneed bastards didn't have the guts to carry it through. Sentences were commuted to life imprisonment. We serve our commitment with quiet dignity in the knowledge that the movement has begun, and it is only a matter of time. Oh, there have been a few incidents. A follower, Squeaky, attempted to assassinate President Gerald Ford, I was burned by a fellow inmate, and a twenty-six-year-old woman who has been visiting me for nine years wants to marry me. I carved an X on my forehead and later completed a swastika. I just completed another parole hearing in which I was denied. I'm eligible to try again in fifteen years, at which time, I'll be ninety-two. It's okay. The plan is working. Blackness is spreading, Helter-Skelter is coming. I am the Devil now, and I will live forever."

A confused Jim Warner awoke with a frightened start. Emergent in the dream, I had assumed the role of Charles Manson. My nerves were shattered so much that I mistook the broken bedside glass for missiles fired from the night itself. I couldn't remember knocking the tumbler from the table, but the evidence was indisputable. Shaking hands removed the glass from worn carpet, and I turned toward the kitchen for a cup of calming tea. The microwave humming as tea water boiled brought the present forth in dramatic fashion. I began to wonder the similarities of the Manson and the Jones backgrounds. There were also differences. They both were from families of modest means. Neither were particularly good students and possibly developed "street smarts" as compensation for sparse education. Neither seemed especially charismatic or handsome. One appeared to have parental support of a parent. Both had an exaggerated sense of self-worth. Both were unable to determine reality. I had to ask myself if these examples of negative leadership are the result of some inheritable mental malady? Or, are each a product of environmental influence? Was the fear of fitting into a world of competitive choices a factor in adjusting to some kind of expected normality so devastating that an unrealistic persona had to be created? This fear, the terror of not measuring up to standards, or fear of the unknown is something I must pursue. In my own case, am I afraid of the "dark"?

In spite of the mellow refreshment, the tea failed to provide answers. I thought of situations that might impact one fear or another. Fear of losing control comes to mind. I think that I might have a fear of losing control. These prescription pills I'm taking for nausea make me forget—not just names but words and concepts. Frightening as it is, maybe it is within the bounds for growing old. Losing control is really a scary condition.

Perhaps Vernon Howell might fall into a different category. He had some of the same delusions as did Jones and Manson but his, it seems to me, was also related to an extreme resistance to authority.

Vernon was born in 1959 to a fourteen-year-old unwed mother. He was reared by grandparents, allegedly raped by older boys when he was eight, suffered from dyslexia, and was a poor student in special education classes.

At the age of 22, Vernon impregnated a fifteen-year-old girl, which led to his being a "born again" Christian in the Seventh Day Adventist organization. He joined the Branch Davidians and later sought to form his own version of the organization. He had an affair with the sixty-five-year-old Branch Davidian leader and proceeded to take charge of the group but was thwarted by the son of the sixty-five-year-old leader. After the son had been charged with a crime, Vernon gained control of the organization. By 1983, he assumed that he had been given the "gift" of prophecy, traveled to Israel, claimed to be a descendant of the house of David, and changed his name to David Koresh. The assumed name, Koresh, was for an ancient Persian King. David now claimed to be a spiritual descendant of biblical characters and declared himself the Messiah.

According to criminal charges lodged, David Koresh married several of the Davidian members, had sex with a thirteen-year-old with the permission of her parents, and had sex with other minor children. He was also charged with beating and abusing others.

After many attempts to arrest Koresh and experiencing armed resistance, local and federal forces confronted the group. There was a fifty-one-day standoff at which time law enforcement moved into the Davidian compound. A fire occurred, and eighty people perished, including twenty-two children and David Koresh.

There seems to be another group that is motivated by a desire to abandon adherence to any authority, to resist any rule that interferes with individual freedom. The various survivalist groups that are not primarily influenced by religion may be bundled in the individual rights movement. Just recently, an individual rights militia group occupied facilities in the Malheur Wildlife Refuge near Burns, Oregon, and refused to leave until the federal government ceded that land back to the people. There seems to have been little thought as to whom would receive it or how it could have been removed from the National Park Service inventory. The incident appears to have been the outgrowth of a contentious feud with a farmer who rejected a fee for cattle-grazing rights on federal land. Armed anti-government Americans held the central park facility for forty-one days in a stand-off that left one person dead and numbers of protesters in jail. The final protester left peacefully, yelling epithets about President Obama and maintaining that UFOs are real.

Recently, I came across a publication by the Southern Poverty Law Center that, for the 2015 year, lists 892 hate groups. Categories are listed as Ku Klux Klan, White Nationalist, Racist Skinhead, Christian Identity, Neo-Confederate, Black Separatist, and General Hate. There is reason to believe that these groups are growing. Sometimes individual members of a hate group are difficult to identify.

In 1994, when I ran for the state senate, Maggie and I were returning from a campaign function in Yalobusha County. Maggie spied a roadside gate that opened to a long lane with a large barn at the end. She became excited at the prospect of a sizable number of potential voters who had parked cars and trucks near the barn. We couldn't resist an opportunity to shake a few hands. I had to turn back and take the dusty lane that parted soybean fields. As we walked through an open barn passage, it was instantly apparent that this was not a family reunion gathering or a church picnic. An open pavilion with tables and folding chairs sat on a grassy plain with barrel barbecue pits in the foreground. Chicken and venison and steak were sizzling on griddles. Country vegetables were steaming on long, clothed planks astride X-shaped wooden horses, and a similar truss held a plethora of desserts shaded by a big oak tree. A large man we assumed was the host stepped forward with a broad smile and a hearty handshake. Although he didn't introduce himself, he welcomed us and insisted that we come and enjoy a drink and food. A rush of white might have assured Maggie and me that we were truly welcome guests. Ankle-length, snow-white robes and tall, sharply pointed hats destroyed any appetite that we may have had. There were no face masks, every cherry cheek and bit of beard displayed. They treated us as respected neighbors who had dropped by for a friendly chat. The voter paraphernalia, lapel buttons, and larger-than-life name tags we displayed on the clothing we wore were ignored. They were a hospitable group that saw their strange dress as that of an ordinary friendly bunch of insiders welcoming a new member. Surely this was a meeting of church Bishops or a civic costume party. But the pointed hats identified these gracious people for what they were. Any doubt was dispelled by banners of emblazoned embroidery dangling from food tables—three large Ks in a neat row.

The host guy never introduced us, but handshakes were spread all around.

Mr. Host spoke pleasantly, "Why don't you guys grab a beer and sit a while?"

"No—no—we have to move along. Just thought we'd stop by. Have to get to Oxford—an appointment. Sorry—food smells so good, but we've got to go. Thanks."

With thoughts of neck ropes being thrown over tall tree branches, we almost backed through the barn. Made it to the car and pulled away as carefully as shaking hands permitted but as fast as I dared. We traveled a full mile before we felt comfortable to talk about the experience.

Admittedly, our KKK friends were, perhaps, pillars of their community. Members of civic clubs, contributors to church and local charities. They probably represented a variety of trades and professions. They seemed to be such ordinary people. They showed no reluctance in identifying with the KKK. Maggie and I agreed that my chances of getting their vote was nil.

Hate groups appear to expand and cement the discriminatory culture. They get in the way of rational thought. If we could only eliminate the group mystique, maybe we could reduce the most radical players. Is generational memory set in stone, or will it crumble with the elements of disuse?

The United States Department of Justice has categorized discriminatory action by individuals or groups. There is a general hate crimes division, religious beliefs category, cases in human trafficking, interference with access to reproductive health care, and a broad area titled "official conduct." Recent cases involve mere threats of violence such as publishing statements of potential violence. An example is the man who sent threatening letters to the head of the Arab Institute and insisted that the "only good Arab is a dead Arab." One woman was sentenced for sending threatening letters to her employer. One person was sentenced for merely displaying a "hangman's" noose to civil rights attendees at a civil rights rally.

Most hate crimes involve actual acts of violence. An example is the Mexican man who died after a beating by a high school football team who shouted racial epithets telling him to go back to Mexico where he belonged. There have been cases of drive-by shootings committed by those of a differing race, gang members murdering blacks, and unimaginable acts by single individuals or small numbers perpetrated simply because of an intense hatred for a particular group of people. Instances of lesser violence fill volumes. Crosses burned on lawns of biracial families, spraying of chemicals on homes and businesses, painting of racist slurs on commercial buildings and the like are too numerous to mention.

I had never thought of human trafficking as a "hate" crime. Nor was I aware that these crimes were so prevalent. Normally these cases involve bringing foreigners into this country with promises and then forcing them to work without pay—as slaves. In some instances, young women, even some mentally challenged, are forced into prostitution as a source of income for their captors.

Reports of bombing and shooting at centers for reproductive health care facilities frequently make headlines. Religious beliefs foster many of these incidents, but the nature of the act and the motivation are such that it has been given a separate listing in Justice Department files.

Atrocities by the religious intolerant make headlines all over the nation. Mass executions, bombings, shootings, and church burnings take place throughout the country. Jewish synagogues, Muslim mosques, black churches, and integrated worship groups have been attacked as have individuals who support these entities. Given the pronouncements of major religious organizations, this hate is, perhaps, the most difficult to understand.

It happened in my other life, a life before Maggie. On a beautiful spring Sunday in 1970, as was our custom, my former wife and two daughters, nine and twelve, drove the two miles to the First Baptist Church. Already cars were filling the parking lot as occupants scurried through double doors to Sunday school rooms. The girls and wife in separate classes, I to lead a class of young adults. As I recall, the topic for discussion that Sunday had something to do with "brotherly love." A shrill bell announced the ending of Sunday school and heralded the time for church service. Entering the hall, I bumped into Andrew Cole, a deacon, friend, and university faculty member. We hurried to the chapel where, as church deacons, we were to usher attendees to seats and later pass the inevitable collection plates.

Six active deacons were on duty in the church vestibule when four non-members quietly slipped past to seat themselves on a back row. African American worshipers had never before crossed that threshold, and for a moment, six deacons were temporarily stunned as if a paralytic breeze had swept itself up those steps and into our sanctuary. One of the six recovered more quickly than the rest of us and began to shout.

"Let's throw out those black sons of bitches."

As he started for the chapel door, Andy Cole, an assistant pastor who happened to be in the area, and I restrained the angry deacon, who continued cursing and yelling racial remarks.

Andy said, "Calm down, Mr. Luckett. We can't disturb the service by turning away worshipers!"

"The hell, you say. Those bastards are not interested in worship. They just want to start trouble."

The assistant pastor also tried to reason with the agitated man. "Mr. Luckett, we can't just throw them out."

"Boy, where you from? You think people will go to church with black niggers? Well, if you think that, you can pack your bags! It will never happen in this town! I, for one, will not sit with them!"

I suggested Mr. Luckett go home and calm down. Fortunately, he took that advice but only for the moment. He became a prime mover in an effort to publish a church policy on integration. He proposed that the church adopt a "closed-door" policy and that members only and invitees be permitted access to church facilities.

Naturally, the full body of all twelve board of deacons was called into an executive session with the pastor, who failed to include the assistant pastor, about whom Mr. Luckett was making all kinds of derogatory remarks. Mr. Luckett congratulated the pastor for excluding the assistant and commented on the assistant's future in Oxford as a representative of the First Baptist Church. "That boy has got to go. He's not one of us. He's one of those 'nigger-loving' Yankees from some place up north. I just know it!"

Pastor Newman sighed and spoke softly. "We'll look at that question later. Right now, we must consider the hue and cry from some of our membership who are calling for a closed-door policy in our church. I assume that we all have prayerfully considered our dilemma and can discuss the matter calmly in the best interests of our faith and the congregation we serve."

Mr. Luckett assumed as pious an attitude as he could but spoke with bridled passion. "Gentlemen, if God had intended for us to mix, he would not have made people of different races. I know the liberal courts say we have to open public facilities, but private church groups have some rights. We can admit whomever we choose. The clamor is to be politically correct, but the Constitution guarantees freedom of religion, and government has no right to enter the church pews. We all recognize that the Negro is different from us, worships differently than we do. I don't want Africa in my church, and I think a majority of our members feel the same way. We know that the rank and file black couldn't care less about being a part of our congregation. It's the agitators and troublemakers who are trying to prove that they can intrude in places where they are not wanted. It's not faith that drives them. They just crave attention and want to rub our noses in you know what."

After a long silence, Andy Cole looked directly at Luckett and spoke in a consoling tone. "Mr. Luckett, I can appreciate your frustration at government intrusion into religious affairs. However, we adhere to the notion that all people are created equal under God and the law. Who are we to judge the motivation of another? Do we question members of our congregation about their faith, require a litmus test as to their motivation for worship? We work alongside minorities; our children go to school with them; our public facilities are open to all; we have laws that reject discrimination; and we possess a basic moral fiber that dictates fairness. As Christians, we espouse love and brotherhood for our fellow man. We are all God's children."

I was the next speaker to address the topic. "Mr. Luckett, I want to agree with you that those who came Sunday had every intention of creating publicity for their cause. They have no interest in joining our congregation. Your reaction is just what they hoped for. No, they came not to worship but, rather, to call attention to our hypocrisy in professing our love for mankind but limiting that love to those who are like us. If this church were to close our doors to others, they will have proven their point, and the world will know where we stand. They will have won."

There was complete silence for at least two minutes. No other deacon spoke. Finally, Luckett made the motion that the First Baptist Church of Oxford adopt a closed-door policy. Hughes seconded the motion. There was discussion as to how the motion could be worded differently but mean the same thing. In the end, eight of the twelve deacons voted for the motion as presented.

For Wednesday night supper and prayer meeting, Pastor Newman announced there would be a short service and then a business meeting. Word had circulated as to the nature of certain items of business to be discussed and voted upon. The church was packed, a noticeable departure from the normally sparse Wednesday-night crowd. There were people who had not darkened the sanctuary door for more than a year. Many in the august body whose regular membership might be questioned.

Brother Newman, after a few innocuous platitudes relating to the family of man and God's love for his flock, introduced Mr. Luckett. Mr. Luckett spent little time discussing the issue.

"I know I don't need to give a lecture on the encroaching federal attack on religious freedom. I also know that you agree with me that government has no right to dictate the expression of our faith. You are aware that our private preference of association is inviolate. Therefore, I am introducing a resolution that can only be instituted by a majority vote of this congregation. It is a very simple proposal we all understand. I move that the First Baptist Church of Oxford adopt a closed-door policy. This expression of the will of the people enables us to continue to exercise our right to choose those with whom we wish to associate in worship."

The floor was opened for audience reaction. Andy Cole, Ralph Collins, and I spoke out against the motion, expressing Christian principles violated by discriminatory practices. Applicable laws inclusive for all people were quoted.

Since no further discussion was forthcoming, Pastor Newman called for a vote. About two-thirds of the congregation voted in favor of the resolution. Only a smattering of the audience cared to demonstrate opposition.

I have often wondered at the way in which that decision affected the lives of those members of the First Baptist Church. The church has grown, expanded, and seems to be doing fine. It remains almost exclusively white. I don't know who coined the phrase, "the most segregated time in America is the Sunday morning church hour," but a majority of churches appears to be divided along racial lines.

I want to think that my own decision to leave the Baptist faith was a result of the First Baptist policy to reject African-Americans who might wish to worship there. In reality, there may have been other factors in play. My disappointment with the policy exacerbated a growing feeling that my marriage was less fulfilling than desired. My wife and I had grown apart through no fault of the wife. I was ambitious and, I must admit, had developed a roving eye. I deeply loved my two daughters but felt trapped in the marriage. I was traveling quite a bit and growing professionally, meeting new and interesting people. Soon divorce proceedings were begun.

After four years as a bachelor and becoming attracted to a more liberal and liberating spiritual experience, Maggie became a part of a new life.

My friend Andy Cole pursued a different and less rewarding path. Andy left Oxford and the university to accept a position as president of a Baptist college in Texas. He had a lovely family and was highly respected in the Southern Baptist community. A year or so later, old friends in Oxford were shocked to hear rumors of financial audits at his new college and charges of misconduct. Andy was always an honest straight shooter who epitomized moral values. So, people who knew him couldn't equate the charges of wrongdoing. Still, he was convicted of using college funds for personal expenditures, including for the services of prostitutes. I still am unable to comprehend this scenario as applicable to the man I knew.

For me, the Baptist experience may have contributed to my reluctance to affiliate with any form of organized religion. A friend did introduce me to the Unitarian/Universalist philosophy, which pretty much espouses my basic belief, but I have never officially joined the organization. For a period, Maggie and I were a part of a local Unitarian fellowship group, but it morphed into a church that we never attended.

CHAPTER 19

Early morning fog hangs low across the lake after a slow night shower spread patches of goldenrod straining to push back invading milkweed by the garden wall. Crown-beard and ironweed limply bowed on an uphill slope. Out front, lantana, American beauty, and knockout roses dripped the refreshing liquid from multicolored petals. I make my way to the shop where sacks of fertilizer and ground-covering mulch cry for distribution. The cell phone jangles, and I squeeze it from my pocket in an effort to keep granules of rose nutriment from spoiling clean jeans. Finally, the damn thing spurts from the slit and skids on the ground. On my knees, I scramble for the phone just as the established ring retreats to silence. By the time I struggle aright, the deep-pocketed instrument plays a familiar tune again.

"Mr. Warner, are you up and about?"

"Walt, are you up and about?"

"Well—yes, hope I didn't disturb you."

"No. Just about to throw some horse shit on my flower bed."

"Good. Say, there was another police shooting in Chicago. Just wanted to assure you that these instances of violence shouldn't affect our case."

"I disagree, Walt. Any widely distributed news of shootings anywhere by anybody has some bearing on our case."

"But these are actions by those who are sworn to protect us, justified or not, public officials."

"And ours is an action by a private citizen, justified or not."

"Mr. Warner, you just will not let this go."

"I can't let it go, Walt."

"Well, we are at the summation stage. I'm working on my summation speech now. Then it's up to the jury."

"Walt, you should be proud of me. I'm working on my summation too."

"Well—alright. See you in court Monday, Mr. Warner."

I carefully put away my buckets, my sprays, and nutrients and head for my study. These actions by police forces all over the country may provide some insight for me. Does my motivation differ that much from these cases? I am determined to find out.

Although the perception seems to be that some cases may not even be reported, various authorities agree that over one thousand Americans each year die of encounters with police. In 2015 *The Washington Post* (December 26, 2015) conducted a year-long study and reported that:

965 were shot and killed by a law enforcement officer

594 of those were armed with guns

281 were armed with another weapon

90 were unarmed

240 were said to have some mental problems (90% armed)

The Post study indicated unarmed black men represented less than 4% of police shootings. They were 6% of the population, but represented 40% of unarmed fatalities. Another interesting statistic quoted is that 25% of all cases involved a car and/or a foot chase.

The federal statistics are dated and may be practically useless. Unreported cases are thought to be ignored, and different groups arriving at varying conclusions depending upon different points of view. Some say that a black male is twenty-one times more likely to be killed by law enforcement while others indicate that numbers are proportional to crimes committed. The Federal Bureau of Investigation reports that black men are nine times more likely to be killed by police than caucasian men. The F.B.I. statistics indicate that African Americans who comprise 13.2% of the population make up 28.9% of police arrests. Some critics gleefully report that 13% of the U.S. population are involved in almost half the crimes committed.

I wonder how statistics relate to the people, white and black, living in poverty with few jobs and little hope.

Killings by officials sworn to protect us is a particularly troubling phenomenon. I was taught to respect the law and grew to appreciate those who were authorized to enforce those laws designed to govern a just society. Because of my real-life experience, however, there is a lingering mistrust and some fear of authority and the fairness of its application. Spotting a police cruiser still creates enhanced adrenaline as I check my auto speedometer. Not long ago, on a return trip from Nashville, a siren suddenly screamed at my back bumper. Pulling over immediately, I stopped a few feet shy of a sign that indicated 55 miles per hour speed limit. I let down the window to a young town cop.

"Do you know why I stopped you?" He asked.

"No, sir." I replied, noting that we were quite past the outskirts of the small Tennessee town.

"You were doing 40 in a 30-mile speed zone."

"I'm sorry, I didn't see the sign. Where was it?"

"Well, it was back a ways."

And, he wrote an eighty-dollar ticket. I could have questioned the sign that was probably hidden in some inconspicuous clump of bush or asked the purpose of a 30-mile speed limit in an obvious countryside, but delay and confrontation was not worth the trouble. I drove on and mailed the eighty bucks to a little town that has a budget to meet.

Outright harassment for any group may, indeed, build resentment. In my experience, black and white persons who drive older, dilapidated automobiles seem to be pulled over more often. Poor people may find it more difficult to repair tail lights, purchase licenses on time, or avoid other violations that attract the attention of police. Add that to specific documented profiling, and reported statistics might better help in understanding that some people have more encounters with police than others.

Drug possession, being drunk, court appearances, probation violations, expired or revoked driving permits, and the like are often listed as reasons for flight. With all the various options, when to pursue a fleeing suspect who may or not be a dangerous criminal is difficult to determine. A quarter of the cases in which a suspect is killed involves a fleeing automobile or foot chase.

Law enforcement is composed of ordinary people with backgrounds, predilections, habits, mental capacity, and prejudices shared with all mankind. One study reported in *Behavioral Sciences and the Law* indicates nine per cent of Americans are subject to what they call "impulsive anger issues." Some have anger issues and also carry a gun. Law enforcement is no different. They also share the bravado, fears, and automatic response to perceived danger. In my eighty-three years, I have observed the finest qualities and darkest objectives of some peace officers. No time frame exists for society's penchant for abusing those who find themselves the object of an invading force, including authorized governmental authority. In the case of altercations between city, county, or federal officers and persons of color in this country, my recollection of widespread publicity for such activity goes back to the early 1990s.

With cameras rolling, back in 1991 the whole world observed the beating of Rodney King by law enforcement officers in Los Angeles. The world did not see a high-speed automobile chase said to approach 115 miles per hour or major resistance to arrest. The amount of alleged alcohol or other drugs involved was not subjected to photographic memory. Nor was the reason an attempt to avoid a speeding citation apparent. What the public did see was violent action visited upon a defenseless victim by a group of policemen. In due course those officers survived the judicial system and were acquitted, resulting in the worst rioting in American history. Seven thousand fires, damage to 3,100 businesses, 2,000 injuries and 53 deaths were recorded. There were over one billion dollars in financial losses, much of it in minority sections of Los Angeles. The public was treated to rioters stealing all kinds of goods when storefronts were breached. Burning vehicles and buildings were the subjects of news shows through the courtesy of all the major networks. The event was a forerunner of what is to be expected when the public views what is considered excessive force used by police against black individuals.

There appears to be no credible records of suspects who die at the hands of police officers. I can remember reading of many in the last couple of years. Names like Keith Childress in Las Vegas, Kevin Mathews in Michigan, Leroy Browning and Roy Nelson in California, Miguel Espinal in New York, Tiara Thomas in Indiana. Always a consideration, prejudice may not have been involved in some of these cases. Not all victims were armed. Some cases involve white on white, which normally suggests instances lacking obvious prejudice.

I read of one situation that involved a Pennsylvania officer who tried to stop a driver for a minor violation. The driver was said to have gone around another vehicle, run a red light to lead the officer on a high-speed chase, ending in the driver's abandoning his car. The police cruiser video camera captured the use of a Taser, placing the unarmed man on the ground. The officer testified that there was hand movement interpreted as the reaching for a gun, and the man was killed. When asked why the car was chased for a minor inspection violation, the officer maintained that it could not be determined why the driver was running, that he could have been an escaping murderer, a bank robber, or a terrorist. That was good enough for the lack of prosecution. The officer was a white woman and the victim a white man.

Possible prejudicial situations involving police or other official or unofficial enforcers have recently grabbed worldwide headlines and resulted in a serious consideration of violence in America. There are many, but I have too few notebooks to contain details of them all. I have studied a few of the hundreds and attempted to summarize what seems to me the salient points. Naturally, I may not understand or, indeed, have all the facts. The result is merely the impression gathered by an old man.

Trayvon Martin, a young, black, five-foot, eleven-inch, 158-pound teenager, was on his way to the home in which he was currently staying. The home was in a multicultural neighborhood, which, according to reports, had witnessed some burglaries. It was late evening; rain was falling, and visibility poor. George Zimmerman, 185-pound appointed neighborhood watch coordinator, observed Martin walking through the complex and determined he was suspicious. He followed Martin in his car, reporting his action to police. He was told to stay in his vehicle and await the arrival of a squad car. Zimmerman ignored the police order, left the car, and followed Martin. While versions of what happened next vary widely, a confrontation occurred. I was not there, and witnesses presented diametrically opposed versions of what occurred. Everyone agrees that a struggle ensued with both individuals scuffling on the ground. There were cries for help but disagreement over who made those pleas. At some point, Zimmerman secured a gun he had been licensed to carry and shot Martin. We do not know who started the altercation, but Trayvon Martin lay dead in the grass.

Zimmerman was charged with second-degree murder but acquitted by a jury for lack of evidence. The defense made much of the Florida "Stand Your Ground" law that gives one the right of self-protection. I can understand that such a defense of self-preservation may be warranted when one has taken every means possible, including flight, to avoid a life-threatening situation. Likely, both participants were fearful. I do find it incredible that one might initiate an altercation, find himself or herself losing the struggle, and then claim a right to kill the opponent. I was not on that jury and did not hear the evidence that was presented to them, but it is difficult for me to understand that fairness prevailed. "Stand-Your-Ground" to me is inherently unfair. Stand with the evidence is a more reasonable approach. Some report this case inspired the "Black Lives Matter" slogan and movement.

Eric Gardner was a six-foot, three-inch, 350-pound black man in New York City. Having been arrested some thirty times for various offenses, he may have felt persecuted and harassed. On the night in question, he was suspected of selling non-taxed cigarettes. A homeless man called police, accusing Gardner of brandishing a gun at him. Police arrived and maintained that he resisted arrest. Gardner was put in what some assume was a "chokehold" and wrestled to the pavement. It was reported that he complained several times that he could not breathe. Unresponsive, he was turned on his side, but no other attention was given at the scene. Gardner died at the hospital by what was termed the result of chest compression, positioning, restraint, and poor health. He was categorized as being obese. The coroner's report indicated no damage to the windpipe or neck bones, and it was assumed the death was caused by other persons, not necessarily intentional or criminal. Others interpreted the the cause to be overzealous policemen's excessive force on a defenseless black man. There were demonstrations, protests, and rallies in various cities throughout the country.

Tamir Rice was a twelve-year-old boy, large for his age at five foot, seven inches and 195 pounds, according to a medical examiner's report. Tamir was in a park, playing with a toy pellet gun that was a replica of a real gun. The toy had no markings to indicate it wasn't real. A call to the police dispatcher indicated that someone, possibly a juvenile, was waving a gun, perhaps a toy, at passersby. According to a dispatcher's radio record, responding officers heard only that someone with a gun was pointing the gun at people. A video showed that within two seconds of the squad car's arriving on the scene, shots were fired, and the child lay dead. A grand jury failed to indict the officers involved. The question remains as to whether this was a terrible accident or a case of gun-slinging policemen who shot first and thought of a reason later. Makes one wonder if skin color was a factor in the exceptionally quick action or whether it was motivated by real fear.

Ferguson, Missouri, is nearer my neck of the woods, and some of the protesters there found the way to Oxford in order to see that justice is served in my case. The death of black Michael Brown at the hands of a white policeman excited passions far beyond the St. Louis suburb. The fact that he was unarmed and a claim that his hands were raised when he was shot have enlisted a plethora of emotional responses. Although there was credible evidence that hands were not in the air, the "don't shoot" gesture is now seen in rallies everywhere.

Disputed facts seem to indicate that a Ferguson police officer was on patrol when he received a message that a customer in a nearby convenience store had stolen a few items of little worth and "roughed-up" a store clerk. On the route to the convenience store, the officer spotted two young men walking down the middle of the street. They were, it seems, asked to get out of the street. Whether it was a nice request or a demeaning order is not of record. One of the young men was eighteen-year-old, six-foot, four-inch, 292-pound Michael Brown. Although this part of the story is disputed, the officer is said to have started to drive on but noticed in Brown's hands the items described as those taken at the convenience store. He backed up the car to confront the two. Communication between the two young men and the policeman has not been authenticated, but physical contact was made, the officer still behind the wheel of his squad car. The officer was able to secure his revolver and fired shots from within the automobile. The friend with Brown testified that they began to run away after the gunshots. The officer left his car, and Brown, who was a short distance away turned and proceeded back toward the officer. The friend indicated that Brown had his hands in the air. The unarmed Michael Brown was shot several times and died at the site.

A grand jury refused to indict the police officer, resulting in extensive rioting in Ferguson and sometimes violent protests in one hundred seventeen cities across America. Television cameras documented autos and buildings being burned. Storefronts crashed, and goods were looted. In fact, many minority businesses in Ferguson were attacked and destroyed.

The Missouri National Guard was called in to quell the unrest. Makes one wonder if violence and lawlessness are sincere or appropriate responses to any form of violence.

A U.S. Department of Justice probe was instituted but found that there was insufficient evidence to indict the police officer involved. The Justice Department was critical of the city of Ferguson, the police department, and racial tension judged to have been promoted by public officials. Minority leadership pointed to discriminatory practices, including the profiling of young black men.

A number of news articles, opinion pieces, and magazines have indicated that we should not make Michael Brown a "poster child" for police aggression against minorities, nor a representative example of civil rights abuses. We do have here evidence of lawless acts and resistance to authority. It does illustrate the underlying mistrust that exists in the black population as well as the automatic reaction that assumes wrongdoing on the part of the police officer. No one wishes to see the life of an unarmed young person taken. Guess we'll never know if the overpowering presence of a potential physical force created a fearful response, or if a young man lost his life due to a non-threatening act that produced the fury of prejudice.

There are some recent troubling incidents that seem more worthy of the indignation produced.

Freddie Grey was involved in twenty court cases, five active at the time of his death, involving drugs. That fact has little to do with what happened on the streets of Baltimore except to provide additional reasons for the black man to run away from a police patrol. He was carrying a knife, but it was not considered a weapon of great concern. At any rate, there was flight and some altercation as he was arrested. He dragged his feet as he was carried to a patrol van and was placed in the van, where he was not secured in the seating. The van made four stops, and at some point, Grey was placed in leg braces. A theory was advanced that Grey may have been exposed to what was termed "rough ride," a practice said to be sometimes used in which erratic driving is employed to frighten a detainee. At the last stop to pick up another prisoner, multiple officers checked on Freddie and found him to have been injured. No medical assistance procedures were administered. The van proceeded to a police station, where paramedics treated Grey and took him to a hospital, where he died.

Six officers were immediately accused of murder or lesser charges. Some disagreements occurred between state and local authorities. The murder charge was first adjudicated, and the defendant was found not guilty. Speculation dealt with the seriousness of the charge and the inability to assess blame. It could not be established as to who was responsible. None of the other officers were convicted. Nevertheless, Freddie Grey died in police custody. Although not bringing charges, the Justice Department has issued extremely strong opinions castigating the Baltimore justice system as corrupt and prejudiced.

An unarmed black man, Walter Scott of North Charleston, South Carolina, was stopped for a broken tail light. He was fifty years of age and had four children. During the process, Scott started to get out of the car but complied with an order to get back in. A few seconds later, Scott left the car and ran. At some point, there appears to have been a short altercation. The white policeman, Michael Slager, claims that Scott grabbed his Taser and that he was struck with the instrument. Although video evidence did not fully record the confrontation, it does follow a foot chase through a parking lot into an open field where the policeman fired eight shots, five of which hit Scott in the back. There was some indication that a Taser was dropped near the spot where the dying man was being handcuffed. Both the state and federal Departments of Justice have indicted the policeman for murder. Friends speculate that Scott ran because he owed child support. That does not provide sufficient reasons for the flight since Scott was leaving his automobile and personal information. Neither does it justify the shooting since the officer must have known that Scott could easily be traced. A trial occurred, resulting in a hung jury. It is anticipated that additional prosecution will be pursued.

Technological advances are beginning to assist the public in evaluating instances in which opposing viewpoints are prevalent. Video cameras are everywhere, and everyone seems to be able to use those fancy phones to produce pictures. It is a good thing that police are now able to document an occurrence. It provides a much clearer picture for prosecution and the administration of justice. Guess some of these complicate the picture when they show only a portion of the action rather than the act itself. Recent incidents showing someone shot at close range while on the ground make compelling views that may or may not tell the whole story.

We tend to focus on the specific act without considering the underlying causative factors. We may know that in a majority of cases involving police shootings, the victim has a weapon. Many involve a chase and resisting arrest. A majority are with one who has a record of law violations. Maybe we should turn our attention to a consideration of why an individual might think a weapon is a necessary companion and the availability of those weapons. Why would one flee a scene? Why would one resist police orders and engage in a confrontation? Why would one trained as a peace officer and promoter of order be so inclined to use force as the primary negotiating tool? How do racists end up in law enforcement? Why haven't hate-related messages abated with the advent of advanced education in such a co-existent world? Why is there prejudice and discrimination?

As an old man having lost any mental acuity to even approach an answer to such vital questions of human nature, I am reduced to simplistic meandering. After all, I am competent only at forgetting things, losing things, dropping things, and falling down. I am a senior citizen.

I believe that the answer lies in fear. Fear of the unknown, fear of safety, fear of mastery, fear of mistreatment, fear of belief, fear of competition, fear of failure, fear of differences, fear of strangers, tribal fear, fear of competency, fear of rejection, fear of the elements, fear of death, fear of the dark, and other fears.

Racial profiling, the exertion of excessive force, prejudicial legal systems in a general atmosphere of racial fear have been well documented. Neighborhood white flight, particularly in larger cities, has escalated an old Southern theme that the Supreme Court sought to eliminate in Brown versus the Board of Education of Topeka in 1954. America has gravitated back toward a separate but equal mentality, as was the case with public schools in 1954 when communities were separate but certainly not equal.

The microcosm of public education might well illustrate my observation of where we are in this post-slavery society. I say, "post" because black and white Americans at this point must get beyond slavery. Having stated such an obviously old man's simplistic homespun philosophy, it follows that some reasoning is appropriate. I've discussed it with Maggie, and she seems to think I should keep my mouth shut. Being a cantankerous sort with nothing to lose, I can pontificate.

Both groups are fearful. The white man is fearful of losing control, fearful that values might be compromised, fearful of competition for jobs and economic resources, fearful of being physically challenged, and fearful of a mystical tribal danger. The black man is fearful of being controlled or manipulated, fearful of bodily harm, fearful of losing his heritage, fearful of losing a fair share of the economic pie, and fearful of losing his independence.

In America, we have lived together long enough to have these fears generate stereotypes. The white man is inherently evil, feels superior, and is determined to keep his foot on the necks of blacks. The black man lacks ambition, is culturally backward, arrogant, and violent. Both groups have good reasons to adopt the stereotypes. Neither has done enough to dispel those notions.

On point, I can envision a confrontation. Let's imagine a night on a lonely road. A white policeman believes there has been a minor infraction of traffic law and stops a vehicle. The officer approaches a darkened automobile, unaware of the number or character of occupants. It could be escaped murderers, robbery suspects, terrorists, or tourists. The two black occupants knew of profiling and harassment of minorities. They had been taught from childhood that there were bad cops eager to shoot black boys. They had learned that they have rights in a free country. It was a matter of pride to "stand up" for oneself. The officer observes two young black men, and a chart of crime statistics from minority communities register on his mind's screen. The automobile window comes down.

"Hey, what you stopping me for. I haven't done anything."

"Sir, you were doing 65 in a 55-mile speed zone."

"I couldn't have been going that fast."

"Well, that's what my radar says."

"Well, the radar could be off. This is the third time this month that I've been stopped for no good reason."

"That's not my concern. Let me see your driver's license and registration."

"You think I stole this car? I have a gun in the car pocket. Want to check that too? It's legal in this state, you know."

"Have you been drinking?"

"One beer."

"That's it; get out of the car."

"Why should I? I've done nothing wrong."

"I'm not going to tell you again—step out of the car!"

This is a recipe for disaster. The policeman is scared and angry. The young man is angry, scared, and determined to uphold his black masculinity in the presence of his friend.

I wonder if police officers and other law enforcement personnel might be required, as are those in many other professions, to acquire continuing education, which could include a healthy dose of anger management? I don't know if there is consistent physical and mental evaluation of these peace officers, but consider that to be a standard procedure. There's been a lot of talk lately about developing national standards for law officers. Some maintain that law enforcement is local. I see that agencies work together, and national laws apply in many instances. The fact that the U.S. Department of Justice may intervene in civil rights or other cases where federal statutes are violated lead me to believe that national educational, emotional, and fitness standards could be implemented. At the same time, I believe that national publicity might be directed toward an emphasis geared toward educating the general public regarding civil responses to police orders. We have empowered airline personnel to give orders relative to passenger safety and regulations for conduct. If we are to eliminate the unfit law enforcement personnel and assure the safety of minority persons, can we not change the attitude that law enforcement is "out to get me?"

Two other factors seem to me to be necessary. We must educate America to consider facts rather than emotion when confrontations occur. We must establish faith in the judicial system. That means that the populous become convinced that justice is handed out in fairness and without prejudice. Each case is different. Wealth, influence, color of skin, and other bias has no place in a democratic system of justice. Let's begin with a war on injustice, which starts with a national panel to identify ways to streamline the judicial process, provide transparency, and treat all with respect, dignity, and fairness. There have been commissions in the past, but little has been accomplished. There must be consequences when public officials fail to uphold standards of conduct.

CHAPTER 20

I have no real conception of what it means to be black in America. From the days of slavery, to what was represented by the demeaning display of a black man with a monkey at the World's Fair of 1904, to the violence of hate groups, to the continuing saga of civil rights, to educational and employment opportunity disparity; status and identity remain unclear. Inequities as debilitating as a plague follow to burden those who have endured unspeakable hardship. A half-century time span and half-hearted attempts at democratization reach the few and not the masses. Even those who achieve what many consider the "American dream" find themselves "kings without clothes" when shedding the environment of societal rank. Even their own tribe tends to abandon them.

My experience with black writers, poets, and philosophers has been extremely limited. I was captivated by the meaningful poetry of Langston Hughes and Maya Angelou. Toni Morrison and Alice Walker filled hours of leisure with exciting stories. My familiarity with W.E.B. Dubois, Malcolm X, and Angela Davis has been relegated to quotations in popular articles designed to attract attention. I have read many speeches by Martin Luther King and related positively to his quest for civil rights. But I have never spent enough time beyond popular media to learn more about black people than the little-associated experiences with those I knew personally. Certainly, I have no knowledge or understanding of metropolitan conclaves with huge concentrations of a single race. Nor can I fully appreciate tribal dynamics of a city ghetto.

My education has been tremendously enhanced by a small volume I chanced to discover while browsing at Square Books, a recognized independent bookstore that happens to be located in Oxford. The book, *Between the World and Me,* by Ta-Nehisi Coats, is an open letter to his African-American son. Mr. Coats is a national correspondent for *The Atlantic* magazine. He is an erudite master of words. He has an expressive and convincing concept of our societal inequities. Any person interested in race relations or who attempts to understand cultural distinctions should study this book. Many will have the open-mindedness and intellectual capability to understand this passionate expression of the minority mystique. I am afraid that I lack the knowledge and sharpness needed to interpret such a talented and comprehensive work. Even at my best mental and physical high, I would have been lacking. Now I am old, infirm, and a shade deficient in overcoming dementia and Alzheimer's. I'll pass on more of my physical and mental shortcomings later. In the meantime, it is sufficient to say that my comments on the Coats thesis are my impressions only and may be jaded and inaccurate. I apologize now for any misinterpretation or lack of understanding.

At the heart of Mr. Coats' philosophy is the "American Dream" he feels is built on the backs of blacks, from slavery to modern domination by a society that feels superior and devalues black lives. He reserves equal venom for blacks whom he considers are attempting to be white by adopting the "American Dream" of nice houses in nice subdivisions, adequate jobs, good education and Caucasian values. He appears to find that this is a myth as a result of the evil of a societal foundation that is centered on destroying black bodies. As evidence, he points to the fear that generates white and black flight, producing ghettos and crime-in-fested neighborhoods. He points to the fact that if one is black, especially a black male, he or she must be exposed to tactics that make one tough to defend the taking of their bodies. Everything from corporal punishment by parents to street fighting prepares one for police brutality that society approves to stamp out black identity. The treatment, arrest, incarceration, and killing of black people is condoned by the search for the "American Dream."

He presents cogent examples of discrimination and prejudice. Coats shows disdain for traditional civil rights tactics and condemns those who sacrifice freedom for a chance to achieve the "American Dream." He is no "Uncle Tom" and makes no case for those who silently opt for the status quo in the hope for change.

My assessment is that Mr. Coats is making a statement lamenting change that diminishes the black culture by forcing it to adopt the ways of the white man, who is seen, perhaps rightly so, as the aggressor who would mold the body of the black man into the image of the "American Dream." He is telling his son to respect his heritage and take pride in who he is. At the same time, he is warning him of the danger of being black in America. He recognizes the different shades of blackness but adopts the idea that all are stigmatized. It is a plea for maintaining customs and identity as a significant tribe.

The black people's fear of abuse and discrimination is well founded in the history of the United States. Others, even white immigrants who are considered different, have experienced similar dehumanization and neglect. As Mr. Coats has pointed out, the difference is that they chose to come, and black people, by and large, were forced to come. Perhaps, because of their history and status as free people, other migrants have become a part of the force with which Mr. Coats wrestles. The fear on the part of that force, well-founded or not, is also evident, and therein lies the rub.

It is my opinion that many of us fail to recognize the contributions that black culture has made to the pursuit of the "American Dream." It almost dominates modern American language, art, and music. In an effort to promote identity, it is difficult to accept that we are a part of the whole. Certainly, with our history and the continuing browning of America, we can never again speak of racial purity. I am aware of at least two examples of the kind of future we might expect.

In 1959 when I was first employed by the university as a field representative, my job was to visit white high schools to recruit students. When arriving in a Mississippi town, I would ask for directions to the white school. The university was popular along the Gulf Coast, which also boasted a strong alumni following. Gulfport, Biloxi, Moss Point, and Pascagoula were focal points for student recruiting. Other, smaller venues along the coastline were also targets. While in the area, I visited other schools located inland. At Vancleave, located a few miles north of Moss Point, one of the teachers asked if I was going to the Acadian School. Observing my puzzled expression, she related that there were four school systems in the area. Public (black and white), private, church supported, and Acadian. Naturally, I was visiting white public, white private, and church, but Acadian was not one I had seen on any listing of secondary institutions. Whether or not it was true, and I was never able to verify it, the teacher told a fascinating and convincing story.

It was a story of pilgrims, of pirates, and criminals on sailing ships plundering the coastal area. Some arrived as survivors of shipwreck in the shallow seas. Some were slaves who found an opportunity to slip away from their masters to swim ashore in the warm gulf waters. Some were convicted felons escaping incarceration back in their own homeland and some simply canceling a debt or avoiding some other obligation. Some may have just had a lust for life, looking for something different.

The one thing these men had in common was their desire for anonymity. For fear of being captured, they could not afford to settle in port cities or towns. So, they, individually and collectively, pushed inward through the pine forests and swampland. Wild game, fish, fruit, and nuts sustained them until many miles lay between them and their would-be pursuers. When they were convinced no one would follow, they discovered tribes of indigenous peoples living along the rivers and creeks that dominate the area.

There were Africans, Englishmen, Spaniards, Scandinavians, and countless others to seek sanctuary in this wilderness. Fur traders, fishermen, and American outcasts may have also had families there. Over time, an amalgamation of cultures and races occurred. Ostracized by polite society, they developed their own governing bodies and institutions. Although of differing hues, most were darker skinned and considered coarse in their speech and customs. As the inevitable advance of civilization moved forward, the Acadians were subjected to laws, regulations, and taxes as everyone else.

I guess, at the time, there was no pressing need to recruit students at a mixed-race school. Integration of schools was at our doorsteps, and the priority became recruiting at black secondary schools. I remember that in the spring of 1963, I made an appointment to visit the Canton Industrial Institute. This was an all-black combined elementary and secondary school located just north of Jackson, Mississippi, the state capital. I arrived to find that the auditorium was completely packed. Every class from one through twelve was seated. As I looked out over the sea of darkness, I had a sense of what it means to be a minority. I was the only white person in the entire building. Evidently, the school superintendent and principal were impressed that the state university was seeking enrollees from Canton Industrial. Perhaps they were simply implying that it was about time.

Some years later when on the Gulf Coast, I asked about the Acadians, this mysterious group of Americans. I was told by a younger generation of teachers that all public schools were consolidated and integrated. They were unaware of any sect called Acadians. I did learn that Acadia was a name given by a French explorer to a French colony on the coast of North America. It was named after a region in ancient Greece, Arcadia. The word means a place of rural peace and simplicity.

The better-documented case of this compatible racial and ethnic accommodation appears in a rural area bordered by three or more U.S. states in the Cumberland Mountains of central Appalachia. Portions of East Tennessee, Southwest Virginia, Southeast Kentucky, and perhaps Southwest North Carolina are the general areas where a group called "Melungeons" settled in early colonial times. Some authorities attempt to trace their heritage to the lost colony Sir Walter Raleigh helped establish in 1584-1599. Others trace their lineage to Sir Francis Drake or Hernando De Soto, who apparently, after leaving North Mississippi in 1540, trekked northeastward through the Smoky Mountains of Tennessee. One theory widely circulated opines that in colonial times a society of Portuguese mariners settled there. Whether the people were sailors, run-away slaves, free blacks, indentured servants, gypsies, or regular migration, DNA samples indicate a mixture of European, black, white, and Indian heritage. Other studies conclude that there is an Asian strain.

The appellation "Melungeon" has weathered many assigned definitions and assumptions. The Virginia term suggested guile, deceit, ill intent, or evil. The Turkish or Persian word was "Malun'jin," which means "damned soul." "Melanin" that means dark or black skin, and "Me'lange," meaning a mixture or hodgepodge, was frequently used. The French "aubergine" expression meaning dark eggplant and the Spanish Portygee were used in derision of these mixed-blood people. They tended to have varying skin pigment, body features, and coarseness of hair. Some could pass for being white, while others appeared to be the product of a darker union. All were discriminated against as a shiftless lot. The darker the skin, the less honest and trustworthy they were perceived. At one point Virginia had a law signifying that if one had a drop of Negro blood, he or she was classified as black. For many years they were denied the vote, even though they were considered free. The Melungeons tended to educate their own and organized traditional religious organizations. They lived in rural, isolated areas.

As some began to expand their world through moving, travel and higher education, more attention was given this group that had found the need to form an integrated society that depended upon its array of disparate cultures and races. With the advent of civil rights and equal rights legislation, the Melungeons have achieved a bit more respect. Those who stay as a fairly distinct group, although some of the poorest in our nation, seem to take pride in the unity that they accomplished. Those who have escaped or chosen to pursue lives outside the geographic area are prone to voluntarily favor establishment of genetic ties to the Melungeons.

It makes one wonder if these people, rich or poor, regardless of skin color, have achieved the "American Dream." To be free and equal under the law may be a large hunk of that vision.

Losing one's body and heritage is a legitimate concern as the amber waves of America apply to more than just grain. I cannot believe that we are powerless to attack the fear that permeates relationships regardless of the great crimes of history that brought us to hate and discriminate. I cannot accept the idea that America must be a tenuously joined association of diametrically opposed units. There must be hope in our unity and civility. There must be a continuity of mankind that is cognizant of connectedness required to perpetrate the future of man.

I am just an old person racked with a lack of understanding and appreciation for the intricacies of international diplomacy or domestic policy. As evident from this trial that I am currently facing for killing another human being, I must be unable to discipline myself. I do know that we must begin a renewed effort at reconciliation, starting at home with our loved ones, friends, and associates. I know nothing of economics, trade, security, education, immigration, or many of the issues bantered about in a current political climate. There are a few things an uninformed, average citizen like me might like to see. There are qualified experts in this country to provide ways and a national wealth to accomplish the means.

Drastic times sometimes call for drastic action. To me, it appears that a serious conversation about freedom of expression versus law and order is essential. I've studied the Constitution of these United States and am convinced that it is broad enough to accommodate sensible rules and regulations. Many have been adopted for the common good. There are limits to free expression, whether it be shouting "fire" in a crowded theater or making a bomb to explode in a crowded theater, church, or school.

The question becomes how much individual freedom should be sacrificed to maintain a civilized society. Is calling in the National Guard to take over a street in a major city to restore the community a violation of the civil rights of gang members that are spreading drugs and violence? Should physical presence and safety measures by law enforcement be established until neighborhood control and trust are established? Can local leadership in neighborhood watch or other programs be adopted without fear of retaliation? Will it be possible to disband organizations that have an avowed purpose to control and wreak havoc on a given population of citizens? Do such organized individuals have an inalienable right to bear arms? Could their right to assemble under the first amendment be considered something less than a peaceable assembly?

It has always been a mystery to me that peaceful assemblies to address social issues attract an element that sometimes overshadows the issue for which the demonstration was intended. For some, it is an opportunity to rob, steal, and destroy. What does burning a car, assaulting police officers, interrupting commerce, crashing store fronts, stealing a television or merchandise, and perpetrating other violence, really have anything to do with exercising a right? Such action creates only fear, a fear that widens the chasm of misunderstanding. Certainly it calls attention to underlying problems, but I question whether solving those issues of discrimination, fairness, and economic stability are made much more challenging. It further divides our nation in a non-productive way.

The bearing of arms always evokes interpretation of the second amendment to the Constitution. While I have always considered the reference was to the people of a state having the right to organize its own militia, I question whether or not a federal legislative body is precluded from regulating gun ownership. Registering guns for sport, personal safety, and for legitimate collectors seem to be reasonable. Assault-type guns with exceptional continuous firing capacity should be reserved for armies or tactical law enforcement. Reform and training of law enforcement are essential. At the same time, civilian purchase of guns might be authorized only at commercial outlets and limited to established categories of safety, sport, or collections, with safeguards to prohibit criminals and mentally ill persons from purchasing. Procedures for gifts, inheritance, or exchanges that would involve re-registration could be established. "Stand Your Ground" and similar laws might be revoked.

Guns are not the only means available to those who would harm others. It seems to me that social media outlets that provide materials on bomb-making or other methods of harming the public could be censored in some way. I guess there is no way to punish all the "hate" literature, but specific means of creating acts of violence should be an affront to all. What is considered freedom for some means the loss of freedom for others.

While government is regulating, there are positive steps it should be taking. My common-man thinking tinkers with established practices and envisions initiatives which, if developed by those with knowledge and understanding, might enhance the lives of us all.

Universal health care should be the right of every citizen, with citizen regulation rather than private, profit-motivated, health care insurance industries and hospitals. Health research and drug production could be a part of a comprehensive federal grant plan where expenditures for investigation might be related to actual need and cost of the end product. I have been advised by my oncologist at Vanderbilt University Hospital that a new drug might slow advancing lung cancer. A quart bag infusion every three weeks is prescribed. The cost is $20,000 per treatment. I've had a few infusions but am waiting to see if limitations will be enacted in the future. Although I have Medicare and a good secondary insurance, my contribution has limits also. I might agree that old men should be sacrificed if younger people have access to more reasonable and affordable medication.

There should be jobs for every able individual. A year ago, I was privileged to go on a cultural exchange visit to Cuba. Communism is not a concept that I could ever adopt, but I found that Cuba seems to have every able-bodied person assigned to a job. While job assignment would not be the goal, I wonder what would happen if the United States would guarantee a job at a living salary for every able-bodied citizen. During the "New Deal" days after the Great Depression, a large effort was made to provide jobs. That effort produced not only a way out of a national financial crisis but also produced goods and services needed by our people. Trees were planted; roads and bridges were built; recreation resources were established; and the arts were included. I remember the Civilian Conservation Corps that gave a teenage school drop-out, my half- brother, meaningful work. A portion of his salary was sent home and may well have kept our family from starving in that difficult period. Those kinds of public works could be useful today to stimulate the economy.

To my mind, immigration continues to provide dynamic opportunities for America. Few would argue that our government has the right to limit an influx that cannot be assimilated into our society. Unfortunately, this involves border security and stringent regulations. My take is that everyone permanently in the United States should have a reasonable pathway to citizenship. Together with world partners, humanitarian immigration speaks to our values as a people. As harsh as it sounds, our first consideration for new immigrants should be that the country can provide jobs and support. It does the immigrant no favor to be admitted without the necessary assistance to ensure a meaningful existence. It is not humanitarian if we cannot provide health care, education, and opportunity.

Education and opportunity are also a problem for Americans. I drive through the Delta section of Mississippi and note paint peeling from giant plantation houses. Among the thousands of acres of cotton, corn, beans, and catfish farms, only a smattering of occupied tenant houses sits forlornly on flat patches of soil. More desolate is the winter season when drab landscapes, void of color, reveal muddy water creeping toward cabin doors. On manufactured mounds of dirt, huge monsters of tin sheds occupy machinery capable of cultivating multiple rows of soil to replace a hundred workers who previously tilled the land. Each machine requires one driver. Absentee landowners have fled to hill country cities; extraneous laborers are left in small communities bereft of jobs or services. Social workers drive through; the U.S. mail brings barely sustenance-level welfare checks. A few larger towns have attracted industry but find it difficult to attract skilled workers. The gap between an educated workforce and quality jobs grows. Those who are qualified might drive long distances to find employment or move to leave the community void of leadership or inspiration. Sometimes I wonder why more would not abandon a dying community for a better life elsewhere. Without education or training, those left behind find it impossible to break away. Technology and automation have outsourced opportunity.

Admittedly, elementary and secondary education is primarily a local concern. The need for an educated society and the investment made by the federal government make standards a national priority. The reasonable assessment of potential continues to be a challenge. However, every high school graduate must be exposed to a standardized body of knowledge. Those unable to navigate such a curriculum for whatever reason should be given an opportunity for technical or other training geared to employment. The dignity of work should be emphasized with the path to a meaningful livelihood. Perhaps free education could be provided through the community college level, both vocational and two-year college years. Qualified workers attract industry, and homegrown businesses flourish.

I understand that trade deficits are a problem. A crazy old man with only one college course in economics can, without question, fabricate crazy ideas. I do adhere to the proposition that in international circles, protectionism does nothing to enhance trade. Tariffs only inhibit the free exchange of goods and services. However, what if there were a producer tax on goods sold to or produced in the United States? An international producer, regardless of point of origin, would pay the difference between the U.S. established rate and that paid its home country. The tendency would be for the home country to collect an amount equal to the U.S. assessment. That would accomplish two things. First, developing countries would have more wealth for their people who, hopefully, would increase pressure for higher wages, training, health care, and other needs. Secondly, it would make location less of an incentive and emphasize quality of goods as the motivation for importing a product. I know that additional agreements would be needed to protect workers and level or equalize pay. Those who fail to adopt negotiated agreements might be barred from importing to coalition partners that have adopted the plan.

My understanding is that terrorism is a global phenomenon and that our country is obligated to be a leader in combating the philosophy both at home and abroad. Also, the U.S. has NATO and other commitments to deal with aggressive states. Difficulties in containment and terrorism are likely to continue for years to come. Perhaps we can find ways to appeal for peace without some of the past mistakes that foment distrust and hate. Attempted nation building is not the answer. Somehow, we must be an active partner of nations without insisting that they become a mirror image of America. In the meantime, we must confront terror at home and abroad. Our leaders must distinguish the difference between our best interests as opposed to pressures exerted to rule the universe. The cautious and careful consideration of pressure and action currently employed seems to lay the groundwork for ultimate victory. In my opinion, vigilance related to outside attacks and more communication and community action for homegrown activists is the key. More attention should be paid to social media spreading hate and instructions for specific acts of terror. Technology exists to block unwanted telephone messages. Would a system of identifying illegal proposals be an intrusive power that threatens free speech?

The jailing of black men out of proportion to their numbers is another question for those far more capable than I. I understand the underlying reasons that our society must change. Education, poverty, discrimination, role models, family stability, history, governmental and people scrutiny are just a few factors in balancing the scale. It does no good to yell that incarceration is proportional to crimes committed. While working to eliminate underlying cause, I wonder if our national policy could be that no one is held in bondage without rehabilitation, education, training, and the assurance of reasonable employment upon release.

Standardized training and procedures for law enforcement are a must. Although each case presents unique circumstances, the justice system has to tackle the problem of sentencing for a more uniform and consistent outcome for all convicted of the same offense. Mandated sentences require little justification and may be unfair in some instances. One answer may take the form of a special sentencing appeals court to examine deviations from normal guidelines. Perhaps judges and district attorney types should have more special training.

I guess it is too sensitive an issue to raise, but I sometimes wonder about involving the entire nation in some sort of service. There seems to be a disconnect between a united nation and our individual pursuits. As I was graduating from high school, the Korean War was winding down. Although required to register for service and indeed examined to be classified as capable of serving, I was not immediately called for military duty. I entered college and, in the interim peacetime, was not asked to be a part of the military. I have, over the years, wondered if I somehow missed an opportunity to experience something that would have contributed to my growth and development. I'm not saying that every male and female should be forced into the military, but suppose that alternate service could be offered before college or prior to the pursuit of permanent employment. Teaching, community action, services for the poor, assistance for people with disabilities, and similar service comes to mind. Associating with those who are perhaps different may foster understanding and learning experiences that create closer ties with others and appreciation for our common values. Perhaps there are other ways to have rich and poor, races and cultures, religious and atheists, environmentalists and developers, LGBT and straight people, farmers and city folk, and other groups become the melting pot of a future America. Just an idea, but the military might be able to have the skilled labor to eliminate contract employees and spend their budget on military matters. We might even redefine the term veteran. I've always wondered how a desk jockey in Hawaii for three or four years could have the same after-service status as one with equivalent time in Vietnam. Just a thought.

Taxation is another concern for those who seek equity. It is also of utmost importance for governmental budgeting and for planners focusing on paying bills. My simplistic solution to the national debt crisis is to collect more taxes. I propose to do that by reducing the tax burden on almost all Americans. It would mean a completely new way of thinking. First, each and every tax exemption would be removed. Interest on home ownership, charitable contributions, farm or industrial subsidies, medical or business expense, and all the political deductions authorized by Congress would be eliminated. Churches or other entities that now claim political anonymity would not be exempt from their fair share of the tax burden. No depletion allowance or environmental or investment allowance would be legal. Not one single individual or entity would bear favor on the federal tax roll. The practice of using the taxing authority to promote any business or individual, regardless of its efficacy, would be prohibited.

And, how will we be taxed, one might ask? I would not consider calling it a flat tax, for under a consumer philosophy, the tax is not flat. It might, instead, be termed a "straight tax." There would simply be a graduated scale tax on ALL income, cash or equivalent. The poor and the rich pay according to their earnings, hiding nothing. Each might share those earnings in any way they choose. They might invest in stock, start a business, build a church, or participate in any activity of their choosing. All would pay tax to the extent of their ability as measured by income. Federal income would inevitably grow to cover universal health care, social services, infrastructure, etc.

Tweaks would surely be needed. Need-based Social Security, for example. Although everyone pays Social Security, it seems ridiculous to waste it on someone who makes $100 million a year. Such taxpayers should be happy to forego such a pittance for his or her opportunity to live in a country where such great success is possible.

This is written with the assumption that insanity on my part would not be subject to taxation.

CHAPTER 21

The cell phone jarred me away from going forward beyond the U.S. to solving problems of all the world. I had just returned from an early morning walk with my dog, Lilly. Lilly is mostly a Great Pyrenees with a spurt of golden retriever. She is all white with a touch of gold when in the sunlight. The only way I keep up with her in the deep weeds is by following that held high, bushy tail, visible through nodding thistles, feather bells, and turnsole—all wildflowers with bending stalks of brushy flowers. Nearer the creek, I spotted a spent Indian blanket, but the dry weather has eliminated spiderwort around the lake, now crowned by a small bald spot of land in the middle.

"Mr. Warner, you do remember we're back in court on Monday?"

"Yes, Walt, I remember. By the way, what day is this?"

"It's Saturday, Mr. Warner. Remember on Thursday Judge Longest gave the jury a long weekend?"

"Yes, now I remember. I've been busy."

"What have you been busy doing, Mr. Warner?"

"Saving the United States. Guess I'll start on the world next."

"Good for you. In the meantime, I'm considering resting our case."

"It's about time. I'm so tired of hearing that crap I could puke."

"Well if you can hold off for a question or two on Monday, we will get on with summations so the jury can do their thing."

"Okay, Walter. See you on Monday."

"Have a nice weekend, Mr. Warner."

"Yeah."

I sit on the porch as cooler evening breeze rustles leaves turning colors early for need of rain. It is my favorite time of day when the western sun sits behind streaks of red, only to suddenly drop beyond the horizon. It is also the time I best share with Maggie. Suddenly, I am aware that I have kept things from her over this past year. Of course, she knows about the trial and has listened to my feeble attempts to validate my dilemma. Slowly, I'm re-capturing visions of the awful thing I did, but why I did it continues to elude me.

My health has never been broached since it is only a blip in the radar of our relationship. In 1990 colon cancer was detected, and after a sectioning of the intestine, chemotherapy was applied with vigor. Maggie held my hand through intolerable bouts of pain and nausea and reminded me of the good life we shared. In 1994, her strength pulled me through a heart attack, where I acquired a couple of stents. Never did we dream that this young, strong, resilient woman would, herself, be struck down. It was an infection that defied treatment as I watched her slip away.

In the ten years since, I have tried to remind myself of the perfect times we spent together. I wrote her a little poem once when she was away on a business trip. I never shared it with her. I told myself that it would only make her sad that she had to travel. Now, I wish I had given her the poem and told her thousands of times how much she meant to me. I never imagined that the writing spoke to the future.

A Day Special

The sun got up early, chasing the dawn,
Filtering rainbow colors beyond lake spray,
Beginning the day in the ordinary,
Little noting that every day is special,
That every breath with you is treasured.

Through the window, life swept away
Over pebbles of limestone, little changed
By the sense of something missing,
A hollow spot of spaceless void,
Until your step echoes again at my door.

Gala parties, fishing on still water, relaxing on the side porch—
small things remembrance stores in satin boxes. It was a good life!

Maggie, we haven't talked about my health. So much has happened.
It seemed so irrelevant to our conversations that brought warmth and
feeling. Nostalgia has been my comfort and filled that spot you left behind. Nothing else has been so important and uplifting.

First came swelling in the groin, followed by a diagnosis of lym-
phoma. Radiation provided a respite until blood appeared in urine. The
old kidney had to go, but the bug traveled to the bladder, where more
chemotherapy was needed. Lastly, spots were discovered on the lungs.
More chemotherapy, yet the cells continue to grow. I'm good at growing
potatoes and cancer cells.

My body, unable to tolerate more chemotherapy, I just couldn't talk
to you about it, Maggie. Then I heard of a trial program at Vanderbilt

University. For five months I tried that treatment, which didn't work out for me. My physician at Vanderbilt is excellent. She is the epitome of the mythical, old-time family doctor who shows empathy with the application of liniment. She recommended that we switch to a new drug that shows some promise. If I can afford the new treatment, I'll travel the four-and-a-half-hour drive to Nashville every three weeks. Maggie, I don't think about what happens next. I am comforted by the fact that I can change nothing. I value quality of life over quantity. I want to live until I die. At that point, I want to join you, Maggie, in the sands of time, scattered over lake and soil of our beloved Wyldewoode.

A valued friend once passed along a statement written by a friend of hers. I understand that it may have appeared in a church bulletin or perhaps in a newspaper, but I have not been able to find where it might have been published. The writer's name was Eula P. Mohle. Although a male is listed with the same name, I've been told that Eula P. Mohle was a Unitarian lay person who was a recognized leader in church activities. She may have written other articles for church literature. According to my friend, Eula contracted incurable cancer and penned the following as a comfort for her many followers. I am not the religious advocate who evokes words like those of Ms. Mohle, but I do adopt the tenor of her article, "Death Will Come When It Will Come."

What shall I say about death? The first point to make is that I should stay too busy living to spend much time thinking about death. The creator has endowed us with gifts too beautiful to ignore: a planet hanging low in the sky, a rose unfolding in the shiny dew, a cardinal calling to his mate, the sweet voices of little children at play, the joys of friendship, the harmonies of a full orchestra, a well-kept home, a delicious meal, a moving sermon, a provocative class discussion, a word fitly spoken, an exhilarating faith in the essential goodness of people and our need for each other—all these and many more should occupy our minds rather than a fear of death. I cannot accept the ecstatic longing of ancient and medieval martyrs to join the heavenly hosts as soon as possible. Life was made too beautiful to cause me to wish to leave it. As long as reasonable health is mine, I don't know of a place I'd rather be than on God's little planet Earth. I shall continue to seek to comfort the dying and the loved ones left behind. I shall freely acknowledge that my own time of death will come when it will come. That the time of my loved ones, too, will come when it comes.

This does not make me bitter. It is merely one of the problems of living that I cannot solve. It is a spur to my endeavors, to prick me into making life count in its own little niche of the universe. Then what? I simply do not know. I have no fear of hell because I don't believe there is one. I have no longing for heaven because again, I doubt there is one. I'll settle for my dust joining the dust of the billions dead before me, to help nourish the earth, to keep its resources supplied for generations after me, to become a part of the livable world for descendants I'll never know. If I've had any worthy thoughts or done worthy deeds, I believe they will live after me in those I may have touched. They will join the unbroken chain that binds each to each. I will become a part of the great world soul and the continuum of creation.

The morning sun skipped through trees as I drove the road made carpet with drying grass showing bits of golden asters lining the ditches.

I have taken this cut-off trail just to appreciate wildflowers and alleviate the monotony of Highway 9. I think my pick-up would have just as soon stayed on the blacktop. It takes only about twenty minutes to the courthouse, and I was early. I watched the people in the benches and the jury file in. I wondered what their day was like and what they are thinking. Walt sat down. Judge Longest came in and swished his robe before taking a seat. The prosecutor was studiously staring at a yellow pad. All was set for a final day of testimony in the case of the United States versus James T. Warner. I was again called to the witness chair. Walt rose to begin the questioning.

"Mr. Warner, how are you this morning?"

"Just fine."

"Mr. Warner, I'm going to ask you some questions about your ethics. Are you comfortable with that?"

"Okay."

"Do you consider yourself a person who has standards of conduct?"

"Well, I suppose so."

"Mr. Warner, are you a person who has adopted moral values?"

"Yes, I guess I picked up some along the way."

"Would that set of moral values lead you to respect and value the lives of your fellow men?"

"God, I hope so—yes."

"Would you willingly harm another person?"

"Heavens no—unless I had to protect myself or my family."

"No further questions, your honor."

Larry Greenwood rises from his seat and comes very close to the witness stand. I know that he is trying to intimidate me. Just for the hell of it, I ignore him and looked up at the ceiling.

"Mr. Warner, you have just testified that you consider yourself a man of principle, one who has developed moral values?"

"Yes, I hope so."

"Were these values accumulated over a number of years, perhaps a lifetime?"

"Yes."

"And where do you suppose those values came from—who taught them or where did you pick up that morality?"

"I guess it started with my parents."

"It started with your parents?"

"Yes?"

"Earlier, did you not testify that your parents had prejudicial feelings toward black people?"

"Yes, but as I grew up, I developed my own values."

"And no person or institution was influential—you just picked up morality on your own?"

"Of course not, there were teachers, church, life experiences."

Greenwood paused for a long time, looking as if he were puzzled.

"Mr. Warner, you mentioned the church as an entity that taught you morality. Are you active in any recognized church organization?"

"No."

"Then when did this religious education contribute to your moral values?"

"I did attend church during childhood and as a young adult."

"How long has it been since your last church attendance, not counting weddings, funerals, receptions, and the like?"

Walter rose to object to this line of questioning. "Your Honor, church attendance is not a qualifying prerequisite to being a moral person. Religion is not on trial in this court."

Judge Longest raised a nodding head and cleared his throat. "The defendant has stated that some of the philosophy to which he adheres came from religious teaching. As a result, this court does not consider it a violation of his first amendment rights to query him as to his religious training. Objection overruled. The witness may answer the question."

Larry Greenwood smiled a crooked smile and said, "You may answer the question."

Don't know why I let him get under my skin, but I snarled, "I know!"

The judge rapped his gavel and gave a deserved admonishment. "The witness is instructed to answer the question without inappropriate remarks."

Greenwood had more of a satisfied smile now. "Thank you, Your Honor. Mr. Warner, shall I repeat the question?"

"No. I haven't voluntarily gone to a church service in probably thirty or more years."

"So, back to moral values. Your moral discipline has prevented you from any act of racial discrimination over the years?"

"I didn't say that."

"Then what did you say, Mr. Warner?"

"That everyone is prejudiced in some way or the other, and black people have been discriminated against from the beginning of time."

"Does that include you, Mr. Warner?"

"I suppose it does."

Walt, on cross-examination asks only one question.

"Mr. Warner, Do you hate any person because of the color of their skin?"

I replied, "as God is my witness, none!"

Walt turns to the jury and then slowly to the judge. "Your honor, the defense rests!"

Judge Longest called for a lunch break and admonished the jury not to discuss the case among themselves or with any other person. Walt had some things to file at the courthouse and decided to skip lunch. I crossed the street to Boure's and ordered my favorite, a salmon salad. By the time it arrived, a young man stopped by my table and asked if he could join me. He had a distinctively British accent. Although I was not particularly enthusiastic for company, I motioned him to sit. He introduced himself as Joel Perkins, a missionary to Africa. He pulled out a chair. I spoke first.

"Well, Joel, what are you doing in Oxford"?

He perused the menu and without looking at me said, "I was just passing through and heard about the trial."

He met my gaze and continued. "I thought that, since I'm going to be a missionary in Africa, I might learn more about how black people are treated in America. I've been in the states for three weeks and attended two protest marches, one in Arizona and one in South Carolina."

"Well," I said, "that's most likely a good idea. Very laudable. It might help to have a world perspective before going to an African nation. By the way, where are you from?"

"Great Britain, Wales, actually."

"I assume that you have researched black/white relations in Europe. What have you learned?"

"Oh, I've lived all my life in the Commonwealth. I pretty much know what is happening there."

"Then, how could I possibly help you, Joel?"

"I've been sitting in the courtroom for three days now and wondering why you would kill an unarmed black man."

"Joel, I've been asking that myself."

"Mr. Warner, I know why you did it."

"My goodness, please tell me. I've been searching for an answer for over a year."

The waiter came with our food and filled our water glasses. "I won't disturb your conversation, but if you gentlemen need anything, just wave." He was about the same age as Joel. I wondered if he was more sagacious than my luncheon companion.

"Your problem, Mr. Warner, is that you don't know the Lord. You are lost and undone. When you find Jesus, the only begotten Son of God, born of the Virgin Mary, you can be washed in his blood and be forgiven for your sin."

"Is that what you're going to tell those people in Africa?"

"Absolutely."

"Well, you're a little late. The Anglicans, Catholics, and others have beat you there."

"That's why I am so desperately needed. Anglicans go only half-way to God, depend on pomp and circumstance. Catholics worship a man, the Pope, and idols. We've got to let the people know the true God. And, there are still humans in the bush who are damned to hell because they have never heard the 'good news' of salvation."

"Joel, let me ask you a question. Do you believe that your religious interpretation is the only way one can come to God?"

"It's not me; it is God's truth, God's way!"

"Joel, if I were a praying man, I'd pray for the people of Africa."

I left a confused young man and went out to observe a bustling town square filled with people going about their business, entering shops and restaurants. I wonder how many of them have differing faiths and blindly follow their own creed of religious belief. Some see little application to personal action or deep-seated feelings. I wonder about religious zealots and the relationship they may have to enhancing lives. Could it be that recipients of this unsolicited fervor might, psychologically, be better served with a glass of wine? Wine goes down better and is not lasting.

CHAPTER 22

Since before recorded history, mankind has shown a continuing propensity to create religions. Fear of other creatures, fear of the elements, fear of starvation, fear of failure, and fear of death continue to feed the development of new ways to allay fear and adjust to life on the planet. Although there are perhaps many more, I was able to find twenty to thirty Greek and Roman gods and goddesses. These mythical deities were worshiped to fulfill a particular human need. Each historic tribe assigned a specific name, and each god was given a functional role.

Each had a King of Gods, Zeus or Jupiter. Love was represented by Aphrodite/Venus, war by Ares/Mars. There was a God of the Sea, God of Harvest, God of Hunt, God of Music, God of Medicine, God of Earth, God of Wisdom, God of Marriage, God of the Forge, God of Wine, God of Messenger, God of the Underworld, and others. Most likely, gods existed for any perceived peril or desire of mankind. Man appears to invent a god for anything man is unable to control.

Eventually, ten or twelve major world religions remain. Those normally mentioned in the literature include Islam, Hinduism, Christianity, Buddhism, Confucianism, Judaism, Shinto, Taoism, and Bahai'. Each has countless numbers of sects and branches. Many are similar in terms of content and purpose. They can't all be the standard bearer for truth, yet man has fought and died and committed the most barbaric atrocities defending a particular religious principle.

I don't rightly understand it, but various religions seem to have a great deal in common. Almost everybody's god has a human representative that is to be worshiped same as the god himself. Many of these humans as god had miraculous births, being born of virgins. My encounter with the young man taking the "good news" to Africa prompted me to do a little search to identify a few reported instances of virgin birth. In addition to Jesus, there was Buddha, Genghis Khan, Krishna, the Aztec god Huitzilopochtli, and others. The impregnation process varied, from Holy Ghost, a great light, to pomegranate fruit, to sky feathers hidden in a bosom. The birth process was normal in some instances, but on occasion the child god emerged from the mother's side or appeared in other ways.

All these stories have been concocted by men whose objective was to organize those seeking to discover a higher power, something that might allay fear of the unknown. Faith requires one to accept whatever provides solace for living and dying. It does not eliminate evil or the ultimate reality of death. Questions remain for that which is unknowable.

Is religious persecution merely seeking power over non-believers? Could it be alleged that religion is the foundation for racism, prejudice, and discrimination? Would it be more appropriate to say that religion is a divisive element in the tribalism perpetrated throughout the history of mankind?

It would be unrealistic to ignore the fact that religion is a strong ingredient in the worldwide unrest being experienced today. The rise of Al-Qaeda, ISIS, and other movements with the attendant violence is of major concern. We have to admit that contrasting philosophies and ideology feed the conflicts. Interpretations within the same basic religious belief create an environment where one feels impelled to label the other as infidels. This gives one the right and impetus to destroy the other. The

U.S. involvement in Afghanistan, Iran, Iraq, Libya, Syria, and multiple places around the world constitutes a desire for conflict resolution. We delude ourselves if we assume that Islamic jihadists are interested only in political power and the acquisition of territory. There may be some who have their own secular motives, but the real motivation driving the movement is religious belief.

The establishment of an Islamist state with a caliph prophet is only the fulfillment of a religious mandate. To serve Allah and Mohammed, they are obligated to kill the infidel in an Armageddon fight between good and evil to usher in the ending of time. To me, it is much like the Christian advocacy for an incendiary end when the faithful rise to meet their maker in the air. The difference may be in the manner in which some accomplish that end.

Since the Crusades much of the world has abandoned theological disputes that led to religious wars. The schism between Shite and Sunni has led to the Shite group's adopting Sharia law, which condemns Sunnis as non-Muslim and, as such, subject to death as are other non-believers.

Hatred for non-believers motivates terrorist acts around the world. From the World Trade Center in New York to Boston, Paris to Brussels, San Bernardino, Orlando to Jerusalem, and places in between, Islamic terrorists have struck. Other groups and individuals commit acts of violence daily all over the world for a whole host of reasons. A religious Muslim contingent continues to degrade a great and respected world religious order. As the world becomes better educated, I would hope that this silliness would subside. In the meantime, we must be diligent and make intelligent foreign policy decisions. The use of technology in warfare and application of negotiating skills rather than "boots on the ground" is preferable to an old man like me. Let us ignore religion and address underlying reasons for animosity among peoples.

How do we ignore religion? While respect is due the customs of others, the separation of church and state in America must be more clearly expressed. The First Amendment to the Constitution of the United States prohibits governmental establishment of religion, the freedom to practice religion, as well as the freedom from religion. With respect to other nations, religion should never be the basis for discrimination, nor should it dominate decisive action or agreement between individual groups or nations. Religious proselytizing should not receive governmental encouragement or support. Such outreach in foreign fields is divisive and has contributed to past conflicts.

Ethnic cleansing, whether it be the elite of Virginia's denying citizenship for those who had a drop of black blood in their veins or "Spanish Bluebloods" asserting purity, to Nazi atrocities, the foundation for ethnic cleansing is well documented. Pagan people, Mongols, Turks, Franks, Muslims, Christians, and others have practiced the art. In many instances, such action was based on religious zeal. In reality, it was for land, power, and economic control. The Crusades, for example, which began in 1269, were ordained as a religious effort to eliminate the enemies of Christ. Muslims had captured Jerusalem in 637, and any people who occupied lands in the path to that city, including Jews, were considered heretics by Catholic warriors. By the fourth Crusade, the fight expanded even within the church when Latin Catholics and their Greek Orthodox brothers disagreed. By the 14h century, these holy wars began to decline, but religious confrontations continue to dominate modern societies.

This is not meant to be an attack on religion that may provide peace and solace for some. I merely point out the fact that religion and morality are not necessarily the same. Great men have been religious but not moral. So have religious orders. Islam, Christianity, and perhaps all great religions endorsed and promoted slavery at one point or the other. That did not make the practice moral in my estimation. Religion and belief may not be a precondition for great moral accomplishments. In my opinion, the idea of a God, not religion, is that speck of humanity that respects others and values the lives of all. That point of view makes it even more essential that I understand why I killed Artise Bradley Washington.

Back in the courtroom on Friday afternoon, Judge Longest ruled in the negative on a petition for dismissal, but discussed other administrative items including the approval of my request to travel to Nashville for medical reasons the following Monday. He announced that summary arguments would begin on Tuesday at nine o'clock with statements by the defense to be followed by the prosecution summary.

On the way homeward, Highway 9-W veers off number 7 to enter a mile stretch bordered by a plant labeled kudzu. It was imported from the Orient to control erosion. The invasive vine attacked trees, telephone poles, buildings, and practically anything upright to push itself skyward. It fills ditches and makes large areas of land useless. It doesn't do a lot to stop erosion but, by killing trees, promotes erosion. After much research, no practical use has been found. I once wrote a little poem for Maggie after she had remarked on the beauty of the giant leaves spiraling up pine trees.

> Stalwart vine, luxuriously soft and supple,
> Rooted in the sands of providence,
> Arrayed in fixed and determined patterns,
> Reasoned with seemingly impeccable patience,
> Growing as if conceived in practicality,
> Spreading its green down the hillside,
> Slender stems reaching and searching.
> Before the miracle of you, I was Kudzu.

Traveling Interstate 40 to Vanderbilt Medical gave me a time to reflect on the story of man, his accomplishments and failures. From the time modern man evolved in Africa perhaps two to three hundred thousands of years ago, to the population of the Middle East, with great empires rising and falling, a steady progression of organized societies have contributed rules and regulations, cultural distinctions and religions, customs, and habits. Europe, populated around 43,000 years ago, emerged after the ice age and included white, blue-eyed mixtures possibly from the Caucus regions and points north. Early tribes banned together, reacting to the elements and forming rules by which a group could survive. If we are to believe discovered artifacts, two thousand years before the Ten Commandments of the Christian era were written, an ancient native African tribe in what is now Egypt developed laws prescribed in forty-two divine principles. Maat, named for a goddess, was based upon justice, truth, harmony, morality, order, and balance. It would appear that societal efforts to regulate after that time have attempted to emulate those principles. From ancient Greece to Babylon to Rome and thereafter, laws express those verities. It is their selective interpretation and application that makes for differences.

Our own system of justice based upon English Common Law has developed around our federation of states couched within a representative constitutional republic. Rules and regulations were designed for the common good. Many local or state laws represent a true democracy where individuals vote directly, but we are a republic in the sense that we generally have a representative form of governance.

Principles have not been uniformly and fairly applied for all. Therein lies the need to interpret our Constitution as a living document for all our citizens. The American justice system must respect and protect the vulnerable and provide fair and equal treatment. A democratic republic is dependent upon citizen participation to ensure competent and dedicated representatives who uphold legitimate and principled enforcement of fair and principled rules and regulations. We must insist on educated and trained professionals in the justice system from law enforcement to prosecutors, judges, and other public officials. Consistent with justice for all, timely and reasonable justice is a requirement with punishment and remediation balanced. We might start with a compilation of consistent procedures to reconcile federal and state action.

There I go, espousing opinions on subjects for which I have no knowledge or understanding. A frivolous undertaking for an old man.

On the way back from Nashville with no confirmation of longevity, I concentrated on driving, for which other travelers were grateful. Arriving home safely, I listened to the message from Walt reminding me that closing arguments would begin next day.

The courtroom was crowded. Valerie, Tom, and Summer sat with Lois and Donald on a front row. Hushed conversations banked against whitewashed stucco. The jury was seated, and folks stood as Judge Longest took his place on the elevated platform.

"Ladies and gentlemen, today we will begin hearing final arguments in the case of the U.S. versus James T. Warner. There will be a summary presentation for the defendant, Mr. James T. Warner, followed by a summary by the complainant, The United States Justice Department. Our justice system dictates the order for these summary arguments. The defense will go first followed by the prosecution. After these presentations, the matter will be given to you, the jury, with instructions, for your careful consideration and the return of a verdict. Is the defense ready for your final argument?"

Walter Dunbar stood in his best dark suit and a bright red tie.

"Ready, Your Honor."

"Then, if there are no objections, you may proceed."

Walt walked smartly to the jury box, stopped and surveyed the jurors.

"Ladies and gentlemen. First, let me thank you for your patience and attention to the procedure of this trial and for your genuine interest in details presented by testimony. I am here merely to synthesize that testimony and to remind you of the facts in the case against my client, Jim Warner.

"Over the course of this trial, Jim Warner has been characterized and pictured as a racist, a murderer, an out-of-control hater of minorities and one who would deny the rights of others to enjoy life, liberty, and the pursuit of happiness. I am asking you to set aside that picture and look at a clean canvas, one that the misdirected artist has not touched. A backdrop that has no angry splashes of black or white, a purity of form and presence as a baby born some eighty-three years ago. Step by step, we intend to fill that canvas with brush strokes that measure his days with good works that slowly fade the picture painted by the prosecutor, a picture that represents darkness and unreality. Our picture is light and filled with hope and truth, with a lifetime of positive experiences lived without prejudice or ill will.

"Jim Warner is a product of the South. While we share an inheritance of gentle regard for our fellow man, we also share a history of intolerance. Jim Warner exemplifies a new South that endorses the fairness and justice inherent in our basic nature. His entire life reflects a picture of growth, enlightenment, and service. I ask that you look at the colors of that commitment as we paint the unselfish contributions he has made to making Mississippi and America a better place, a place of peace, harmony, and justice for all.

"You have, over the course of this trial, heard ordinary people testifying to the character of this man, Jim Warner. How he has spent his entire life helping others, particularly minorities, the downtrodden and hopeless. How, as a child, he empathized with those who were mistreated, spoke for those who were powerless, related to the poor and disenfranchised. We see him recognizing injustice and the need for societal change. We see him struggling to become educated and to be in a position to be of service. He learned to work hard on the farm and in menial tasks to achieve his goals. Pulling himself up by the bootstraps, he gained the respect that empowered him to help others. He took advantage of every opportunity to learn and serve.

"You heard how this son of sharecroppers, the poorest of the poor, was himself subject to discrimination. You realize that, in addition to racial and other forms of discrimination, class discrimination exists in our society. If our picture of this man reflects a color for this, it enhances our understanding that Jim Warner can relate to those who face a different treatment because they are different. How, then, could he act based upon a hatred for the very people he knows, understands, and appreciates?

"You heard testimony as to his kindness to minorities and others who just needed a boost to achieve their dreams. His work to provide funding for needy students to pursue education, his voluntarily giving of himself to achieve positions of leadership to be in a position to design and influence programs that target those who need assistance, were highlighted in testimony. Real people illustrated the hiring, recommendation, and promotion of minorities in the workforce. Acting as mentor and friend to those in need of encouragement, Mr. Warner provided hope and inspiration to many. His support of religious freedom and inclusion is well documented in the testimony. His openness and support of political equality and work with such groups are of record. Assisting in the integration of public schools, working for equal treatment for all citizens, campaigning for open meetings and governmental transparency speaks to his desire for inclusivity.

"I know that each of you has endured hardships in living your lives and that you can relate to those faced by Jim Warner. You have confronted those hardships and now are citizens on this jury with the power and experience to sit in judgment of one lucky enough to be a part of your community. Jim Warner is us. Like the rest of us, Jim Warner is not perfect. Despite all that he has done in his eighty-three years, he still has the warts and frailties we all share. He makes mistakes. In this case, his mistake was to assume that his granddaughter was being raped. He reacted as many of us may have reacted under the circumstances. He acted without thought, just as we all may have acted at times. Without warning, he came upon a scene where his granddaughter appeared to be wrestling with an attacker. He did not know the victim. The victim's race did not register with him. It was a tragic event that has greatly affected Mr. Warner. In fact, he still is unable to recall details. The event was that traumatic for him, the kind of person that values all lives.

"As you may recall, at the opening of this trial, I indicated that the hate crime charge must establish beyond a reasonable doubt that the perpetrator was motivated by prejudicial hate toward the victim. We have shown that Jim Warner had no motive to act on the basis of race, creed, or color. He did not know the victim. Nor did he process the color or physical characteristics of the victim. He had no intent or purpose based upon race. His action was race neutral. He had no pre-planned result. No harm was contemplated, and no thought of injury to anyone was planned. His was an automatic response, a tragic accident.

"I would ask of you, the jury, to look at the completed picture of Jim Warner and to the totality of his life and service to others and ask yourself if this is a man who would hate, hate to the extent that he abandon his entire record of dealing fairly and without prejudice. I would ask you to remember that picture painted by his granddaughter, Summer, who testified, "Poppy is one of the most tolerant people I know." The bright picture of integrity and decency.

"You will be asked to form an opinion of the quality and worth of the picture we have painted. There will be various degrees of guilt offered according to the charges listed. I would hope that you will see the man and reject all charges. I would hope that you see the hope and purpose to which Jim Warner has dedicated his entire life. Thank you!"

M y attorney stood looking from one juror to another, down the line of seven men and five women with the same concentration for each, black and white, men and women.

There was a stillness in the courtroom that could be cut with a knife. For a long moment, the only sound was Walt quietly making his way back to our table. The audience mumbling was low but strong as people looked at one another. I couldn't determine if they were impressed or if they thought the outright hyperbole was indeed over the top. I leaned to the ear of my lawyer and whispered. "You forgot to mention what a son of a bitch I really am."

The ensuing lunch break gave me the opportunity to chastise Walt for his excessive praise. "You made me sound like a saint. Even the jury knows that isn't true. They are smart people. They'll know the stuff is just window dressing. How can they believe anything you say if you stretch the truth like that? Not that it makes a difference now."

"Mr. Warner, the only thing I didn't tell was that you are an ornery old unappreciative cuss."

We jawed a while about the effect his oratory might have on the jury. In the end, we slurped our soup and inhaled a sandwich with an exotic name listed on Newk's menu.

Themed for the afternoon session had doubled. Guess they wanted to gander at a certified saint. Except for the judge, all were seated when we returned to the courtroom. Judge Longest appeared hesitant when approaching his perch on the bench. After a moment, he cleared his throat and spoke.

"The court will come to order. As I indicated this morning, the final argument by the prosecution follows that of the defense. Mr. Greenwood, are you ready?"

"Ready, Your Honor."

Lawrence Greenwood walked leisurely to the jury box and surveyed the body.

"Ladies and gentlemen. I, too, would like to congratulate you for persevering thus far. I would be dishonest if I told you the easy part is ahead. The hardest part will now be on your shoulders, the administration of justice through your decision making. It is a difficult undertaking, but I know you will undertake it with the dignity, seriousness, and consideration that you have shown already. You will be presented with a number of questions or charges to which you will vote guilty or not guilty. I would hope that you will answer guilty to all charges for the reasons I will now address.

"Let us not forget Artise Bradley Washington. It is easy to dismiss one with whom we may not have been acquainted—one who possesses no power, wealth or influence. In our society, it is especially easy to ignore one that happens to be black. Who will speak for him? I'll tell you who speaks for him! Ladies and gentlemen of the jury, justice cries out for him! Justice screams out for one, even those who may be labeled the lesser among us! Artise Bradley Washington did not have eighty-three years to amass a fancy resumé. He was born to an unwed mother and never had the opportunity to know either of his parents. He was shuttled from one foster home to another until rescued by grandparents. This transition validated the fact that he was a bright young man, a leader, and one with unlimited potential. All that potential was snuffed out in an instant by one person who had no regard for the life of another. That person, despite a public show of good works, did not see a human in his rifle sight, he saw blackness. He saw a lesser being through the mirror of years of degradation and slavery. A spark of indignation and hate overcame his plastic image of liberality. His only thought was an obligation to protect his lily white granddaughter from voluntary violation by a lowly black.

"Ladies and gentlemen of the jury, James T. Warner is a coward. He will not admit to this horrendous act. He claims that he cannot remember. We presented expert testimony that a loss of memory, in particular for an extended period, is highly unlikely. We know the gun belonged to James T. Warner. We know that there were only three people present and the granddaughter has not been charged with pulling the trigger. That leaves only James T. Warner and Artise Bradley Washington who is dead. So, we have no doubt and can remember that James T. Warner shot and killed an unarmed black man. The only question remaining is why he did it.

"During the trial, we learned a great deal about James T. Warner. His ancestry is filled with avowed segregationists. From their histories and positions in society, we might assume that some were slaveholders.

He admitted that he grew up in an environment where prejudice against blacks was rampant. He admitted to experiencing violence against blacks. You heard him testify that everyone, including himself, holds prejudicial tendencies. There were other witnesses who corroborated his admission to prejudicial acts. It is our contention that when he looked down the barrel of the murder weapon, the veneer of liberality cracked as he pulled the trigger.

"In this trial, we have heard hours of testimony extolling the virtues of James T. Warner and all he did for minorities. We might want to ask ourselves why his association with black people had to do with business and not social involvement. Could it be that he worked with blacks but chose not to have close relations with those he considered inferior?

"But this case is not about mere feelings. It is about the actions of the defendant. He shot and killed Artise Bradley Washington. This is plainly a case of targeting an unarmed black man to commit a crime that would not have been visited upon a white man. The defiling of a white woman by the unclean required retribution. Long-repressed laws of Southern manhood demanded it.

"Ladies and gentlemen of the jury, I submit to you that James T. Warner saw a black man with his white granddaughter and was incensed. Racial prejudice and hatred led him to level a gun and kill Artise Bradley Washington, whose only sin was being black and participating in a consensual act of love with a white girl.

"Thank you for listening, ladies and gentlemen. I urge you to carefully consider the evidence and bring in a verdict of guilty on all counts."

When Greenwood sat, there was a stunned silence from the audience. It was sensed and felt as an unseen breath. Time hid among courthouse rafters and in wall crevices. The moment was finally interrupted by Judge Longest, who cleared his throat with a gentle cough.

"Ladies and gentlemen of the jury, it has been a long and emotion-filled day. I am delaying my instructions until tomorrow, at which time we will reiterate the solemn duty of rendering a verdict. There will be some specifics relating to procedure and order in the jury room. You will be given the charges and burden-of-proof requirements. In the meantime, I ask that you return home for overnight items and return for transportation to the Conference Center Hampton Inn. I take this unusual sequestration measure to give you an undisturbed opportunity to consider the facts presented in this case. You will still be under the admonition that the case not be discussed with anyone. Food will be served in a private dining room, and phone contact is discouraged except for emergencies. A deputy will be available to assist you in any way. This measure is designed to lessen the temptation to seek advice. We desire that you enter the jury room at 9:00 o'clock tomorrow with only your impressions, which will then be shared with other jurors in arriving at a verdict. I know that this request comes as a surprise to you at such short notice. I will be happy to hear special circumstances that may make it difficult for you to comply. Please relay those concerns to the official who returns you to the holding room. Court dismissed."

I sat like a zombie trying to assess what had transpired and determine if I could move from a frozen position. Walt had his hand on my arm and squeezed to get my attention. "Mr. Warner, don't let that summation get to you. It was just a lot of words—the kind of words that we might have expected."

"But, Walt, a lot of it was true."

"Mr. Warner, what we said was also true. Truth is on a sliding scale depending on one's perspective. You are a good and fair man who had no malice, had no intention of harming anyone. That is the picture I see."

"I just want to go home, Walt."

I had to get away from it all. To push myself past physical endurance. To not have to think. I walked the dry trail, crossed Tarvers Creek to the higher elevation. Tall pines reached skyward and then the downward plane where mist flower brushed my legs and pineweed and joe-pye struggled with dog fennel for space in red clay. Not the most beautiful of wild plants but among the most prolific. They fit my feeling of nothingness while passing among great oaks. Realizing I was out of breath, I threw myself into a space between roots of a huge red oak shedding fall color. The leafy display outlined my presence in due course, exacerbating my feeling of smallness in a universe of giants. The limbs filtered sun shifting toward a horizon in blazing red. For some reason, I patted a tree root and then remembered why. It reminded me of life's journey.

At the age of eighteen, I had never been outside the state of Mississippi, and I was leaving. Having hitched a ride to just south of Kosciusko, I was going beyond the Leake County line on the way to Nashville and to what would be a Bible-selling summer job in North Carolina. I stood in the shade of a tree and stuck out a thumb. A farming family invited me to ride in the back of their pick-up truck. Looking back, the tree was my last remembrance of leaving. For years thereafter, upon reversing the route to visit what was once my home, I looked at that tree as the door to my new world.

The white oak tree is dead now,
With withered branches, sap ran out.
But it once marked the county line
With all its lofty arrogance.

It could never last as long as stone,
Nor spend the day surveyors iron pipe.
Then, could not make a legal stake;
Now, provides no shelter from the sun.

It did not lose its grayish bark
To spend its plank as drinking keg.
No beams as oft for sailing ship,
Instead, made old with passing time.

It gave itself my trusty knife
To carve my childish mark
As I prepared to leave the womb
And pass the way of man.

But I recall how strong it was,
So solid it would never change.
That in a space my cup be full,
Alas to grow and strive again.

I left my leafy bed, bid goodbye to the accommodating oak, and made my way homeward in invisible light.

CHAPTER 23

I skipped supper. Just wasn't hungry. I sat on the deck in harvest moonlight. House lights were extinguished, and I was in the middle of two hundred and sixty acres. There was no artificial illumination. The lake was highly visible as was the row of crape myrtle lining the spillway. The brightness was such that it would not be an exaggeration to say that one could read and write out here. Lightning bugs flitted, and crickets sounded for mates. Somewhere deep in the woods, a screech owl howled. I had a vision of Maggie's ashes floating in on the western breeze to settle beside me. It was perfect timing for a visit.

Maggie, I heard some awful things today—all about me. I'm beginning to face me—the person I really am. My understanding of prejudice has always been colored by my own experience, not that of others. I was a skinny, non-athletic kid in high school. In sweeping floors and working cafeteria lines in college, I felt shame. I still meet, from time to time, a classmate who became a college president. He never fails to remind me that he remembers me from the days I ladled gravy on his potatoes at the university cafeteria. Several law school friends were sons of successful attorneys and politicians. They had served as Washington aides to Congress persons, traveled to exotic places, and had summer jobs in prestigious law offices. I was jealous. I did reconcile somewhat in that I immersed myself in theatre. There I could play roles from sophisticated diplomats to low-life bums. Perhaps I have simply played roles all my life. Was my role as a liberal the most perfect of my theatrical accomplishments?

How can I know how a black person feels? How can I even compare my own small slights to a minority who is excluded from a respectable role in society? Maggie, I take no comfort in the fact that great men have been racist or sexist or xenophobic or whatever. Aristotle defined a woman as an inferior man. Abraham Lincoln was said to consider blacks inferior to whites. Martin Luther said Jews were second only to the devil. Of course, they were products of their time, Maggie. Am I just a product of my time? Can it be that time is neutral, that a neural circuitry governs what we think and how we behave?

I never told you about our mutual friend, a university colleague who was the epitome of circumspect behavior. A dedicated churchman, he was socially conscious and considered a strong supporter of civil rights. Black and other minorities as well as white students flocked to his enlightened personality and read his humorous articles and followed his pithy comments. Once, we attended the same meeting in Jackson and returned to the hotel where we were to spend the night. After we had a nice dinner and a couple of drinks, the discussion turned to race relations. We talked of miscegenation, and the general topic of the mistreatment of black women was broached. My learned friend leaned forward and lowered his voice.

"You know, I could have sex with a black woman, but I could never kiss her."

As I recall, I had absolutely no reaction to that statement. But I never forgot those words and later tried to relate them to the fine gentleman I knew. He had grown up in Iowa and pursued higher education at Princeton with a post-doc in Oxford, England. After a meritorious career and a spotless human relations record, there was still a tinge of thought in the recesses of his being that considered some things unclean.

Maggie, I think that's where folks of my generation are. No matter our geographic location or environmental influences, we still are apprehensive of strangers, suspicious of anyone different. Reaction to color may be the most glaring manifestation of tribal differences. We grew up in America where the Western hero wore a white hat; the villain wore black. There were ghosts and goblins hiding in the night that dissipated with morning light. With light we can see; the darkness holds danger. God is light; the devil is darkness. We fear the dark because we cannot see.

This brings me to the end of my journey to understand myself, Maggie. I know that I hold in my soul that tinge of prejudice. It is manifested in thoughtless actions and repressed feelings. I don't appreciate obese people for who they are. I just see them as invading my space in a tight seating arrangement on a plane or in an auditorium. Tight dresses and gargantuan legs exposed almost to the crotch offend me. If I park my car in an area where Mexican or other foreign workers are present, I lock my automobile, a habit I don't normally practice otherwise. I do pay more attention to driving violations or discourtesies committed by black or other-race drivers. If I see kids running wild in Walmart or hear overly loud and irritating music from a car or boom box, I tend to suspect that black people are responsible. When in Memphis or other major cities, I sometimes avoid going into a neighborhood with mostly black or immigrant populations. I am suspicious of panhandlers or beggars, particularly if they are people of color. I seem to expect more minorities of leaving kids unattended, of abandoning shopping carts in parking spots, of breaking in line, and of littering. Although I support people to love whom they will and consider private the right to a chosen lifestyle, I have an aversion to seeing same-sex couples kiss. I support one's right to marry whomever they please, but I wonder about the ability of children of mixed race to straddle two cultures.

As I consider these feelings, I know they are ridiculous, but they and others I fail even to remember are a part of my being. A basket of impressions without thought or reason. Maybe it is like a habit—alcoholism, that must be admitted, controlled and massaged with time. Perhaps, as with many people, it is not bigotry. If I understand the word, a bigot carries an element of hate. I don't hate anyone. But, if Artise Bradley Washington had been white, there might have been a hesitation of my finger on that trigger—a moment to reason. I wonder if it had been a poorly dressed white person, the result would have been the same? Perhaps it is class rather than race that is in question.

Regardless, deep within my soul, I know that I retain discriminatory thoughts.

I don't understand why I keep using that term soul. I have difficulty reconciling the concept of soul in the absurdity of my humanistic philosophy. Then where do kindness, faith, justice, hope, belief—our humanity—come from? In life, we encounter unconditional love and unapologetic hate. We see compartmentalized violence contrasted with sentimentality. We see great sacrifice and insidious greed, ugly devastation, and wondrous beauty. We see fear and courage. We see hope and hopelessness. We contrast ambition with morality, right versus wrong, ignorance versus knowledge. We see belief overcoming reality. We see talent juxtaposed with principle. Perhaps being able to distinguish differences between those emotions is the truth we fail to see. It is the length and breadth of a light spectrum that is confined to black and white. We fear the darkness and embrace illumination.

Where do we go from here, Maggie? The road is shorter now, but we still have a ways to go. I see young people, like granddaughter Summer, who have embraced change, and I am encouraged. I see young black people pursuing careers in every profession. I see a diversity that cannot be fathomed by my generation. Education is the key. Some will continue to embrace the fear. Others will find it difficult to wait. Still, I have faith in the future. With the browning of America, the tolerance of a majority and the patience of all, the fear will dissipate. It will not be easy. We must resist the fear mongers, reject those seeking to spread division and instead promote fairness and equality. The remnants of xenophobia and color will fade with the ashes of old codgers like me. Well, I have a bit of time left. Now that I've looked at me, maybe I can look more clearly at others. Thanks for listening, Maggie!

Morning slips into my bedroom, and beyond my open window wild geese honk as they prepare to leave the placid lake. Although the weather is still mild, it is an early stop-over for an instinctive journey south. Nature has a way of anticipating a wintery blast. I watch as they rise in the form of a "V," and I marvel at the beauty of life.

Judge Longest was reading from pages of jury instructions. I was absorbed within myself and not burdened with the burden of proof and other nonsense that was being proclaimed. Actually, it's not nonsense. The process is meant to keep everyone on track to reach a reasonable decision according to law and evidence. Reasonable or not, I am at peace with myself and resigned to whatever happens to Jim Warner. I suppose I heard some of the conversation but none registered. After a period, I realized that the jury was filing out and the court room audience leaving.

Walt was gathering his materials.

"Well, Mr. Warner, the jury is out. All we can do now is wait. I do feel good about the outcome. How are you doing?"

"Fine, thank you, Walter."

"Good. What are we going to do to celebrate our victory?"

"As I've told you before, Walt, it really doesn't matter. I'm happy."

I left Walter Dunbar with a quizzical look on his face. The crowd had dissipated, and my family was nowhere in sight as I made my way to my car. The CD auto player resounded over speakers a favorite song by a friend of mine, Tricia Walker. It is a Bigfrontporch Production written by Tricia for some friends who were dying of cancer.

What a Wonderful Day

Did you see the sun rise this morning?
Did you hear the mockingbird sing?
Did you touch the hand of a good friend?
Well, that's a beautiful thing.

Did you taste a strong cup of coffee?
Did you smell the freshness of hay?
Did you sing I'm alive, I'm alive, I'm alive?
What a wonderful day.

If you feel the road you've been walking
Is a little too lonely and dark,
I will walk here beside you
And I will listen with my heart.
I may not have all the answers

But I thank God when I pray,
That you're alive, you're alive, you're alive.
What a wonderful day.

What a wonderful day, what a wonderful day.
You're alive, you're alive, you're alive.
What a wonderful day.

There'll be moments of laughter
And there'll be a time for tears,
But when you need a shoulder,
I will always be here.
We've been through this together,
Now we all can say,
We're alive, we're alive, we're alive
What a wonderful day.

What a wonderful day, what a wonderful day.
We're alive, we're alive, we're alive.
What a wonderful day.

What a wonderful day, what a wonderful day.
We're alive, we're alive, we're alive.
What a wonderful day.

I was listening to the amazingly clear tonal quality of Tricia's voice and enjoying a cool breeze from open car windows when topping the hill preceding a descent to Yokna River bottom. With the winding curvature of highway, it is almost impossible to determine exact locations, but slightly southward toward where my property is situated, a huge cloud of billowing black smoke rose high above the tree line. Five minutes later, I was at a battered lane gate. It had been locked tightly, and for some crazy reason, I wondered if it had produced a scratch on the bumper of our new, red volunteer fire department truck.

I arrived in time to see the roof implode inside a cavern that exploded to chase smoke with streams of flame spurting burning sparkles of Cyprus timber. Thunder rolled with each falling piece of fuel drawn into a circular mass. Someone had dragged a smoke-filled couch, apparently the only item rescued, some fifty yards up the driveway. I sat mesmerized as volunteer firemen and one firewoman stood and watched the blaze. I thought of voluntary firefighters as one of the few legal machismo opportunities left in our community. And now they had women. The men must now watch their language, refrain from touching or even telling a female that they look good. And, I guess, the opposite gender has the same restrictions. Being socially and politically correct is necessary, but it sure can ruin positive relationships. Thinking such crazy thoughts at a time like this is insane, but they did cross my mind. A captain of the force, Gene Boatright, came over to where I sat.

"I'm sorry, Mr. Warner, we only had the one pump truck, and our hose couldn't reach to the lake."

"Couldn't be helped, Gene."

"Mr. Warner, there were two five-gallon gas cans laying around. Do you have any idea who?"

"Doesn't matter."

"Well, I'm awfully sorry."

"Thank you for coming, Gene."

"We'll stay around and make sure the woods don't burn. Got a Water Valley tanker on the way."

The house I loved is gone, the flower beds, the workshop. But, there are many things, family and other people to love. My daughters are still here for me, daughters who have been steadfast and loving. They are a source of pride for me to love and appreciate. They are good people and represent a sentiment I am unable to express. Suffice to say, I truly love them.

The land, a permanent tie to earth, is intact. I can love the trees and wildflowers, the animals that share this space. We are all one with nature.

Once, I would have thought of this fire as a devastating tragedy. Today, it is just one of the vagaries of existing. Living with oneself is vastly more important than where one lives. I thought of my life, how fortunate have I been.

An afternoon ago, running on wobbly infant legs to keep in time, I dreamed a crystal dream, assured that it was not my lot to stand by the road, disoriented as the lost bee whose role is distanced when the farmer moves hives, the bee left for yet another day to draw liquid gold from different flowers, weeds, and trees. I yearned to be thoughtfully contemplative, not as when I was a child and the sow under the back step wallowing only enough acrid mud for newborn pigs, so near the smokehouse, failing to see predestined fate, ordered and changeless as mine seemed to be.

I know that life ends too soon. Far too soon, like unwelcome news or the end of a perfect day that fills the shadows and falls equally on every blade of grass. Life creeps on spindly legs of a praying mantis with halting step, making the way on my deck boards, grayed also with passing time.

An age I never thought I'd reach, despite a desperate urge to live forever, stop the clock hand, cheat the lock of fate. It was not as if I slept, oblivion left alone with the thought of suddenly awaking to find purple asters picked that very day. Shrinking with neglect, I try to recall the hours and urge a kaleidoscope of colored fabric, now frayed like trampled grass on which I lay awash in first love, knowing only that time stood still with ripe apples and every moment with Maggie a pleasured step.

As early Thrift in spring, Maggie spread her splendor strewn in patchwork patterns on winds of changeless time, though blossoming and wilting in winter's sway. Buddha has said, "Each morning we are born again." And I now have thoughts more real than feelings when the day did start—same needs and hopes when leaving as when I first began. Beyond the garden wall, there is a field of brilliant moss, a resurrected womb embroidered by warm hands of constant care. I see myself in mellow bloom, a daffodil, the fullness of all time.

Abruptly, the cell phone jingled in my pocket, and the beauty of the moment left as if the last run of the day.

"Mr. Warner? Walt. The jury is in."

ACKNOWLEDGEMENTS

There are numerous people to whom I am indebted for their support and encouragement. My readers provided insight in attempting to make the story readable and understood. Millie McAuley, Mary Beth Montgomery, Laurie DuChaine, and Jo Ann O'Quin were liberal in their recommendations but kind in expressing shortcomings. Taylor Brame suffered through hours of additional proofing.

Mary Ann Bowen, an excellent editor, placed a spotless reputation in jeopardy by accepting the fact that I was reluctant to accept so much good advice.

The staff at Nautilus Publishing were outstanding. Sinclair Rishel and Carroll Moore were more than generous in applying their considerable talents for layout and artistic design.

Finally, the publisher, Neil White, is an amazing person and friend. His advice and inspiration is sincerely treasured.

Needless to say, I owe most to my loving wife, Margaret, for her understanding and patience.

About the Author

University of Mississippi Juris Doctor in Law, dean of admissions, and registrar at Ole Miss, Ken has a long career in higher education. He was a leader in educational policy on the, state, regional and national level including:

> Trustee, College Entrance Examination Board, New York.
>
> One of founders and first President of National Association of Student Financial Aid
>
> Administrators, Washington, DC.
>
> President, Southern Association of Student Financial Aid Administrators.
>
> President, Common Cause Mississippi
>
> President, Oxford/Lafayette County Chamber of Commerce
>
> President, Oxford Rotary Club
>
> President, Oxford Civic Council
>
> President, Law School Graduating Class
>
> President, Yoknapawtapha Arts Council
>
> President, Theatre Oxford
>
> Museum Board of Directors, Library Board of Directors
>
> Past college consultant for colleges from New York to California. Consulted for North
>
> Carolina Board of Higher Education, National Merit Scholarship Service, U.S. Office of Education, U.S. Justice Department. Testified before U.S. Congressional Committees.
>
> Founder, President and CEO of manufacturing company.

Publications include *Tests: The Foundation for Equity, Josey Bass*; *Americans With Disablity Act Compliance Manual*; and a novel, *Blackberries*, published in 2013.

Ken lives near Oxford, Mississippi on a 15 acre lake in a 260 acre forest with his wife, Margaret Wylde, a Great Pyrenees, Lilly, and a fat cat called Cheddar.

www.ingramcontent.com/pod-product-compliance
Lightning Source LLC
Chambersburg PA
CBHW020935260626
47169CB00006B/1737